WHAT WE DID THAT NIGHT

MARNIE VINGE

TRIGGER WARNINGS

- A negative portrayal of BDSM due to lack of consent
- Animal cruelty (only briefly mentioned, the animal survives and is okay)
- Rape
- Murder
- Gaslighting
- Physical assault
- Choking
- Brief discussion of a suicide attempt

FOREWORD

This might be one of the darker books I've written, and I'd like to give some special insights into this book for those of you that pre-ordered directly from me!

I wrote this book in 2016 as an assignment from my therapist. I had always wanted to be a writer and my favorite genre of all time was thrillers. In my teens, I'd also written romance novellas every week that I'd give to all my girlfriends on Fridays. They loved the characters and the stories and I'll never, ever forget that feeling. But it wasn't until 2016 that my therapist encouraged me to really go for it with my writing. To try to write something long form, which I'd never been able to do before.

It was daunting to think about trying to write a full-length novel again. I'd tried many times and stalled out somewhere in the murky middle, as they call it.

But I was determined this time.

Not only because I wanted to finish a novel, but because I wanted to exorcise some demons of my own.

When I was 20 years old, I was raped at a party by someone I considered an acquaintance. I passed out alone, completely clothed, and woke up to the sensation of this person violating my body, which I could not full control due to how intoxicated I was. But I screamed and I kicked as well as I could and finally got him off me. The damage was done at that point, though.

I spent years pretending it hadn't happened. But the trauma stayed in my body. Unfortunately, I was retraumatized several times in similar situations. All the while, I wasn't talking to anyone about it or even acknowledging to myself what was done to me.

During the six months it took me to write this book, I really dug into that experience. And what it was like to live with both PTSD and complex PTSD. Many of the experiences in this book that deal directly with how Tash processes her trauma, or looks at her abusive relationship are drawn from my own emotions and feelings and the way I handled myself following the rape.

When you are traumatized, your brain takes a snapshot. You may not be able to tell anyone these details verbally, but your body knows what time of day it was, what time of year, the barometric pressure, the precipitation, the temperature, the sights, smells, and sounds around you. And it stores all that information so that hopefully, it can protect you from ever being in that situation again. But sometimes, that backfires. It tooks years and years and years of therapy for me to get to the point I'm at now with what was done to me, and I'm not nearly where I want to be. But this book was my first best effort at healing.

I hope that for those of you that read it in a similar place, it gives hope. As I was editing this book, I saw a quote in it where Tash is describing not being able to even imagine what it would be like to feel safe and loved. I used to think I'd never experience that either, but I have and I do. And if you're in that dark place thinking things can never change, I promise they can and they will. Just take that next step forward on your healing journey, whatever that looks like.

Thank you all for taking the time to read my stories. I love you from the bottom of my heart. This one is a special one.

A NOTE ABOUT THE TIMELINE

I wrote this book in 2016 when victims of revenge porn did not have much in the way of legal recourse. At the time, there was no law surrounding it in Tennessee. Thankfully, there now is. I believe the laws everywhere should be stronger, though. If this has happened to you, consider checking out this guide from HelpGuide.org.

https://www.helpguide.org/relationships/domestic-abuse/dealing-with-revenge-porn

ONE

Nashville Dec. 2016

People who preach forgiveness have never done something unforgivable.

The cold air sets my lungs on fire as I inhale deeply, my body desperate for more oxygen as I strike the bag. *Jab, cross, uppercut, ridgehand.* With each exhalation, a cloud of humid breath expulses into the air from deep inside my chest, warming me up more and more, starting a fire inside of me. The same fire I stoke every morning in this ritual, trying to burn away the things that left me so tired the night before. With each strike, I steel myself for the battles of the day: the push and pull of socializing in polite society, going to work and teaching jiu-jitsu, going to class and trying not to scream when the guy who always sits next to me touches my shoulder to ask me what the last slide said. Easy things. Things that shouldn't bother other people. But they bother me.

In the dim light of the garage, I can make out Sue's gray fur near the corner where his bed lays. He only uses it when I'm working out here. Currently, he's snoozing despite the blaring music and my grunting. Named for both the Johnny Cash song and the largest Tyrannosaur ever found, Sue is my guardian angel. An addition to our household after I returned from Los Angeles. He cured my loneliness and gave my roommate and best friend, Dan, a project to work on when it came to training him. He sleeps in my bed with me at night though his hulking Irish Wolfhound frame makes it seem like I'm sleeping next to a person instead of a dog.

Jab, cross, backfist, ridgehand.

The door leading from the house into my makeshift garage gym swings open and smacks the wall loud enough to sound like a car backfiring. Dan stands there, darkening my doorway like an omen. I ignore him in my peripheral vision, imagining that he's going to bitch about the stereo at 7am. He shouts my name, and I hear him clearly, though I pretend I don't. Maybe if I ignore him, he'll go away.

He doesn't.

Dan marches across the garage and over my freshly cleaned mats.

"Hey!" I shout. "I just mopped those last night!"

He reaches for the stereo and hits the power button. Suddenly the music stops, leaving only the sound of my heavy breathing and Sue's snoring. I turn to him, an animal with its hackles up. "*What?*"

"There's something you need to see," he says, running a hand through his bed-head of brown hair. He stands taller than me, broad-shouldered and intimidating. He looks like he could be ex-military, though he isn't. In his green eyes, I can tell that he's serious. Without any further cryptic instruction, he walks back past me, once again treading on the mat.

"I really wish you wouldn't do that, asshole," I say as I

follow him. "Come on, buddy," I say to Sue, waking him from his slumber. He groans in resignation, unhappy to terminate his early morning nap, but he slowly gets up and follows me into the house.

The warm gust of air from the laundry room hits me as the dryer spins.

In my drenched sweatshirt and leggings, I march down the hallway after Dan. Sue follows as he turns into the office that we share and sits down at his massive desk. He pauses as though thinking of what to do next. I notice a small dot above the mail tab, indicating that there's an open email.

"What do you want?" I ask, reaching to my side to stroke Sue's massive head. "This better be good."

"Tash, I think maybe you should sit down," he begins, looking at me like he's about to brief me on national security.

I feel my stomach tighten. Goosebumps rise all over my skin. Whatever it is, it's bad, and my reaction is instinctive. He looks like he's in pain and angry at the same time. I recognize the juxtaposition from seeing it staring back at me in the mirror each morning.

"I'm going to read something, and I want you to stay calm, okay?" he says, going for the mouse. He moves the cursor over the mail tab and maximizes it.

There in the subject line it says, "Hello."

It's when I read the information in the sender field that my stomach plummets.

krothpenderg@gmail.com

The combination of initials and names is familiar to me, stirring a coldness in my gut. I know the man who uses that handle.

It's a combination of his late brother's first initial and last name along with an abbreviation of the last name of his favorite fictional character growing up. That character was an FBI agent always specializing in cases that seemed to involve serial killers, something that had always fascinated him.

The dread creeps up my spine and wraps its hands around my throat, squeezing, constricting. Its old familiar grasp takes my breath away. It's been so long since I felt it so intimately.

I swallow and read the three words in the e-mail.

Ha. Ha. Ha.

My hands tremble as Dan reaches for an attachment with the cursor. It's named SeasonsGreetings.jpg. He clicks it.

There, on his twenty-four-inch screen, is a picture of me in a see-through lingerie top and a thong, lying on my side in the bed that I had once shared with the sender of this picture. I look dead. My eyes hold no light, and my skin looks corpse-cold to the touch. My chest aches at the memory of the day he took those pictures. I know this is one of many.

I feel like someone landed a sidekick not just on my stomach, but somewhere between my belly button and my spine, rearranging my internal organs. I reach for Dan's shoulders for support. He reacts, turning and steadying me.

"Tash, breathe," he says.

I didn't realize it, but I stopped breathing. I gulp for air. This familiar dynamic clenches my guts in a vice. It's been three years since I've had any kind of word from him. He made it clear that I was nothing to him—*worthless*. The word rings in my ears every time things get too quiet.

"I'll do whatever you want me to do. We can fix this," Dan says with resolve. He wants some kind of direction from me. He wants to do something.

I steady myself for a moment, reeling from the blow. Sue nuzzles my hand with his snout. My fingers hang limply over his muzzle. My vision begins to tunnel, going in and out of focus. With my voice shaking, I speak.

"Book a flight to Los Angeles. I'm going to kill him."

Dan does nothing. He only stares at me.

"You're not going to L.A. That's insane. It's too dangerous. There are things we can do from—"

"I am going," I cut him off. I turn from the room, the nearly-nude picture of me still sitting on his desktop. I go towards my bedroom and Dan and Sue follow me. Dan reaches out and grabs at my arm. Sue tries to step between us, ever the peacekeeper.

"Don't touch me," I say, my voice on a razor's edge of panic.

He pulls his hand away.

I hate to be touched by just about anyone but Sue. I could stand it inside the jiu-jitsu studio, but that was it. In this moment, the idea of another person's flesh against mine makes me ill.

"Tash, you're not going to Los Angeles," he says.

"What? Are you going to stop me?" I spit. "And why did you even open that e-mail? Were you talking to him?" I ask. Rage clouding my logic.

"Tash, listen to yourself."

"Or did you like that picture, and you wanted to keep it?" I shriek, suddenly aware of my body and wanting to cover up every inch of it. I cross my arms over my chest, my sweatshirt no longer enough of a barrier between Dan's eyes and my breasts.

"Tash," Dan murmurs. "Listen to yourself. You know those things aren't true. This is exactly what he wants!" His speech speeds up. "He wants you right back under his thumb! This is just—"

"Stop," I say.

Dan takes a deep breath, shifting his eyes around the room, finally landing them back on me.

"I have to go," I reiterate. "You can't stop me. This isn't your fight, so don't get involved. I don't need your help or anyone else's. I going to take care of it. I *can* take care of it." I say the last, not sure if it's for my own reassurance or for Dan's. I try to sound as calm and rational as I can, even though inside a storm rages. My mind races at breakneck speed in at least nine different directions.

Dan says nothing. He knows when I make up my mind, there's no changing it.

I've become a woman that can't be stopped. I've spent the three years since I'd heard from Alex making sure of that. Making sure that I'd never be back in that apartment with him. Never back on that boat with him. That I'd never let any of that that happen again. This is just a minor setback. It's harassment at the very least and it has to be illegal. I try to keep any creeping thoughts of the power that Alex has from extinguishing the flame of resolve that I've built in the last few moments. I've mustered the courage to deal with this. I can't think that I am the underdog, my chances worse than a chihuahua in a dog fight with a pit bull.

I have to believe I have a chance.

Dan turns and goes back into the study. For a moment, I imagine him looking at that picture, saving it, touching himself. My stomach turns. I find my trashcan and dry heave into it, no breakfast on my stomach. Sue comes up and nuzzles my face, giving me a lick. I reach out and stroke his head and meet his big brown eyes. There's nothing but compassion there.

I spit what bile I do purge into the plastic container. On my knees, I think of praying for the first time in years. Three to be exact.

This can't be how the story is going to end.

I calm myself, breathing in and out. I dress without showering, grab only my purse and I head out the front door to my car parked in the driveway. I'm going to the airport.

The drive is surreal, both tangible and not. The thought of what I'm about to do hasn't fully coalesced in my mind. I don't think I've completely grasped exactly what flying back to Los Angeles will mean. I don't think I've fully imagined encountering Alex again. I haven't imagined his hot breath on my neck, me cowering to him like a beaten dog. It's all so far away, such a nightmare. A dream from a lifetime that belonged to someone somewhere else.

Nothing rational comes to my clouded brain on the drive to the airport. All I see is the blackness on the outskirts of my field of vision. It tunnels as I'm cut off by another driver. I speed up, flip him off, and cut him off in return. I don't care about getting a ticket for reckless driving, or worse, triggering the road rage of someone far less stable than me.

My life has been shaped into the form that I've wanted it to be all along. I've worked so hard to make it what it is. To make the jiu-jitsu school and the women's program my life. To imagine all of it being ripped away because of the repercussions that will inevitably ensue if those pictures are circulated. Not the one he sent. The *other* ones. It's unfathomable. I picture Alex in his office, not seeing me in the doorway, as he reached a hand down to touch himself while he looked at pictures of girls whose ages I dared not guess.

My stomach turns, flipping the thoughts of Alex and the pictures over like hotcakes, trying not to let any of them settle for too long, lest they burn indelibly into my brain.

Vomit scorches the back of my throat and I try to hold it down, swallowing and swallowing again. A gagging sensation grips me, and hot tears sting my eyes as I wheel off at the exit ramp. I swing around the turn on two wheels, ready to be getting on the next plane to Los Angeles, not that I've stopped long enough to know when that will be taking off.

Once I get off at the exit, I go into autopilot mode. My tears stop, and my face and chest, red from anxiety, cool and regain their natural color. My car makes the trip to the airport that it has made so many times before during those few months when I was getting situated in Los Angeles with Alex. I drove this route so many times. It was familiar. Comforting and frightening in its familiarity. Comforting because I know each step along the way. And frightening because I know there is no doubt that if I follow through, I will land on Alex's doorstep in a few hours.

The idea of getting on the next plane to Los Angeles is almost enough to make me puke again. I haven't seen him in three years and I don't know what to expect, except I do.

He is the same person I left. The picture in the e-mail tells me that much.

My mind drifts into the darkness, and I reel myself back when I find a parking in the garage. I hop out and grab my purse, the only bag that I have with me. I'm not planning on this visit being long. Honestly, I haven't put much thought at all into this visit. I just took what I knew I would need to purchase a ticket and board a plane. My thoughts hadn't been interested in what I might need once at my destination. All I can think about is wrapping my hands around Alex's throat and squeezing until he stops breathing.

The fantasy tids me over on the shuttle ride to the terminal.

"Which airline, miss?" the driver asks me. An older man with black hair graying at the temples, his breath forms clouds inside the unheated shuttle bus.

I realize that I don't know which airline. I haven't thought that far. Somehow, the idea that I need to get to Los Angeles was going to be enough for my addled brain. Somehow, I thought my need would summon up a pilot and a plane specifically for my cause. I didn't think about logistics. Perhaps that's one of the things Dan was yelling about as I peeled out of our cul de sac.

"I—uh—American," I say.

I go with the first name that comes to me. The man smiles and wishes me happy holidays as I disembark from the bus. Strangely, I was the only person on it this morning. With no bags except my purse, I throw my scarf over my shoulder and step out of the cold into the warmth and humidity of the airport.

People bustle to and fro, some saying goodbye at the security checkpoint, others trying to make sense of the self-service kiosks that seemed to plague every airport in the nation. I do what seems most natural and bypass the kiosks and go straight to the counter. A girl with blonde hair and a sharp American Airlines uniform greets me with a plasticized smile with one slightly chipped front tooth that makes her beauty all the more charming for the fact that it isn't perfect.

"How can I help you?" she chirps, her voice straining behind gritted teeth that reveal how much she hates her job.

Before the words can come out of my mouth, I am seized by paralysis. Terror claws its way to my heart, burrowing through my sweater and into my skin, ripping a wide hold in me. My mouth opens but words do not come out. I try to force the air from my lungs, over my vocal chords, trying to vibrate them to make any sort of sound resembling human speech, but nothing happens.

"Miss, are you alright?" the girl asks, her tone suddenly much more alive. She has a look of concern on her face, but also a look that say, *Please, God. My shift is almost over. Don't let this bitch faint on me.*

My mouth hangs open and I gawk at her. I don't know what I was trying to say. I can't form the words to tell her that I need to leave this place and get to another. I try to make her understand by using sheer willpower.

"Miss, calm down," the girl says, more of an order than a suggestion at this point.

I realize I can feel a sticky dampness in my palm, my hand balled into a fist at my side.

I look down and shut my mouth, seeing blood pooling in four little letter *c*'s across the heel of my palm. The blood flows into the wounds and begins to drip from my hand onto my jeans and down onto the floor beside me. I look back at the American Airlines girl and see horror in her eyes.

I can only imagine what she's thinking, but her face betrays it to be some combination of *What the fuck?* and *I don't get paid enough for this bullshit.* Those thoughts and others flash across her face, but something in my eyes must make her call for help instead of security.

"Sandra!" she shouts to another woman standing further down the counter helping other customers flying with American. Sandra is a woman of about forty and she looks up, her black ponytail bobbing vivaciously when she does.

Sandra comes marching down after she slings two bags onto the conveyor belt with a grunt. She surveys the scene and finally her eyes land on mine, which I realize now, are stinging with the threat of tears.

"Are you okay?" Sandra asks me, reaching a hand out for my arm.

I recoil on instinct. In a moment like this, when I feel like a cornered animal, snarling a warning to anyone who dares to come near, being touched is unthinkable.

"It's okay," Sandra says, much more calmly than she posed her original question. I can tell that she's doing her best to soothe me, having probably had training on how to handle an explosive situation like the one I am sure she thinks she's found herself in now. For a few moments, I lost myself. I fell apart from my body, unaware of my nails digging into my palm and unaware that my mouth has gone parchment dry. My heart is pounding and I can hear the sound of my own blood pumping dangerously close to my ear drums, which feel like they might rupture at any time without warning. My hand is still clenched and I can still feel the wetness of the blood. My face is fraught with alarm, my eyebrows doing their best to touch one another.

And still I cannot speak.

"We'll get someone for you," Sandra says, now stepping out from behind the counter.

"Please don't," I croak somewhere deep inside my throat. It's a voice I haven't heard in a long time and a phrase that I haven't used in just as long. It's foreign and yet familiar and makes my stomach uneasy.

Sandra looks relieved that I've begun to speak. I'm sure that I'm relieved at all. The voice that came from inside of me isn't mine. It belongs to a stranger that I haven't seen in three years. That strangled voice only reminded me that even halfway across the continent, Alex still has a vice-like grip on me, silencing me now as he so expertly had then.

So I run.

I run until my legs go numb in the cold. I run until it feels like my lungs bleed inside my chest, aching for me to stop drawing in breath after icy breath, the fingers of the air probing deeper into my chest cavity with each inhale/exhale cycle. I run until I see the parking lot. I run past cars that honk at me. I run in front of cars that slam on their squealing brakes to avoid splattering me across the road. I run until I'm in that lot full of cars, and then I stop.

I fold my body in half, almost collapsing but not ready to give in yet. I still have to find my car before the airport authorities are alerted to a woman acting strangely at the American counter. I try to catch my breath, slowing my inhale and exhale, counting in my head, trying to remember everything I've ever learned about breathing during a fight.

I stand once more, a stitch in my side cramping and causing me to reach for my waist.

I start to walk. I see a light pole that looks familiar and then realized that the same familiar-looking fixture is in about thirty places throughout the lot. I walk on past car after car, searching for the back of my RAV4.

At last, I spot it.

I dig for the keys in my purse and for a horrible moment I think I might have dropped them on my race from the terminal. I find them, though, and unlock the doors, shoving them into the ignition and starting the car. The leather seats are cold on my thighs, heated from their little sprint.

My muscles jump, electricity still pumping through them, adrenaline keeping me afloat at this point. I reach for the gear shift, and it becomes sticky. I looked down to see the congealing blood on my palm and for a moment, I can't figure out how it happened. For a moment, I am not entirely sure why I'm here to begin with. For a moment, everything in the world is just as it was earlier this morning when I was doing bag work.

Reality cascades over me as the damn of truth breaks under the weight of my circumstances.

My stomach contracts and my esophagus follows suit. I throw the door open and lurch to the side, vomiting directly beside my car. Twice.

I wipe my mouth with my bloody hand, leaving red streaks around my lips and chin. In the rearview mirror, I look like a vampire that just got a bad case of food poisoning.

I laugh.

My chest heaves as hysteria begins to take root. I pound my hands against the steering wheel and scream. And then I begin to sob. I let myself have only a few moments and then I throw the car in reverse and hit the gas.

Shaking, holding back the hysteria, I drive home.

TWO

Nashville Jan. 2008

I crossed the street and walked up the sidewalk that led the building my Spanish class was being held in. The cold air nipped at my nose and stung my cheeks, giving them a rosy redness. I was twenty-one, on track to graduate with a paleontology degree, and nothing stood in my way except a couple of Spanish classes and a few more science electives.

I grabbed the cold door handle of the old building and went inside. Students bustled about, talking to each other about events on campus, how their winter breaks had been, and other topics that disinterested me. I wanted to get to class on time and find a good seat. I wanted to ace it and never look back.

Once at my classroom, I took a seat in the front row and waited as the minutes ticked by before the professor showed up. He came in silently and went to the front of the class. The room filled up, leaving only one empty seat next to me on the front row. Finally, he shut the door and walked back to the front of the room to begin his first lecture.

"Good morning," he said. "Or should I say, *buenos dias*?"

There was a little tinkling of nervous and unamused laughter throughout the room. I looked over my shoulder and smiled at the girl behind me when there was a knock at the door. The whole class turned, and the professor went back to open it, obviously annoyed at the person's tardiness, but not as annoyed as I was that I was going to have to move my backpack so they could sit next to me.

When the door swung open, a tall, blonde guy stepped through. His eyes were piercingly blue as they looked around like a hawk, trying to find a seat. I reached for my bag instinctively, knowing that this was the only seat in the room.

His nose was long and straight. His hair was swept out of his face, a little longish, and he wore a black sweater and jeans that looked like they cost a fortune. With them he wore dress shoes, which I found alarmingly sexy. I found myself wondering what he'd look like in a finely tailored suit, and from the look of him, I imagined that he probably had one.

He locked eyes with me and my stomach jumped, suddenly filling with butterflies. He made his way towards the seat next to me as the professor went back to the front of the classroom.

The stranger took the seat beside me and scooted his bag under the table. Before the professor could begin again, he looked at me and whispered.

"Alexander Roth." He stuck out a hand to shake mine.

"Natasha Davis," I said. "I go by Tash."

"I go by Alex," he smiled.

We sat silently beside each other, each of us aware of the movement of the other's body throughout the rest of the class. Afterwards, when we were dismissed, everyone hurried to rush out of the classroom, but Alex and I both lingered. Neither of us wanting our first encounter to be over.

"Hey," he said finally. "Maybe I could get your number, and we could be study buddies or something like that."

I smiled, blushing, and looked down.

"That would be nice," I replied.

I scribbled it onto a piece of paper and watched as he dug his flip phone out of his pocket, getting ready to enter the data into the device.

"Or maybe we could get coffee sometime," he said with a smile. His eyes flicked downward towards my lips. My face flushed again though my eyes never left his.

"That would also be nice," I said, smiling.

"You're goddamned beautiful," he said under his breath.

I was taken aback by his statement. I brushed my blonde hair back behind my ears. I looked around but there was no one else in the classroom.

"I just thought you should know. It's nice to hear that sort of thing sometimes," he said.

His confidence was intoxicating. And with that, he left me in his wake.

How was I to know then that he'd always be doing that? How was I to know that the waves would become more and more ferocious and eventually I'd been pulled into the undertow?

THREE

Gulf Shores, Alabama Mar. 2009

Waves lapped at the sandy shores of Fort Morgan beach as my hair gently whipped at my face in the sea breeze. My eyes were shut to the sun and shaded by a pair of Ray Bans that Alex had bought me in honor of our little spring break adventure. I lounged on a towel as he went out to swim in the ocean.

"Don't be long," I said to him, not wanting to be separated from him a moment longer than necessary.

He smiled his characteristically winning smile. The way his dimples puckered on his tan cheeks sent a lightning bolt through me.

"I wouldn't dream of it," he replied, turned and took off at a jog for the waves.

I leaned up on my elbows and watched him, his perfect body soaking up the rays and tanning to a beautiful bronze in the last few days. We had rented a house on the beach away from most of the other college kids. Alex was a little older. Twenty-six at the time. He'd taken some time away from school after his father's death, an event that he'd taken hard but never wanted to talk about. He had returned the year before to complete his business degree though with his family's money, it was an unnecessary ornament to his success. Despite that, he wanted to be a lawyer and had started law school last fall.

He splashed into the sea, his blue trunks soaking up the salt water and turning from a baby blue to a deep cerulean. He dove into the next crashing wave and soon was up to his chest. A pang of nervousness hit me, wondering if there could be sharks in this water. I knew it was a possibility. Danger lay at every turn in the real world, but at that point in my life I hadn't learned to worry the way that Alex would one day teach me to.

Instead, I reached into our beach bag and grabbed the book I'd brought to read. It was a romance about a small Scottish village, a former rock star and a down and out divorcee. It was just the kind of thing I needed for spring break. A vacation from reality. Alex had teased me about it on the drive down.

"Do you really enjoy those?" he'd asked in the car.

I'd paused and closed the book over my thumb, looking up at him from behind my Ray Bans. With a stunning pair of his own, he looked out over the open road.

"Enjoy what?" I'd asked.

"Those books. Aren't they a little vapid?"

They'd never struck me as vapid. They always struck me as the kind of thing one should read when one had given up hope of finding the good in people.

"Not at all. Quite the opposite, I think."

He'd chuckled.

"Whatever," he'd said.

It was the first bitter taste I ever got of his disposition. It was a taste that I'd become so familiar with that it would cause me to cringe when I identified it in his words.

I'd brushed it off, but lying on the beach, the words came back to me. I tried to ignore them and enjoy my book, but it was near impossible. The way he'd laughed. I closed the book and put it away, a little embarrassed that I'd brought it to begin with. Someone with him should be reading Malcolm Gladwell or Mary Roach. I hadn't picked up a non-fiction book that wasn't a textbook in years.

I sighed and crossed my arms, lying on my stomach, I rested my chin on them and looked out over the sand into the water but didn't see Alex. I sat upright and my heart beat a little faster.

Suddenly, his head popped up out of the water.

I breathed a brief sigh of relief and reflected for a moment at the terror that had seized me at not seeing him. It was intense and powerful. I had no idea then how intense and powerful and fucked up the feelings between us could get.

He came bounding up the beach, his chest heaving as he breathed rapidly. An athlete's pant. He dropped his hands to his knees and bent at the middle with a huge grin.

"How was it?" I asked, looking up and squinting even though I had my sunglasses on.

"Colder than I thought it would be," he said and stood up. He stretched his tall body out. I marveled at the fact that this man would be sharing my bed tonight.

"Need something to warm you up?" I asked and gave him a wink.

"I could always use something to warm me up," he said and positioned himself on the blanket next to me. He leaned in and cupped the back of my head with his hand. He pulled me into him and pressed his sun-warmed lips against mine. I tasted the salt water and felt the tiny granules of sand that clung to his damp lips. His tongue danced across mine as the kiss deepened.

"Get a room!" yelled a passerby hanging out of his friend's Jeep as they drove down the beach. Alex and I pulled away from each other. He flipped the guy off and then looked back at me.

"Maybe we should take his advice," he said, his voice low.

"Maybe so," I agreed.

He trailed his thumb over my bottom lip, and I kissed it. His eyes locked with mine. They were a deep blue, like a storm over the sea. It was a storm that I wanted to lose myself in and soon I'd be searching everywhere for a compass to navigate me out of it.

CHAPTER 4

Nashville Jun. 2010

Alex twirled his spaghetti like an Italian cuisine connoisseur, the way that someone would who had gone to finishing school. I cut mine up in pieces like the Southerner that I was. He glanced at my plate and then at me and smiled.

"You're so funny," he remarked in the way that he might have about his favorite dog's charming eating habits. I crinkled my nose.

"Why?" I asked, knowing it had to do with manners. He was obsessive about them. He knew what was ladylike and what wasn't and relished the chance to inform me about the differences.

"You're cute, too," he said as he put his fork down and raised his glass of red wine. We sat at a candlelit table in his apartment. The dim lights gave the place the ambiance of a restaurant. He'd wanted to go out, but I was exhausted from working. I begged him to stay home, and he'd surprised me with this.

I rolled my eyes like I always did when Alex complimented me. He had a way of insinuating sarcasm in every kind word. I never knew what was serious and what wasn't. Instead of making a fool of myself, I resorted to self-depre-cating. I acted as though anything nice he had to say couldn't be true. I had been conditioned.

We'd been together long enough for me to know that I was in love with him. Madly, insanely in love with him. Dan hated him and I didn't know why. My parents hadn't warmed up to him either. I thought it had to do with the difference in how and where we were raised. I thought that maybe he made Dan feel inferior. Not through any effort on Alex's part, but just by virtue of the fact of who he was: a senator's son from California. He was ivy league material, not Volunteer material. Sometimes I wondered why he left Los Angeles, but he would dodge the question with the kind of ballerina-like grace with which George W. Bush dodged that reporter's shoe. I let him off the hook. He didn't talk about his past very much, but when he did, a cloud passed over his face. I hated to see him like that, so I avoided it. He didn't mind.

"I have something I want to talk to you about," Alex said, bringing his napkin up and sitting it on the table. I put my fork down and chewed and then swallowed deliberately. I washed it down with a big gulp of wine.

"I'm about to graduate, as you know," he said with a proud smile. He ran his index finger around the rim of his wine glass in the same way he might have run it down the curve of my hips. I sat, hypnotized by him even still, months into our relationship. "I'm going back to Los Ange-les. That was the plan all along. You know that don't you?" he asked.

So, this was it after all.

I nodded and felt the sting of sadness against the rims of

my eyes. I didn't blink, not wanting to let a tear slip past the edge and run down my face, betraying my feelings.

"I do," I said, trying to keep my voice strong and steady. Alex had come to mean everything to me. My friendships had drifted apart. It was like no one was willing to accept that I was happy. Alex was different. He was from California. He was an outsider. The very thing that most people resented about him was what drew me to him. I was a moth, and he was a bug zapper, though I couldn't see it then.

Alex looked at his glass of wine. The silence was excruciating. He smiled cautiously.

"I want you to go with me," he said, his voice low.

"What?" I asked, blurting it out without an ounce of grace. The harshness of my voice contrasted with the gentle ambiance of the candles.

He chuckled.

"Will you go back to Los Angeles with me?" he asked. He looked me right in the eye. He commanded the room anywhere we went and when we were alone it was no different. His eyes were black pools with a single flame reflecting off their wet surfaces.

I swallowed. I processed what he was asking me to do. He wanted me to leave behind everything I'd ever known for him.

I couldn't wait to do it.

Everyone had left me behind when I'd met him, and now it was my turn to do the same to them.

"Of course," I said. "Of course I'll go with you," I reiterated.

Alex's somber visage cracked and broke into a huge smile. He clapped his hands together like a billion-dollar business deal had just been closed in a restaurant in the Hamptons. I couldn't help but grin right back at him. The idea of starting our life together so far away from Nashville was exhilarating. I'd lived there my whole life. My entire world was in Tennessee. It occurred to me that there was an entirely different world out there, just waiting for me to come and stake my claim in it.

I was young. I was dumb. And I was in love like I'd never been in love before. I would have thrown myself in front of a freight train barreling down the tracks at eighty miles per hour for him then. He was it for me. Everything. And I was his. I belonged to him.

And it wouldn't be long before I'd forget how to define myself by any other means.

CHAPTER 5

Nashville Dec. 2016

I press a napkin from my console onto my palm once I get home and into my driveway. I put the car in park and sit, letting it idle for a few minutes. Lost in my thoughts, my reverie is broken when Dan pokes his head through the curtains in the study. He doesn't look surprised to see me back which irritates me. I'm spoiling for a fight.

I grab my things and go in, crashing loud as a plane into the crowd at an air show. I let everything cascade across the counter and onto the floor, making a mess that I know he will resent. He loves for the kitchen to be clean, saying that it's the first impression that people really get of our house. For a guy who lived most of his life like a frat brother, he's surprisingly fastidious.

I want to make an impression. I want the kitchen to reflect the mess that I am inside—torn apart and unable to even begin to put the pieces back together or even sort out the edges like you do with a puzzle when you first take it out of the box. My edges are ragged and indistinguishable from the rest of it.

I hear him open the study door and pad down the hall. I turn, ready to say the first vile thing that pricks my tongue, ready to hurl. The intended target of my rage just happens to live 2,006 miles away in a bungalow in the Hollywood Hills. I failed to reach that destination this morning, so Dan will have to do.

He comes around the corner into the kitchen, his hair still a mess. He folds his arms across his chest. Sue wanders up beside him, his eyes searching mine for some explanation of the discord in our household.

"What?" I bark, my voice as threatening as a junkyard dog's first warning. I beg him to ask me why I didn't make it to Los Angeles, wanting so desperately for him to make some verbal misstep so I can justify reaming him.

"Tash, there's more," he says, his voice soft.

His words stop my train of thought in its tracks.

"What the fuck are you talking about 'more'?" I demand, throwing my arms skyward, wishing so much that the confrontation would get physical though that has never happened between us. I want to feel a limb break against the twisting of my body, it doesn't matter if it's his or my own. The sound itself would be cathartic.

"Just come in here," he says. "There's another e-mail and I kind of fucked up."

"What do you mean you 'kind of fucked up?'" I ask, my head ready to spin around like Linda Blair's in *The Exorcist*.

"When I opened the first e-mail, I sent a read receipt," he says evenly.

There is a silent gorge between us. The girth of what he's trying to pass on to me is enough to choke on. Alex knows, then that we have read the e-mail. It wasn't just lost in the void that is the World Wide Web. He has confirmation that it had reached its intended target. In a way, Dan has allowed him to have the tiniest peephole into my life. I feel betrayed. Right now, I want to kill them both. I want the whole thing to be over and if I had a gun, I might stick it deep into my mouth and pull the trigger.

It's only then that I realize Dan said the first e-mail, implying that there is a second.

"The first e-mail?" I ask. "Did you not show me everything?" I accuse him outright of keeping something from me, of conspiring against me. A dark part of myself reminds me that he's a man and even though I've known him my whole life, he's not to be trusted, no matter what he's done to prove himself worthy of it. "Have you been talking to him behind my back?" I ask, my eyes widening wildly with confusion and fear. I feel like a tiger, caged and cornered, prodded and ready to explode into the next of my captors who comes too close. It's a feeling I'm all too familiar with.

"Tash, breathe," Dan says, taking a step towards me and reaching his hands out to take mine. Sue whines standing beside him.

"Don't touch me," I say, guarded and vicious.

"I won't," he says, raising his hands up like he might have if I was a cop, ready to blow him away. "I'm not the enemy here," he says very evenly, convincingly even, and I try to breathe, to force air into my lungs and down into my chest. I try to remind myself to keep breathing.

"Was there another e-mail?" I ask, reframing the question.

"Yes," he says. "After I sent the read receipt and you left, there was another one. He must have seen the read receipt and responded to it."

"I want to see it," I demand, pushing past him and going towards the study. He grabs me by the arm and I defend his grasp, breaking it satisfyingly with a twist of my wrist. I head on.

"Tash!" he calls after me. "Just calm down! We can handle this!"

I storm down the hallway and into our shared office. I sit down at the computer and the newest e-mail is already pulled up on the screen.

http://j6h23hjwiu38dedn555.onion

https://www.torproject.org/download/download-easy.html.en

That's all it says. Two links.

I stare at the screen, puzzled by this new information. I look over my shoulder as Dan walks into the room.

"What does this mean?" I ask him.

"I've heard of this thing," he says. "Tor. It's a web browser for the deep net."

"What the fuck does that mean?" I ask.

"The websites that you can access with Google make up a small percentage of the internet. There's a shit load more out there that can't be accessed on a normal browser like Chrome or Edge. Most of it is totally normal, but there's some fucked up shit, too. I've heard horror stories about it on the gaming forums I'm part of," he says.

I click on the .onion link.

A page from our internet provider pops up.

Sorry, the url http://j6h23hjwiu38dedn555.onion cannot be found.

I go back to the e-mail and click the link to the Tor website.

The description of the web browser reads:

Tor prevents people from learning your location or browsing habits.

There is a tab on the side describing the types of people

that use Tor. It shows a picture of some kids, saying that friends and family of yours probably use it. That military and law enforcement use it and activists and journalists, as well. I click to download it.

"Don't do that!" Dan says.

"Why not?" I ask, giving it permission to install on the computer.

Dan groan.

"I've yet to hear a good story about someone down-loading this thing," he says.

I wait until it's finished and opened it up. I key in the .onion address into the search bar.

In a few seconds, a website pops up. The title is Blue Heroin and there's a picture of a scantily clad girl posing for the camera in what looks to be an amateur shot. I scroll down, seeing that the first entry on the page is a girl's name. Madison.

I click on her name, and it takes me to a page that looks like your average porn site's page. There are pictures of her in various positions. She looks kind of high in some of them, though, something that I don't know to be typical of porn actresses. Some of the shots look blurry and were obviously taken on a cell phone camera. I scroll down and see some information at the bottom.

Madison Reynolds, 24, Cleveland, Ohio
1254 Pershing Blvd.
Cleveland, Ohio 44115
(216) 405-7180
mreynolds92@yahoo.com

I back out of the page and go to the next entry. A girl named Arianna. It's the same thing. Amateur looking shots. They are all candid. A few of her in various sexual positions. And then at the bottom, her information.

I back out again and scroll down the page. About five names in, I stop.

Natasha

I look at Dan who is glued to the screen. I click.

There in full color is the picture of me that Alex e-mailed to Dan. Along with it are others from the same night. Most of them are of me on the bed, wearing lingerie and posing for the camera even though I hadn't wanted to. I thought at the time that I'd do anything for him to save our relationship. I never intended for anyone to see the photos. I scroll down. There are so many.

There are pictures from another night. I'm tied up and naked. I remember the cold flash of the camera blinding me and making me cringe, imagining my flesh forever documented in pixels. Alex laughed at me, telling me no one would ever see them.

I scroll to the bottom.

Natasha Davis, 29, Nashville, Tennessee

602 Sycamore St.

Nashville, Tennessee 37203

(615) 580-9184

admin@redtriangle.com

"Oh my God."

The temperature of my skin plummets, matching the coldness outside. I feel myself grow dizzy and I inhale sharply. I inhale again, not getting enough oxygen. And again. And again.

"Tash, breathe!" Dan says, grabbing me by the face and turning me towards him.

"Oh, fuck," I say between labored breaths.

"It's going to be alright!" he promises.

Vomit crawls up my throat and I lurch past him, puking into the trash can.

I begin to shake.

"Tash, we have to go to the police," Dan says.

I snort with laughter.

"The police?" I bark. "Dan, this is the tip of the iceberg. He's a fucking psychopath! He put my home address—he knows my home address and put it on the internet!"

"Which is why we have to go to them," he says calmly.

He doesn't understand. Fear chokes me. Alex is a monster. I know that. And I know the kinds of things he's capable of, but this has never entered my mind. And the e-mail address. My stomach does another dip on this roller coaster. It's the username for the staff e-mail at the jiu-jitsu school. Whatever is sent to that e-mail went to everyone.

I should jump on the landmine. I should have the guts.

But there is something niggling in the back of my mind that neutralizes any knockout punch I could throw at Alex. I feel paralyzed.

"No," I say quietly.

"What do you mean 'no'?" Dan asks, incredulous and echoing my tone from earlier in our conversation when I asked about the second e-mail. He's stunned.

"Exactly what I said. We're not going to the police," I say evenly.

"Tash, listen to yourself! This guy is sending you naked pictures of yourself and posting your fucking home address and phone number and work e-mail on the goddamned internet and you're just going to let him?"

I am silent.

He stands in front of me, his arms outstretched with his question, waiting for me to give him something, anything, to work with.

"You can't let him do this to you," he says, as stern as my father.

"And what the fuck am I supposed to do?" I ask. "You don't know him, Daniel," I say. "I just need to ignore it and let it die down."

"You really don't get it, do you?" he asks.

"You don't get it," I say.

"No, I get it completely!" he shouts. "What's happening is that you're going to give in to him. You're going to contact him and you're going to be begging and pleading, just like you were three years ago. You're going to let him slither back into your life like the snake that he is, just like he did the first time. You're about to be right back where you were when you begged me to let you come and stay here!" He says it all so bitterly. It cuts.

"And you resent me for that?" I ask. "For asking you for help?"

"I resent you for being weak enough to let it all happen in the first place," Dan says.

I'm shocked into silence. I never thought Dan felt that way. I never thought he could say something so cruel.

"Well, be my guest to walk out the door, Dan. Just like you did before," I say, the words firing out of my mouth as retaliation for what he just hurled at me. I aim for the heart and hope that I'll hit my target. He walks out of the room. I wonder if maybe this is the end of me and Dan. For real this time.

Sue remains. He looks over his shoulder to see where Dan has gone and then looks at me as though he wants some sort of explanation.

"I'm sorry, buddy," I say to him, reaching out a hand. He steps forward and receives my gesture of goodwill. It looks like at least he is willing to forgive me.

CHAPTER 6

Nashville Apr. 2010

"I just don't think he's a good friend to you," Alex said as he grabbed a container of hummus from the fridge in our little apartment. The money was there for a much more lavish living situation, but the agreement he had with Sharon, his mother, was that he didn't get to touch most of it until he graduated.

"We've been friends since we were kids, Alex," I said with conviction. Dan was my oldest friend and had always been there for me, until recently.

Earlier in the week, we'd all gone to dinner. Just the three of us. Dan had always felt awkward not having a date since I was usually his date in cases when he didn't have a proper one.

We'd gone to a little Italian restaurant near Music Row. I'd ordered spaghetti with marinara, and Alex had a salad, ever conscious about his health. The conversation was dull and needed resuscitation after they delved into their political differences. I prodded it onward like I was driving a cow home that refused to go to the barn.

"So, Daniel," I said, using his full name. "Why don't you tell Alex about the photography project you're working on?" I asked him, sounding more like a mother than I'd ever sounded in all my twenty-one years.

Dan fiddled with a breadstick, dipping it into the alfredo sauce that he'd ordered specifically for that purpose. That was his—our—habit when we went out. It was something Alex forbade me to do. He thought it made me look like I'd never been anywhere in my life. I eyeballed the alfredo sauce jealously, wanting desperately to slather my bread in it and stuff it into my face. Instead, I delicately twirled just enough pasta onto my fork. Never too much, that was also something Alex considered crass. Just enough for a tiny bite.

Dan looked up at me like an insolent teenager on a date with his mom and her new boyfriend. He wasn't over Alex's comment when they'd first met at one of Dan's shows. Alex had looked around the exhibit and remarked, "It's amazing that you can make a living at this."

I tried to convince Dan that Alex had meant it was remarkable and wonderful that Dan was able to make a living doing what he loved. Dan didn't believe me. I didn't really believe myself either.

"I don't think he wants to hear about that," he said, sighing and looking around the restaurant like he'd rather be at any other table and with any other couple.

We sat in awkward silence for a moment and then Alex spoke in his most condescending tone. It was the tone he took whenever I needed reminding that I was just a girl who grew up in Nashville.

"No, Daniel. Please, tell me what you're working on. I'm sure you're really excited about it," he said. He sounded the same was a part-time father would sound talking to a child that he never really wanted.

The tension between the three of us was palpable. I could have taken its pulse and felt it racing, waiting for the perfect moment to explode in a fit of rage.

In an unprecedented move in their relationship, Dan took the reins.

"Well, Tash is involved in this one," he said, smiling at me.

It was news to me, and I dropped my fork, letting it clang loudly against my dish. I didn't know where he was going with this, but I knew it wasn't somewhere good. I chewed my food quickly, hoping to be able to interrupt him before he said something both of us would regret.

"Oh, really? She didn't tell me that," Alex said, looking from Dan to me with an amused smile.

"Oh, yeah," Dan said, leaning forward as though he was about to let us in on the nuclear codes. "It's a series of photos of women in shitty relationships. I was thinking about superimposing the crazy shit these assholes say to these girls on their skin. Kind of like bruises. Just showing what it does to a girl when she's stuck in that kind of relationship."

Dan leaned back and took a drink of water, happy with himself.

I inhaled sharply, waiting for the hammer to drop. My stomach flipped and I felt nauseated. I thought I might throw up. I wanted nothing more than to disappear. Instead, I sat in stunned silence. Angry at both of them.

I chanced a look at Alex, and he was smirking but there was vitriol in his eyes. I knew that whatever came out of his mouth next would be horrible. But he surprised me. Instead of shooting back something at Dan that would bring him to his knees, he simply reminded him who was leading this parade by pulling out a crisp one-hundred-dollar bill and laying it on the table.

"Tash, we're leaving," he said with authority.

Without thinking, I got up from the table. I grabbed my purse, and I turned for the door. Before I did, I looked into Dan's eyes. He was hurt and angry. He felt just like I did. My anger overcame my empathy, and I looked away.

"I know you've been friends since you were kids, but that doesn't mean you need to be friends as adults," Alex said later that week. "People change and sometimes those people become toxic."

In a sick way, what he said made sense. Alex provided for me and could provide for me for the rest of my life. I was happy. He loved me, even if he didn't show it like other people. If Dan couldn't accept that, he didn't have a place in the new life I was building with Alex. Maybe he had become toxic.

"He's just bitter because he's alone," Alex said philosophically. "Some people can't stand other people being happier than they are. Maybe that's how it is with the two of you. Haven't you always been there to support him?"

"Yeah, I have," I said.

"Well, there you go," Alex said, concluding the matter as though it were as cut and dry as that.

I ruminated on Alex's words for the rest of the week and didn't talk to Dan. I wanted to see him and smooth things over. I wanted the man who I trusted most and the man that I loved to be able to be in the same room without wanting to kill each other. But I wasn't sure that was going to happen. I was going to have to make a choice if Dan forced my hand.

That weekend, I asked Dan if I could come over and talk to him. I went to the house that we had once shared earlier on in college before I had moved in with Alex. Dan came to the door and stepped outside like I was a stranger trying to sell him my kid's chocolate bars for a school fundraiser.

"What do you want?" he asked without much emotion aside from irritation.

"I wanted to talk to you about the other night," I said.

"Oh, you mean the truth?" he asked, riling a little.

I laughed.

"Alex isn't shitty to me," I said, saying the word like it was dirty and it was the greatest insult that Dan could have thrown at my relationship. So far from the truth.

"Tash!" he shouted. "Wake the fuck up! He treats you like some kind of nineteenth century prostitute that he can order around. It's like watching a sicker version of My Fair Lady that was written by the Marquis de Sade!"

"He isn't abusive," I said, my voice wavering. The truth of what Dan said seeped into the cracked edges of what I'd built with Alex. At every place that had been chipped away by demeaning conversations, Dan's words permeated the surface like water rushing over a porous rock.

"Listen to yourself!" he shouted. "You're defending that asshole just so you can go home, and he can treat you like shit! Don't you get it? I don't even know you anymore."

"Well, you don't have to," I said.

"What?" Dan asked, affronted.

"Know me anymore. I'm done here," I said. "Don't worry. I won't bother you again." I got into my car and slammed the door. I looked up to see Dan standing in his doorway thunderstruck. I felt a sense of pride swell in my chest, adrenaline racing through my system. I knew what I'd done would make Alex proud. I felt like I'd done the right thing in the face of adversity. I told myself that the sinking feeling in my gut was just the old me dying away so something new could be born.

I had no idea how right I was.

CHAPTER 7

Nashville Dec. 2016

My head pounds as I hear Daniel slam the door on his way out to go to work. Our argument is echoing throughout the silence in the house. I hate to be at odds with him but he doesn't understand. He can't. Going to the cops isn't an option. I know Alex and I know that pissing him off will only exacerbate the situation. My best bet is to lay low and try to not let it get to me. I can talk to Heather about any e-mails that the staff received at jiu-jitsu. That will be easy enough to smooth over. I lay in bed for a little while giving myself a pep talk. Sue lays in the bed with me, taking up his half. It's like having a human being beside me.

At last, I get up and mill around the kitchen, putting the dishes up and loading the dishwasher again. Things that have to be done regardless of what's being sent back and forth on the internet right now. I try to find things to occupy my mind and almost forget that I have a private lesson.

I look up at the clock on the microwave and see that it's ten till nine. I remember that I have a private lesson with a woman named Angela. She's in her fifties. A domestic violence survivor. She has a restraining order against her ex-husband but she's afraid of what he might do to her even still. I can relate. Helping women like Angela is what I'd dedicated my life to since I left Los Angeles three Christmases ago. I still fear him, though. He hadn't made a habit of hitting me, but he was capable of far worse things.

He was always creeping in the shadows for me, waiting around every unilluminated corner and in every alley. There was one night when Dan was out of town, and I pulled up into our driveway after a girl's night out with Heather. I'd had a few drinks, and I thought I saw someone standing in between the two of the pampas grass plants. Immediately I thought it was him. I hadn't seen him in two years at that point but still, there he was. The thought of him haunted me throughout the night. I didn't sleep and kept looking surreptitiously out my window, monitoring the cul de sac. Nothing ever happened and I knew he wasn't really there, but it didn't stop me from feeling like he was.

I always felt like he was.

After I left Los Angeles he didn't reach out to me. I assumed he knew why I'd left, and he knew he was wrong. He was so determined to have whatever he wanted, and it puzzled me that he didn't come after me, so I spent a lot of time pondering why he hadn't. It played havoc on me. I didn't want him to pursue me, but why hadn't he? I would have preferred it if he'd come after me back then. And in some sick way, it made me think he was right about me. That it was the reason he hadn't come after me.

You're worthless.

I knew why.

But now, with the pictures on the internet and my home address out there for the most depraved users of the internet to see, do I really know what lengths he is willing to go to? And after so much time. Can't he let it go?

These thoughts haunt me as I scramble around to get ready. Sue tries to help by nuzzling my gi and my gear as I lay it out next to my bag. He hates for me to leave and begins to whine as I get ready.

"I know, boy," I say. "I'd rather stay here with you."

I throw my gi in my bag and don't bother with a shower. Usually, the idea of rolling without bathing would repulse me. This morning, I don't seem to care. Nothing is at the forefront of my mind except those pictures and the people who are looking at them. I remember when they were taken, the night emblazoned on my brain with a branding iron, never to be forgotten.

Alex had begged me and begged me to let him take some pictures of me. He'd gotten a digital SLR for Christmas and he wanted to practice with it. He'd pull it out every time things got hot and heavy between us, and I'd gently force him to put it away, pulling the covers up over myself in an act of modesty. He would protest and I would withhold sex until the camera was off and in a bag under the bed. It became a ritual.

In the end, though, when I knew that he'd cheated and I knew that we were in a downward spiral, I was willing to do anything. I was weak and a prisoner in that house. I depended on him for everything, including, mistakenly, my self-worth.

One night, he brought the camera out. I didn't protest. Instead, I just watched as he got it out of the bag. I had on see-through lingerie and instinctively covered myself. He coaxed me out of the covers and begged once more to take my picture.

"No one will ever see them," he said. "I promise."

His promise echoes in my mind, and I didn't ever see the pictures after that night. Not until this morning when Dan got one of them in his e-mail and then a link to the site with the rest of them. I know there are more, though. There had been another night. A night when he'd used his cell phone as we had sex. I shudder at the thought of those pictures seeing the light of day. What happened that night shouldn't have been documented.

On the drive to the jiu-jitsu school, all of these thoughts compete for first place in my brain. It's a blur. I'm not sure exactly what to do with the information. At least inside the wall of Red Triangle, I'm safe. It's a studio that was designed to teach jiu-jitsu to women. We have one male instructor, Henry. With Heather and Henry I am safe. It's a place that I've always gone when I didn't feel safe. The following night after I thought I'd seen Alex in the bushes, I slept at the school and had brought Sue with me. It was and is my haven. And when I pull into the parking lot, I feel a wave of relief wash over me, cleansing me of my stupidity and my sins and allowing me to breathe deep into my lungs once again. I put the car in park and sit behind the steering wheel, listening to the disc jockeys on the radio for a moment, even though I'm running late. I lift my hands and see that they're shaking. I clasp them together and rub them, hoping that the friction and the heat will bring me back to life—back to my former self before Dan stormed into the garage. I marvel at the way a single file can change your life. How an arrangement of pixels in a digital format can shatter everything.

I get out of the car and go in. As I walk by the office, Heather pops her head out. She's about my height and has straight brown hair that falls below her shoulders. She has a straight, angular nose, and her skin is a gorgeous tan all year round. Her green eyes stand out from her complexion in an almost startling way.

"Hey, come here," she says.

I need to talk to her about the e-mail address thing. I don't want to, but Heather and I have grown quite close in the last few years and it shouldn't be a big deal. She'll understand.

I turn and walk into the office that has become my second home. She walks around the desk and sits down at the computer.

"Hey, I don't want to freak you out, but I need to show you something," she says.

I imagine the kind of lascivious e-mail that's waiting for me. Something disgusting potentially housing dick pics from some guy who lives in his parents' basement.

"I know already," I say. "It's a long story, but basically my ex posted the jiu-jitsu school e-mail address to a forum full of creeps, so don't be surprised if you get some gross e-mails."

"That's not it," she says.

"What?" I ask.

"I got this this morning," she says, maximizing an Outlook window on her screen. I look and see that it is the same e-mail Dan had gotten, complete with the link to download the Tor browser. "I downloaded it and looked at the website. He's a sick fuck, isn't he?" she asks.

"You have no idea," I say. "Oh God. So, everyone has seen this?"

"I'll delete it. As soon as their phones sync, it'll be gone," she says.

"What'll be gone?" comes a male voice as Henry pops his perfectly gelled head into the office. He smiles brightly, his white teeth contrasting with his brown skin. I return his smile, but only with great effort.

"Nothing," I say. "Girl stuff," I add with another fake smile.

Heather gets up from the desk and walks towards Henry.

"Hey, I wanted to show you something about the new A/C system," she says to him and shoots a look over her shoulder protectively. I nod at her as she escorts him out. Henry is a friend, but somehow, I don't feel like sharing this with him if I don't have to. Once they are out of the room, I sit down at the desk that I've sat at so many times, having people sign contracts and discussing problems with parents and students. I hover the cursor over the delete button on the e-mail and click it.

Heather comes back into the office.

"Your private lesson is here," she says, all business, as if nothing is wrong. "When you're done, can we talk about New Orleans?" she asks.

I smile, all business, as if nothing is wrong.

"Of course," I say.

I stand from the desk and go into the lobby to greet Angela.

CHAPTER 8

"I really don't know if I'm ever going to get the hang of all this," Angela says, sweat beading on her brow in the humid gym. She reaches up a hand and wipes it from her forehead back into her short pixie cut that's wild now from all the rolling we've just done.

"You'll get it," I say. "Your rear naked choke sank in pretty deep on that last roll. I'd say you're already doing great." I smile at her. This one is genuine.

I take pride in passing along my knowledge, especially to women who I know are in desperate need of it. I think about the girl I was three years ago and how much I could have used all of it.

The first thing I teach my students is to never close the Triangle of Victimization.

There are three things required for a sexual assault to take place: a victim, a predator, and an opportunity. As long as one of those is missing from the equation, you never have to worry about being raped. I love to think that I never have to let my triangle close on itself ever again.

I've managed to focus my attention on Angela somehow for the last hour that I've had her as a student. Other students for the morning class are beginning to file in and put their gis on. There are more students in the morning class today because of Christmas break. Students that normally have college classes or are in high school are able to come to classes that they normally can't attend. I crack my neck nervously, looking at all of them, turning it side to side almost violently. It's a tic that I developed when I was with Alex. I haven't done it in years.

"Are you okay, Natasha?" Angela asks me. She's always using my proper name. Alex was never a fan of the nickname 'Tash.' He said it sounded cheap, like a prostitute or a stripper. I always hated that he connected my nickname with those things. It was like taking my autonomy wasn't enough, he decided that he'd take my name, too.

"I'm fine," I lie. Angela is always so nice to me. I hate to rain on the image she has of me. She thinks I have my entire life together in a neat little package, jiu-jitsu the bow on top that held it all together. Shattering her idea of who I am, even though it isn't real, means that version of me doesn't exist at all, not even in someone else's mind.

"Sure," Angela says, drawing out the word, making it clear that she knows I'm anything but fine. She leaves the door open for me to correct myself but I don't.

"Same time next week?" I ask.

"Same time," she confirms. She and I walk off the mat and I wave at a couple of the morning students. They greet me eagerly.

"Hey," says a deep voice from behind me as a hand grabs my shoulder. I flip around and instinctively brush the hand off with more force than necessary. It's a friendly hand —Henry's hand.

"Hey," I say, almost as out of breath as if I've been running.

"You okay?" he asks me, tilting his head like a dog.

"Yeah, why?" I respond, forcing a smile.

He smiles back impishly as though he knows better but doesn't want to get into the details of everything.

"Whatever you say," he says, the words melodic. He winks.

It's been so long since I've flirted with anyone seriously that Henry catches me off guard. He isn't normally like this and usually treats me like a sister. I'm not sure what to do or how to respond. My body goes rigid, my bones seeming to convert the muscle tissue around them into hard, calcified flesh. Goosebumps prickle my skin, even though the studio is a balmy 78 degrees. I'm suddenly aware of all the private parts of my body. I can feel Henry's eyes on them like they're his fingers, caressing the outside of my clothes as my skin crawls beneath.

"Wanna roll?" he asks. "I'll go light on you. Promise."

Henry backs off the mats in the central part of the gym and walks towards the private room. I find my feet carrying me forward. I long to destroy myself. Anything to get me out of the nightmare and back into a workable reality.

"Yeah," I say. I do want to roll with Henry, but I want to roll hard. I don't want him to hold back on me. I want him to sink in his rear naked choke and make the lights go out. I want him to squeeze the life out of me. I want him to snap my arm in half. I want him to break my body because I'm going to try to break his.

He leads the way to the private room and I follow. Usually when we roll, it isn't too aggressive. We get competitive with each other, but neither of us ever try to hurt the other. I wonder if he has any idea of what's about to happen. He pulls back the blue curtain and we step into the room that's always a little warmer than the rest of the studio. The humidity feels good on my dry skin. It always cracks and flakes in the winter.

He goes to one knee, and I shake my head. He raises an eyebrow and purses his lips as though stunned and impressed. He furrows his brows.

Henry doesn't set a timer and I don't care. I want to go until I can't breathe or my muscles give way. I dive for his waist and take him to the ground. He goes easy on me at first. We become a tangle of limbs, rolling this way and that, me trying to submit him and him escaping with natural, fluid ease.

I go in a kimura and submit him, bringing his hand dangerously close to his head.

"Hey! I tapped!" he growls. I finally let go. He looks shocked when we sit up and pull away from each other. There is always an awkward moment just after finishing a roll when you and the other person realize just how close you are to each other. "What was that? You know better than that."

I look at him with a blank expression. I would never try to hurt one of my training partners, but something is different today. I'm fueled by anger in a way that I'm normally not. Normally I use my anger as fuel, but today, I'm just acting out what I feel inside.

Adrenaline surges throughout my body.

"Come on," I say, demanding that we roll again. I get up from the floor and motion impatiently for Henry to stand and he does.

"If that's how you wanna play, we can do that," he says, as though he really would rather not hurt me, but he will if he has to.

This time Henry goes for my waist and flips me over his hip. I hit the ground with a thud and feel the air rush out of my lungs, temporarily immobilizing me. Breathless, I scramble, grabbing his foot and trying to put a joint lock on him but he beats me to it. He twists my ankle and I hear it pop. The muscles and tendons strain but I didn't tap out. I want him to keep going. I want him to snap it right off. I want to go to the hospital and be so doped up on morphine that I don't know my own address.

"Tap!" he growls.

I don't. I only struggle against him.

"Tash, tap! Goddammit!"

I keep struggling like a fish on a river bank in the paws of a bear, gasping its last. Finally, though, I succumb and do as he says with great regret.

He lets me go and I lay there on the mat panting, staring at him. Our bodies are still entangled and I wish that I hadn't tapped out. I wish I could have felt my tendon snap. The bigger the better. Whatever would put me out for months or give me an excuse to hide from my entire life. Whatever it takes.

"What the hell is going on with you?" Henry asks me. "You've never rolled with me—or anyone—like that." He pulls his legs to him and wraps his arms around his knees like he's ready for story time at the library.

I'm not about to tell him any stories. I just pull myself up and sit cross-legged in front of him.

"Just want to get ready for the tournament," I lie.

There's a tournament coming up in Dallas and it's true that I want to go. It's also true that I've never competed before. Heather and Henry have been pushing me to since I got my blue belt a year ago. Something has always kept me from it, though. Maybe it's that it would feel like a real fight, and if it's going to feel like a real fight, it needs to be one because I won't stop.

"That's news to me," Henry says and shakes his head with a little laugh.

"Well, unlike you, I don't post my every move on Facebook," I say, mustering a little smile.

The king of social media just grins.

"Hey, you wanna get a drink sometime?" he asks me.

I only stare at him.

"I mean, we just never hang out outside of here. We should, you know?" he says, trying to make it less weird.

Suddenly, a thought seizes me. The last person I've been with was Alex. The last hands that have touched my naked body belonged to Alex. I don't want that to be the case. I want it to be anyone but him. I don't care who. Anyone who can touch my skin and erase the marks that Alex left there would do. Here is my opportunity.

"Yeah," I say.

"Bye!" I wave at the students filing out of the studio and I walk into the office. Heather has just come in, fresh off the mats, and is changing clothes.

"Hey!" she says, always in a good mood when she's fresh off of a roll.

"You wanted to talk about New Orleans?" I ask.

We have an upcoming trip. Heather and I have started taking the women's program on the road this last year. We've gone to San Francisco, Seattle, and Orlando. It's exciting and intimidating. We are going to be teaching at Hernandez Jiu-Jitsu in the Crescent City. It will be a weekend of chokes and drinking. I'm looking forward to it.

"Yeah," she says. "I wanted you to check out the hotel I booked. See if you think it's okay."

I nod and she pulls on a fresh t-shirt. She steps around the desk and pulls up her internet browser. She enters the address and the hotel pops up on the screen. It's nice. A lot nicer than anywhere I would stay on my own. It's right in the French Quarter. The room that she booked for us has a balcony that overlooks the Quarter on French Street.

"Damn," I say.

"I know, right?" she squeals. "They have everything. There's even a courtyard with a sauna and a hot tub. Oh, and a bar. That's important."

I smile at Heather.

Since I've become friends with her, we've had a lot of nights where we've gone out drinking. I'm almost always the designated driver and when I'm not, I don't drink that much. The idea of blacking out terrifies me. It was something that when I was younger, didn't make me bat an eye. Dan and I have gotten black out drunk several times. But the idea of it now is too much. It's different than being choked out. Being choke out here at the gym is safe. Blacking out from alcohol was something else. I don't want to lose control of my body. Heather, on the other hand, knows how to take her liquor and can handle it. I have a feeling that there will be a lot of drinking on this trip.

"It's nice," I say.

Heather closes the browser.

"So, do you want to talk about your ex?" she asks me, cutting straight to the point, as she is wont to do.

I sigh deeply. I knew that it was going to come up, needing to be addressed sooner or later, as our conversation from earlier were been cut short by Henry. It doesn't make it any easier to talk about.

"I guess I shouldn't be surprised," I say. "He's a fucking psycho."

"Yeah, from what I gather, he's definitely a psycho."

"I never thought this was a possibility, though. I had totally forgotten about those pictures," I say.

Heather has a look on her face that screams, *Only a dumbass would let a guy take nude pictures of her with her face in them.* But she's too kind to say that, instead, she offers a sympathetic smile.

"It could happen to anyone," she says.

"Only morons who let people take naked pictures of them," I retort.

"You're not a moron. You were in love with him, weren't you?" she asks.

"Madly," I say.

"Would you have done anything for him?" she asks.

"More than anything. I would have given him the world if he'd asked for it," I say, the truth of my statement like a knife in my gut in light of what happened between Alex and I. The idea that he's only an e-mail away from me at this point is both terrifying and something that I am curious about. I know that I have to contact him sooner or later.

"Have you talked to him?" Heather asks, reading my mind.

"I don't want to," I say.

"You're going to have to," she says.

"I know. I just don't want to have to face it. It's like if I don't contact him then maybe it's not really happening."

"But it is happening," she says.

I sigh.

"He's just so scary," I admit.

Alex scares me. He always danced on the razor's edge of

what was acceptable to say or do. I never knew what to expect from him.

"You can do this," Heather advises me.

I sigh and rub my temples.

"I hope you're right," I say.

CHAPTER 9

Los Angeles Oct. 2010

After I got with Alex, we were incredibly close without indulging equally in sharing our pasts with each other. I felt like I knew him, but I'm not sure that I ever really did. I had told him everything there was to know about me, but he had never really told me anything substantial about himself. I knew that his father was a senator for a number of years and that his mother stayed home. I knew that he felt like he lived in his father's shadow and that he'd never escape it, but I didn't know any more than that.

When we first moved to L.A., we spent many nights driving through Beverly Hills, hugging the curves and parting the fog. On a particularly foggy night during that time, Alex was driving faster than he normally did, taking the curves without quite as much care as I would have. I tried to remind myself that he knew the roads and that he was in total control. He didn't do anything without being in total control.

As we drove, I clutched the passenger side door handle of his Audi until my knuckles ached. It was brand new, a purchase that he made on a whim. That was the kind of money he came from.

"Sometimes when I drive these roads, it reminds me of my brother," he said.

I sat in silence. The topic of his brother was completely taboo between us. I knew that he had died, and Alex had glossed over most of the details. I didn't even know how it happened. I chalked it up to the subject being so painful for him that he balked at remembering it.

"Why's that?" I asked.

"My dad drove these roads after Killian died. Sometimes he would make me go with him. He would be drunk, take the curves too fast—" like Alex was doing. "I would always be so scared that we would die. I was so afraid of dying when I was young," he laughed. "But part of me wanted to die after everything."

I didn't say anything. I knew better than to prod him, but I also knew that Alex was the kind of person who would take it as a personal insult if I didn't ask for more information. I wasn't sure what to do. He was a Pandora's box of emotions. Sometimes my inquisitiveness didn't bother him, other times it made him cruel. I let him continue, uninterrupted.

"I've never really talked about it with you," he said. "I don't really tell most people about it. I don't like to talk about it, but it, y'know—it happened. There's nothing I can do to change that."

I looked ahead and saw headlights peeking through the fog, creating an ethereal glow between the trees as the car raced through the hills. I clenched my fist around the door handle, hoping he would slow down, but he only accelerated through the curve and deeper into the fog, passing the car too quickly for my liking. I tried to reassure myself that he knew these roads the way he knew each curve of my body, navigating them effortlessly.

"When he died, I was only eight. We had a huge swimming pool at that house—the first house I ever lived in. After everything, we moved, of course. But it was a great house for two boys to grow up in. It was here, in the Hills," he said, gesturing towards the road ahead of us. "We had a game room that all of my friends loved, and we had our own bedrooms and bathrooms. My brother was five."

He paused and looked in the rearview mirror. I glanced at the side mirror, trying to see what he saw, ghosts as tangible as the fog, but I only saw my own disturbed reflection.

"My brother had been taking swimming lessons. My dad wanted both of us to become swimmers. He thought we could become Olympians. I sucked at swimming," he said with a bitter laugh. "The first of many disappointments I would bring my father."

We continued through the hills and came to a stoplight. Alex turned left and navigated us through a neighborhood full of fancy houses. We passed celebrity home after celebrity home. The higher the bushes, the bigger the star, they said in L.A.

"That day, my mom had been swimming with us. She went inside to get something. It was strange. Usually, she would have asked our housekeeper to do it, but I guess she wasn't around. Or she was busy or something. My mom went inside. Killian and I were swimming in the shallow end. He was tall for his age, and he could bounce up from the floor of the pool and keep his head above water. He wasn't the best swimmer yet, but he was better than I had been at his age. I kept teasing him, jumping off the diving board, telling him that he would never be able to dive as well as I could."

Alex got quiet for several moments and gunned the engine. We flew through the curving neighborhood full of houses that probably belonged to the rich and the famous.

He continued.

"I dove in headfirst. I touched the bottom with my hands as I reached it. I felt like I really could be an Olympian then. I kept diving and Killian kept edging out of the pool, egging me on. I told him to stay where he was, but finally, I came up from the bottom and he was standing on the diving board."

I felt my stomach knot up, thinking about the trauma Alex was revisiting.

"I yelled for him not to dive. I told him not to," Alex said, nervously, rapidly. "But he dove. He dove and he didn't come up. I saw blood and I tried to swim to the bottom. I don't think I knew about blowing all the air out of my lungs because I kept floating to the top. He didn't come up," he said, having regained the composure in his voice. Without tears, he said, "He never came up."

We sat in silence in the car, and I reached a hand cautiously over the console to touch his on the steering wheel that he now clutched with white knuckles.

"It's not your fault," I said, the only appropriate thing that I could think to say. Alex had never been so vulnerable with me before. I treasured the moment like an oyster holding onto its pearl.

Alex looked over at me, quickly turning his vulnerability to vitriol.

"Whose fault was it then?"

The question was loaded. I knew the answer and he knew the answer, but speaking Sharon's name would make me the villain in this poorly drawn cartoon. His mother was sacred to him. I never fully understood the dynamic of their relationship, but I knew that the bond was strong. I tried to tip toe around the answer and found myself stammering.

"It was my fault," he said. "And that's what my father believed from that day forward."

I got quiet again, not sure what to say, letting him have his moment. I felt an outpouring of empathy towards him and an utter helplessness as to what to do with it. He never let me in this closely. I feared that one wrong action would see me sealed out forever. I would have done anything for him. I wanted to sacrifice myself at the altar of his suffering, take it from him and hand it over to the gods that might have been.

"We moved shortly after. My father started drinking. He started taking me on these drives. He started coming up to my room at night. He'd wake me up and slap me around. It was our little secret," he said with a venomous smile.

I tried to imagine that Sharon didn't know about this, and I couldn't.

"Didn't your mom know?" I blurted out, outraged at what I was hearing. Disgusted by her antipathy.

He shot a look at me, his eyes like swords, pinning me down like the man on the tarot deck.

"Of course she didn't know," he said, mustering conviction that I was certain he didn't feel. How could she not have known? Her son bruised and tired waking up with new marks each morning, her drunken husband leaving their bed in the night. There was no way she didn't know.

I remained silent, unsure of what he wanted from me only sure of what I wanted to give him. Solace in the fact that it wasn't his fault, that his father had been wrong. I knew, though, that those were things he couldn't have heard even if I'd said them through a bullhorn. But maybe one day, he would be able to hear them. Maybe one day, I could help him heal.

I held onto that idea. I thought for so long that I could fix what was the matter with him. I thought that surely, I could make everything alright for him and tame the snarling demons that lurked behind his eyes. I thought for certain that love would be enough. I had no ideas about the way that demons were born at that time. And I had no idea that Alex made a great sire.

He would go on to give life to the demons that danced on my shoulder and told me things about myself that I'd rather forget. That I'd tried so desperately to put to bed, but couldn't. They would tell me things about my worthiness. Things about my appearance. Things about me being trash. Being cold. Being a monster.

At the time, all I could feel was pity for him. Not in the sense that he was a pitiful creature, but as though he were something broken that I could reach down, pick up, and piece back together. I didn't know then that I would cut myself on his most jagged edges and that with one shard, he would stab me more deeply than I thought possible.

Maybe in some fucked up way, we were meant for each other.

CHAPTER 10

Nashville Dec. 2016

I pull into the driveway and gather my things from the car. My gi is drenched in sweat from rolling with Henry. I know that if I don't put it in the washing machine, bacteria would start to grow and the stench will be unbearable.

I go inside and open the door slowly, carefully, wishing so badly that it won't make that horrid creak that it's known for. Not one to disappoint, it does what it does best. I cringe and close my eyes only to open them to an empty house. There is no music coming from the study. Daniel has surely gone to the gallery by now. I breathe a sigh of relief, not ready to deal with the field of emotional landmines he laid out before me. And I'm not about to apologize. If anyone is going to apologize, it'll be him.

Alone in the house, I flip on the TV, trying to occupy myself. I plan to spend the rest of the morning and afternoon working on homework that's due tonight. My paleontology courses will be my refuge. I can bury myself in school work and real work and numb myself to what is going on around me. I'm a master at juggling too much at once and distracting myself from bleeding wounds.

I settle into the couch and get to work. Sue joins me, taking up one side of the L-shaped piece of furniture. He sighs contentedly and begins to snooze.

As I climb up the steps of the earth sciences building, I put everything away. I put it all out of my mind and ready myself for study. We're discussing Cambrian fossils and my attention needs to be there. Paleontology has been my passion since I was a little girl and saw *Jurassic Park* for the first time, sitting on my daddy's lap with his jacket pulled up over my eyes, scared and fascinated by the creatures Stan Winston had created.

In Los Angeles, I worked at the Tar Pits Museum. Until Alex asked me to quit.

He didn't want me to work because his mother hadn't worked. His father had provided more than enough for both of them and their children. Their family had very conservative values behind closed doors, even by my Tennessee standards. I didn't have it in me to argue with him then. The idea of being a kept woman was intoxicating when I was twenty-one, setting out for California, leaving behind my family and my education.

That kind of lifestyle was so far from what I'd imagined for myself growing up. I'd always thought I'd be Dr. Ellie Sattler, out in Montana or Utah, Dr. Alan Grant at my side, digging up the biggest T. rex to ever be discovered. I had no idea that instead, I'd be a prisoner in a mansion.

Walking into the paleontology department is usually enough most days to make me forget about whatever is bothering me, and this day is no different. I successfully push Dan from my mind and Alex even farther away. I just want to focus on the lecture. I want to soak up everything that I can from Professor Reid. I love him.

He's young, maybe thirty-five. He's good-looking and can carry on a conversation that doesn't revolve around sports or the Nashville music scene. He's been on digs across the world and knows his shit. He actually persuaded me to go on my first dig.

There's a little town named Kenton in the panhandle of Oklahoma. It's not known outside of the circles of people who either have family there, are looking for fossils, or like to stargaze. There are so few lights in town that it's perfect for both amateur and professional astronomers. It's a haven to those who want to disconnect and get away from the world. You can't get a cell phone signal or high-speed internet. It's always a chilling thought to me that you could have a minor mishap out there and die simply because no one could get to you for at least an hour.

Over the summer, I went and worked as a research assistant for Dr. Reid. He was my professor for a course on dinosaur behavior and another course on the Jurassic period. He also helped out with the Paleontology Society, which I've been very active in after I came back from Los Angeles. Dr. Reid doesn't have children and so he can dedicate much of his time to his students. He has a wife, but he cracks jokes that she wanted kids and he was depriving her of that; however, there's always a little truth in his humor.

One day last spring, I came to his office to ask him some questions about a passage from the textbook that had to do with pachycephalosaurs' mating habits. He looked up from the student newspaper and smiled widely. He always greeted me as though his whole day was made by a student expressing more than a passing interest in his classes and their materials.

"Hey, Dr. Reid," I said.

"Tash," he beamed, folding his paper over and leaning onto the desk. "What can I do for you on this lovely spring afternoon? Why aren't you out enjoying the day?"

"Oh, you know. I have this professor that thinks we should study night and day for his exams about dinosaur behavior," I offered with a smile.

Dr. Reid looked away almost like he was embarrassed. He looked innocent and warm. Friendly, even.

In those days, I'd found myself thinking of Alex less and less. He'd become a mirage on the horizon. Something I only saw in moments of tired desperation. His memory didn't haunt me the way it had in the beginning. Now it was a matter of enough time having passed without an incident. I felt close to Dr. Reid, but he didn't know me. He didn't know that I'd been engaged. He knew that I'd lived in Los Angeles and worked at the museum, but that was where the explanation of my backstory ended for him. I'm sure he guessed that I'd left school for a while and had decided to come back. I assumed that he was smart enough to put that together himself. Some days, I couldn't put it together myself why I'd come back to school. On the days that I was exhausted from teaching or rolling hard, or the days when that mirage did darken my memory, a beast on the horizon, it was hard to remember my purpose. It was hard to remember that this is what I wanted to do with my life, but this wasn't one of those days.

"He sounds like a monster," Dr. Reid said, leaning back away from his desk, assuming a more causal position.

For a moment, I thought he was talking about Alex, and it caught me off guard. I quickly regained my composure.

"Eh, he's not so bad," I said with a shrug.

Dr. Reid laughed.

"Hey, Tash," he said. His tone of voice allowed that he was about to ask me for a favor and my body tensed. "I have a dig coming up this summer in Kenton. You ever heard of it?"

"No," I said, unsure of where he was going with this.

"It's this tiny town in BFE, Oklahoma. No internet. No cell phone reception. Lots of dinosaur tracks and bones."

I stared at him, wondering why he was giving me this information.

"I want you to be my research assistant," he said, as though it were the most obvious conclusion that I could have drawn.

"Oh," I said, stunned. I'd never been asked by a professor for anything like this. It was a huge responsibility, and I balked at it.

"You worked at the museum in Los Angeles. This will be a piece of cake," he said, urging me to accept, seeing my hesitation. "I know you've got a lot on your plate, and this would require you to leave the jiu-jitsu school in the capable hands of your friends, but I assure you it's something you'll want to be part of," he said.

I smiled.

"I realize it's not Montana or Glen Rose," he allowed, holding his hands up as though he were surrendering to an invisible opponent. "But it will still be fun, and you look like you could use some fun," he concluded, looking up at me with his friendly eyes.

I looked away at the floor. I shuffled my feet and the papers that were in my arms. I hadn't left Tennessee since I'd gotten back that day in late December three years ago. I wasn't sure if I even knew how to anymore. Suddenly, fear clenched my gut with an iron fist.

"I have to go," I said, turning abruptly.

"Tash, wait!" Dr. Reid shouted after me, standing up from his desk. I looked back to see him standing in the doorway to his office as I marched out onto the sidewalk.

I didn't see Dr. Reid over spring break. In the last couple of years, I'd spent my spring breaks helping him catalogue research. That year I laid low. I distanced myself from him. The following week, I could feel his eyes on me every time I entered the lecture hall. I sat in the back, not my normal routine, and it wasn't until a couple of weeks had passed that he was able to catch up with me.

I had dropped my pencil bag on the floor as I was packing up and it stalled me in getting out of there. He climbed the steps quickly and bent down to help me gather my things.

"Tash," he said, a little breathless from his hike.

I said nothing and only stared at him.

"I know you've got a lot going on, but I want you to consider this opportunity," he said as though he'd rehearsed the line in his head, trying to get it as succinct as possible.

I sighed. It had been all I could think about since he'd mentioned it. I knew that I wanted to go. I knew that leaving the jiu-jitsu school would be hard, but it wasn't my school to worry about. It would survive. And so would I. Leaving home would be hard, especially the first time since I'd been back, being away from Dan who had become my comfort blanket, but I could do it. I knew that. I broke into a smile, throwing caution to the wind.

"I want to go," I said, my breath barely above a whisper.

Dr. Reid's face broke into a smile. His worried look was vanquished by sheer elation.

"Excellent!" he said. "Come with me to my office and I can give you the details on everything." He turned and hopped down the steps, not even checking to see if I was in tow. I knew he was excited, and I could feel his giddiness transferring to me as if by osmosis. I'd never been on a dig before and even though, like he said, it wasn't Montana or Glen Rose, it was still a dig, and I would still be a research assistant. That was something I could put on a resume.

I followed him down the hall to his dungeon-like office. No windows, only posters from various dinosaur movies and some figurines. It looked sort of like a shrine to his childhood. I could appreciate the comfort that had to give him. I wondered what he needed to be comforted about. My mind drifted to my ideas about his wife, begging for a baby while he wanted to be the next Jack Horner.

"Here," he said, after a moment behind his computer screen. I stepped around the desk and looked over his shoulder. What I saw were images of a practically barren landscape. It was peppered with tumbleweeds and brush, some trees. It looked like there was a cow in the background. A man was standing next to a huge femur of what I thought might be an Apatosaurus.

"They found this bone a long time ago, but it's one of the most famous ones that they ever found there. It's in the Sam Noble at OU now. You can pose and take your own picture with it," he said, smiling up at me as though he hoped desperately that I would be impressed. It was almost sad.

I smiled back at him, and he looked away, clicking through the pictures on the Google image search. There were dinosaur bones and mammoth teeth that had been discovered by ranchers. He showed me the tiny general store that sold gasoline and hamburgers, and he showed me the town square which measured only about a block in distance.

"That's it. That's the whole town. Everyone else lives on ranches outside of there," he said. "It's amazing, really."

"And how do they feel about people coming out there and digging up dinosaur bones?" I asked.

"Pretty paranoid," he said. "The local don't really trust outsiders. Not most of them anyway. There are a few people that welcome it and are pretty proud of the little collection of bones that they've got going on. I guess you'll just have to see for yourself," he said, beaming at me.

"I guess so," I smiled back.

CHAPTER 11

Kenton, Oklahoma Jun. 2015

A little less than three months later, I was unpacking my suitcase in the upstairs bedroom of a ranch house that had more character than it had amenities. The three guys that had come with us had fought over who would take the couch and who got the two twin beds in the bedroom downstairs. Dr. Reid took the other bedroom upstairs. Sometimes being a girl paid off.

"What do you think?" came Dr. Reid's voice from the other room. I stepped out into the hallway.

"Cute," I said, and he popped his head around the door frame.

From the top of the staircase, we could hear an escalating argument that had to do with the bathroom and who got what drawer. My guess was that there were only two drawers to be argued over. I was relieved to be sharing a bathroom with Dr. Reid upstairs.

Dr. Reid shrugged his shoulders.

"It's an upgrade. I'm used to sleeping on the couch at

home, so a tiny upstairs bedroom meant for a mouse should be fine," he said with a smile.

I watched him turn and go back into his bedroom, wondering how much truth there was in what he said. Sometimes in class he made jokes about his marriage, but I could never tell how serious he was. I wondered now if maybe the stage presence he brought to the lecture hall was a little more real than I'd once thought. I wondered why he'd gotten married if he was so unhappy with her.

Sometimes I oversimplified marriage that way. Why would you get married unless you loved the person? I almost married Alex and for an entirely different reason. I felt bound to him without a choice. It wasn't until he forced my hand that I had to leave and never look back.

I turned away from Dr. Reid's door and went back into my bedroom. My immediate thought was to pull out my cell phone and snap a shot of my quaint surroundings to send to Dan. It wasn't until I hit send on the message that I realized I had no service. I groaned and tossed my phone to the bed. It was a bummer to not be able to share it with him. Our relationship had gotten so much better after I'd left Alex and come home. Dan and I had made up and things went back to the way they were before everything. Before Alex had tried to ruin our friendship. Tried and succeeded.

He'd controlled my life in so many ways beyond who I was allowed to be friends with. I saw that now. I'd seen it then, but didn't act on it until it was far too late. For a moment I wondered where he was now and marveled at the thought that he couldn't reach me by any means unless he wanted to track me down out here and physically come and find me. The thought comforted me.

"Tash?" Dr. Reid knocked on the door.

"Yeah?" I responded, spinning around, caught up in the

moment with a very private thought, suddenly feeling as though he could read it by looking at my eyes. I felt exposed and vulnerable, like he'd just caught me stepping out of the shower, so I looked away.

"I'm going downstairs," he said. "I think everyone probably wants something to eat. You hungry?"

"I'm starving," I said.

It was a couple of weeks into our trip when the rains came.

The panhandle wasn't a stranger to rain, but it was unexpected. We were out at the dig site when it started pouring down. Dr. Reid helped us cover up what we could and pack away our tools. Soaked and tired, we went to the Merc for a drink.

The guys who came with us were from the Paleontology Society. One of them was a freshman, so wet behind the ears that I was surprised he didn't pack baby powder for his ass. Their names were Mitch, Connor, and Zeke. The last was unfortunate to me because when he said it, I thought he'd said 'Zach.'

I hadn't encountered a Zach in the three years since I'd left Los Angeles somehow. I was grateful for it, though, and didn't look a gift horse in the mouth. When he'd first told me his name, the similar sound cut me to the quick. It was like jamming my finger and having my fingernail bend backwards halfway down the nail bed. The pain and emotion was that raw and real. My nerves still tingled at the thought of his name even though I never let myself speak it.

The five of us poured into the Merc, sopping wet and dripping everywhere. The guy at the counter was nice enough to oblige us with drinks, all on Dr. Reid's tab. Suddenly, the topic of conversation shifted to video games.

"You played the new Walking Dead yet?" Connor asked Zeke.

Zeke shrugged his shoulders.

"Yeah, but I'm not a huge fan," he admitted.

"Oh, come on!" Mitch chimed in.

I felt completely out of my element. I was a fan of *The Walking Dead* but not a fan of video games. Especially those that involved anything that might jump out and startle me. Just watching Dan play them at home was enough to creep me out.

I didn't know what to add to the conversation, so I sipped my beer, peeling the label.

Dr. Reid sat down and ran a hand through his spiky, wet hair. He took a swig of his beer.

"Cold out there now," he said, faking a shiver and smiling.

He was completely in his element. He was so much happier than I'd ever seen him back at home.

I smiled and the guys continued their conversation about video games.

"I take it you're not a big video game player?" he asked me, segueing into our own conversation.

"No," I said. "My roommate plays them. I watch sometimes."

Dr. Reid chuckled.

"Believe it or not, my wife's a huge gamer," he said, admitting it as though it was some kind of dirty family secret, leaning in to tell me conspiratorially.

"Really?" I asked, trying to imagine Dr. Reid in his parents' basement playing WOW and meeting a girl.

"Yeah, we actually met at that gaming café downtown," he said.

"No shit?" I asked and quickly apologized for my language. He waved it away like an annoying fly.

"No shit," he repeated, though affirmatively.

I raised an eyebrow and smirked, taking a swig of beer.

"Don't judge," he said, squinting and looking at me over his bottle.

"Hey, Dr. Reid?" Connor said.

"Yeah," he answered, looking to his right.

"We're gonna go back to the house and play some video games if it's cool with you," he said.

"Cool with me," Dr. Reid said with a smile. "Good work today, guys."

The three of them got up from the table, chugging down the last of their beers. They'd walk back to the house. It wasn't far since the town square was only a block.

"I'm gonna get another," I said, standing and walking up to the counter. I returned with another beer for myself and another for Dr. Reid. "Here you go," I said. "You've earned it."

"You didn't have to get that," Dr. Reid said.

"I know," I said. "Think of it as a thank you for asking me to come and be your research assistant. I really can't thank you enough. It's been a great experience. All of it."

"Of course," he said. "I wouldn't have wanted to bring anyone else."

I sipped from the new bottle, enjoying that first swig of beer. Everything after that was just a disappointment to me. Nothing beat that crisp carbonation and flavor when you first cracked it open.

"What's on your mind?" he asked after a moment of silence.

"Oh, nothing," I lied.

"You looked like something was on your mind there for a minute," he said, pressing the issue.

"I was thinking about how good the first sip of beer is," I said. "And I guess I was lost in thought about how sad it is that every sip after that is just a cheap imitation of the first."

He laughed and looked down at his beer. He finished it and took a sip of the new one. He paused and took another.

"My God," he murmured. "You're right."

I laughed.

"I don't think that's what you were actually thinking about, though," he said.

I felt sadness overtake my features as my mind drifted to someone, I'd tried to forget a long time ago. Despite my efforts, I'd never been successful. I watched the downpour outside.

"This conversation is going to require more alcohol," I said, partially joking and partially not. I hadn't ever really had much of a conversation with Dr. Reid that wasn't about my job at the jiu-jitsu school or my duties in the Paleontology Society. It made me a little queasy to think about bringing this to light since I'd never done it.

Dr. Reid stood and went to the counter. He returned with a bottle of tequila, and I grimaced. My least favorite of the hard liquors.

He poured a little into a shot glass that he brought with him and passed it to me.

"You first," he said.

I looked it over and felt my stomach turn, ready to lurch the second the amber liquid hit it. I sucked it up and threw the shot back, fighting the urge to vomit.

"You look like you might have done that before," he said.

"A few times," I said with a laugh, wishing desperately that I had a lime. I chased it with a swig of beer.

Dr. Reid took the shot glass for himself. He poured a shot and took it, chasing it with the beer. He poured another and placed it in front of me.

We passed a little time like that, passing the shot glass back and forth, Dr. Reid the bartender for both of us. Our conversation picked up and idled and picked up again. I hoped that he'd forgotten the direction he'd been taking it in.

Dr. Reid had an elephant's memory, though. Even with the tequila.

He poured another shot and handed it to me.

I glanced at the amber liquid and felt my stomach turn, knowing that I was getting dangerously close to my tequila threshold.

"So tell me what it was you were really thinking about," he said.

I sighed, resigning myself to the fact that Dr. Reid wasn't going to stop.

"His name is Zach," I said. "He was a friend of mine before I left Los Angeles. Great guy. Good sense of humor. Kind," I went on.

"So, it wasn't your ex-fiance you were thinking of?" Dr. Reid said. "This is getting good."

I smiled.

"Not really," I said. "I just didn't treat him the way you should treat a friend."

Dr. Reid looked a little disappointed.

"Nothing ever happened between you two?" he asked. "I thought this was gonna be good!" he joked.

"No. Nothing ever happened," I lied. Shifting gears, I asked him, "What are you thinking about?"

He took the bait and began to speak.

"Wouldn't that be inappropriate for your professor to complain about his personal life to his research assistant? It seems so cliché," he lamented.

"Not anymore cliché than you trying to project a love story onto my past," I said with a smile.

"Allison wants kids," he said after a long pause. "She's always wanted kids, and I knew that. I'm an asshole because I married her anyway. I was young and I thought that she'd change her mind. That she'd come around. Now she's thirty-four and I haven't given her any children and I don't plan on it. It's just a matter of time before she realizes what a piece of shit I am. Our marriage is a ticking time bomb."

I stared at my beer. I hadn't been expecting quite that level of honesty and transparency from Dr. Reid.

"I don't want kids, either," I said, trying to reassure him.

"It's just so much goddamn responsibility, you know?" he asked, taking an angry swig of beer.

"I totally agree," I said. "I can barely take care of myself," I added with a lighthearted chuckle. It was the truth. I could barely keep myself going some days. How I hadn't self-destructed by now was a mystery.

"Hell, if it weren't for Allison, I wouldn't take care of myself," said Dr. Reid. "I'm still so in love with her, but we've become different people. Sometimes when I look at her, I see that same girl that I fell in love with so many years ago. But sometimes when I look at her, I see someone entirely alien to me. She might as well be another man's wife. And she deserves to be another man's wife. Another man who would appreciate her and who would want a family. That's what she deserves, and I just have to find the courage to give it to her."

We both remained silent for some time. I wasn't sure

exactly what to say. I used to be good at that. Finding just the right words. For the last three years, I had struggled to even find an accurate description of my breakfast. Words didn't come easy anymore. It was like there was a fog that had settled in my brain, preventing me from viewing the most damaging of my memories, but in the process, it prevented me from seeing the good ones, too, or communicating how I truly felt because I couldn't even see it clearly in my mind. Not for all the fog.

I didn't offer Dr. Reid any words of advice, but only the solace of my silent presence. Sometimes the best thing to say is nothing at all. When words fail us, the heat radiating off our living bodies has to be enough. I hoped that my presence was enough for him that day.

"So why didn't you get married?" he asked me.

The question was so direct that I fumbled it like it was a football thrown to someone sitting in the stands reading a book. It landed without any grace beside me, and I didn't want to pick it up.

"A lot of reasons," I said, my guard starting to erect itself.

"There's always a specific moment, though," Dr. Reid said. "With any breakup. There's that moment when you've had enough, and you have to walk away."

I knew that he was right, and I knew exactly when my moment had been. I also knew the moment that came before that that should have been enough. I knew exactly when Alex had gone from being the man I loved to being the monster that I lived with. I also knew that I was not going to talk about any of that with Dr. Reid because I'd never talked about it with another living soul. Instead, I pulled my shirt down to reveal my collar bone where I'd gotten it broken in jiu-jitsu.

"He hit me," I lied. "Finally hit me hard enough to break something. Seeing myself in the hospital with a wristband was my final straw." Part of me wanted to protect what had actually happened. A part of me felt that it, too, was sacred and it belonged only to Alex and I and that letting anyone in on it would somehow break the bond we shared because of those two awful nights.

Dr. Reid sat there, speechless.

It was exactly how I wanted him to react.

"Let's go," I said, drinking the last of my beer and sitting it down on the table. I didn't wait for him. I walked out the door of the Merc, hearing the bells ring, and stood on the porch in the rain.

Chapter

Nashville
   Dec. 2016

After I park my car, I walk in the chilled winter air towards the lecture hall that holds Dr. Reid's classroom. I can't wait to get there, in out of the physically cold outside world and away from Dan's icy cold shoulder. It'll be an hour and a half that I'll have to myself. I don't have to think about the pictures or the website.

I find my usual seat and smile at the guy who sits next to me, praying in silence that he won't touch me tonight. Dr. Reid isn't in class yet, which isn't unusual. He's typically a little bit late. When he finally steps in on the floor, he looks strange. His hair is disheveled and his shirt looks like it needs ironing, like maybe he'd pissed his wife off, and he couldn't figure out how to work the damn thing.

I give him a smile when he finds me in my usual seat

and his eyes linger there for a moment. He doesn't acknowledge me like he normally does. He only stares and parts his
lips as though he's about to say something and thinks better
of it.

I shrug it off as part of his pouting for being made to
sleep on the couch.

Dr. Reid starts his lecture without much fanfare. He
takes the position of professor to mean that he not only is
there to educate us, but to also entertain. I guess he thinks
people learn better when they are having a good time, and I
can't disagree.

We go through the last slides on the mating habits of a
specific species of dinosaur and move on to their seasonal
behaviors outside of mating. This is where he does most of
his research. He always says you can listen to the bones and
they will tell you a story. I remember him craning his ear
down towards some fossils in Kenton and saying, "What
was that? Listen to them, Tash. They're talking to you!" as
he chuckled to himself and went back to his research.

The lecture is as boring as watching paint dry. I
continue to take notes, but my interest is lost about halfway
through. Dr. Reid isn't in his element. His mind is else-
where. I want to stop him after class and ask him what's
wrong. Part of me just wants to go home and sleep for two
weeks, wake up, and have never met Alex.

He concludes the lecture and I begin to gather my
things up. A girl beside me is in a hurry and huffily asks if
she could get by me. I watch as Dr. Reid quickly gathers his
things and turns for his office. I let the girl by and get my
stuff together.

"Dr. Reid!" I call out but he doesn't turn.

I scurry down the steps and into the hallway that leads
to his office. I get there just as he's about to close the door.

"What?" he asks, obviously irritated. His face reddened when he sees that it's me.

"Dr. Reid, are you okay?" I ask.

"Tash, this is wildly inappropriate," he begins. I'm puzzled. "I don't know what kind of ideas you got into your head, but that wasn't my intention."

"What are you talking about?" I ask him.

He stares at me dumbly.

He opens the door and goes to his desk, he turns his laptop around to face me. An e-mail is open. I walk closer and take a look.

The sender field reads:

Natasha Davis <ndaviskitty1987@gmail.com>

In the body of the e-mail is the link to download Tor and the link to Blue Heroin.

"Dr. Reid, I didn't send that," I say, pointing at the e-mail.

"Tash, I think you'd better go," he says.

"I didn't send you that! You have to believe me!"

"I'm sorry if I gave you the wrong impression, but I'm going to have to drop you from my class. It's not personal, but this is entirely inappropriate. I could lose my job if I don't. I'm sorry, Tash," he says.

I stand there, dumbfounded.

It isn't until I taste salt that I realize I'm crying. I clap a hand over my mouth to keep from making an animalistic sound. I feel like I've been punched in the gut all over again. The one place that's left for me to seek refuge in has been jerked out from under me like a rug in a cartoon. Alex knows exactly what he's doing.

I've played his game before, and he always wins.

CHAPTER 12

Los Angeles Oct. 2013

"It's just part time. It's not like she's going to be my secretary," Alex said, annoyed that we were even having this conversation. "She's just going to be doing filing for all of us."

I rinsed out the bowl that I'd been eating ice cream in. I placed it in the sink. I turned and crossed my arms over my chest.

"It just seems like she's becoming a pretty big part of our lives," I said.

"Well, it's not like I can just tell her to fuck off," Alex said.

He walked out of the kitchen and into the living room where he promptly plopped down on the couch. He grabbed a magazine and began leafing through it, obviously not looking at the pictures, only looking for something to keep him from losing his cool with me over this disagreement.

"I know," I finally acquiesced.

He looked up as I walked into the living room. I swept

my long sweater jacket out from under me and took a seat on the leather loveseat adjacent to the couch. I grabbed the remote and flipped the TV on.

"I wish you wouldn't do that. I'm trying to read," he said.

I prickled at that. He wasn't trying to read. He was flipping through an issue of Men's Fitness. He was looking at pictures and trying to think about anything but the fact that he had no choice but to hire Amy.

By turning on the television, I was doing the same thing.

Amy's presence in our lives had become a point of contention in our relationship. In the last month, she'd appeared more and more. We'd run into her at parties inside and outside of the Sanctuary. She'd started calling and texting Alex at all hours of the night. I hated it but I let him take the calls and field the texts, feeling powerless to do anything.

I resented him for not standing up to her, but I knew he couldn't. I knew that I couldn't either, so I just took it as best I could, trying to keep it from grinding me down every day. Our lives had changed so much in such a short period of time.

Even though Alex didn't want the TV on, I flipped to the news. It had become habit in the last few weeks. Watching the headlines and seeing what was and wasn't important to people comforted me. As long as they didn't talk about what was important to me, I was safe.

I had flipped it on in the middle of a story.

A blonde reporter that couldn't have been more than twenty-five was talking and there was a picture of a girl with black hair and blue eyes, smiling from beside the reporter with the word MISSING above her head.

"...reported missing two weeks ago. There are no new

leads in the case, but investigators are asking anyone in the public to come forward that might have knowledge of what happened to Samantha Logan. Any tips are appreciated."

I flipped the TV off and looked at Alex. He was still concentrating hard on pretending to read and didn't seem to have been disturbed by my nightly check in with the news. There was nothing new to talk about and that was fine with me. I wanted our lives to be calm instead of feeling like the calm before the storm. It felt every day as though we were just waiting for the other shoe to drop.

The image of the missing girl haunted me as I, too, tried to lose myself in a magazine. I wouldn't forget how happy she looked in the picture they showed of her in the news. It always seemed that way, though. No matter who it was, they showed the most heart-wrenching picture of them. Maybe it was with their family or their dog or just of them looking happy, but it always made the whole damn thing seem so tragic.

And it was tragic.

I put down my magazine and walked back into the kitchen. I grabbed my bowl out of the sink and filled it with another scoop of ice cream. I poured myself a glass of red wine and went to bed to watch TV in there.

I glanced over my shoulder one last time to see Alex sitting on his side of the couch, the magazine in his lap, his hands cradling his face. He was rocking slightly back and forth, and I knew there was nothing I could do to comfort him.

Normally, the Sanctuary held two parties a month. It was an off weekend, but they were throwing a party anyway. It was in honor of the missing girl, Samantha Logan. She'd been a member of the club. Not for very long and not too many people knew her, but those who did felt an obligation to try to help find her.

We arrived and entered the normal way, through the back of the huge factory building that had been bought and renovated by the Sanctuary's owner. Whoever owned it kept their identity a secret. At the club, everyone went by an alias, including the owner.

I went by Kat and Alex went by Pendergast. It was a Saturday evening ritual that, though I didn't particularly enjoy going, I found comfort in it.

Alex had first taken me to the Sanctuary sometime when we'd moved to Los Angeles. It was something we'd done on a whim. It sounded exciting. He'd heard about it at work in murmurs in the break room. He'd tracked down Alan, one of his fellow lawyers, and had asked him for more information. Alan was happy to vouch for us and we went to our first party.

Now veterans, we checked in at the back door and entered the strangely lavish building. The lighting was red, making the walls look like they were bathed in blood. It had an open floor plan. No walls had been erected in the large warehouse building. St. Andrew's crosses lined the walls. They were stations that people used to play. You could sign up for whatever station you wanted and reserve a time.

I hated it.

I had let Alex top me and dominate me only a handful of times, each occurrence worse than the last. I hated seeing the look in his eyes when he was drunk with the illusion of power over me, though the more entwined our lives became, the less of an illusion it was.

Maybe that was what I hated about it so much.

He had begun playing with Amy, a friend of the missing girl's. She was there and I rolled my eyes when I saw her in a fancy leather corset that probably cost a small fortune and thigh high leather boots. She looked like she belonged in a German dungeon.

"Hey," she said, much more chipper than I felt that night.

"Hey," Alex said, his voice softening to a degree that made me shoot him a look. He didn't notice.

"How are you guys?" she asked as though we were her parents on the edge of a divorce.

"Fine," I said tersely. "Why wouldn't we be?"

Amy looked from me to Alex and back at me again.

"I just thought—"

"Save it," I barked, annoyed at her very presence. I didn't want to be here tonight or ever again. If I never saw the inside of the Sanctuary again in my life it would have been too soon. I walked away from them, leaving them to their conversation. I went over to the table of refreshments where there was a huge poster-sized print of the photo of Samantha Logan that the news had used.

I grabbed a glass and got some alcohol-free punch. I sipped it, staring up at the poster into her blue eyes, wondering what she was thinking when the photo was snapped. I wondered if anyone actually still thought she was alive. There hadn't been a lead in the last week, and I knew that if the police didn't locate the person within forty-eight hours the chances of them finding that person alive decreased dramatically. I wondered how good of a chance they had at finding her at all.

"Excuse me," said a girl who pushed past me to get a drink. She startled me from my meditation on the nature of a missing persons case. I forced a smile and stepped to the side.

I looked over my shoulder to see Alex lost in conversation with Amy, both of them laughing, him, I was sure, turning up the charm and her flirting her brains out. I rolled my eyes for the second time in less than ten minutes.

I went to the back patio to get some air.

Fairy lights ringed the pergola that was set up above stained concrete and wrought iron furniture. I took a seat at an empty table for two, the absence of my partner only made more apparent by the vacant seat across from me. Cell phones were forbidden inside the Sanctuary, so I sat with nothing to occupy me. No stimulation from Facebook and no conversation with a stranger.

I watched a couple at a table across the patio. The girl was nude, covered in a blanket and sipping some water out of a Dixie cup. The guy rubbed her shoulders, guiding her gently back to reality after a scene, I was sure. She was probably in subspace. That state of bliss that you supposedly could achieve only after feeling a certain amount of pain. I wondered if it worked on emotions, too. So far it hadn't.

The guy smiled at me but I didn't recognize him. I only looked away and back into the main part of the building where a few people had gathered around the refreshment table. They all looked at the poster of Samantha, wondering like everyone, I was sure, what had happened to the girl.

CHAPTER 13

Nashville Dec. 2016

Exhausted and emotionally drained, I drive home from school. I feel defeated, as though there's no way that I can escape Alex's grip, no matter how much time or distance is put between us. The image of Dr. Reid's face, so contorted with disgust and contempt for me is emblazoned onto my brain as though put there by a branding iron.

He's one of the few men that I have truly begun to trust after coming back to Nashville. I hold our relationship sacred and the idea of me crossing such a line makes me feel sick. I wonder at how well Alex knows me to know just what would get to me. I wonder briefly, feigning being dumb about what he wants from me.

Darkness falls early as it's winter and I find myself on the highway in rush hour traffic. I combat my sadness and emptiness by putting on some music. "Fourth of July" by Shooter Jennings comes on. I quickly turn the station. It was one of my favorite songs when Dan and I first started college. It was something we would listen to on repeat, having gone to see Shooter every time he was in Nashville. The memories make me sick tonight, so I skip the track.

An old George Jones song comes on, and then something by Merle Haggard. I listen to the latest Eric Church song and switch back to the radio.

I get off the interstate and make my way to my neighborhood. Once I turn down our street, I notice taillights up ahead in the cul de sac. They're sitting directly in front of the house I share with Dan.

Our neighborhood is relatively new and there are two vacant houses across the street from us. Once, kids were caught partying there, but there's never been any other activity that wasn't on the level. It's a nice neighborhood. Mostly full of parents with young children and older couples.

I pull down the street, slowing as I pass the car. I turn into my driveway and look in my rearview mirror. The driver rolls down the window low enough to flick his cigarette and then rolls it back up. He shifts into drive and pulls down the cul de sac, turns around and slowly approaches my driveway.

I watch in the mirror as his car creeps by. I can't see into his tinted windows. After a long and awkward moment, he keeps going. I watch as he pulls around the corner and hear his car disappear into the neighborhood. It's odd.

I turn the car off and get out, bending down to gather my things from the passenger seat. The cold air is refreshing on my flushed cheeks. I slam the door and go to the porch where I fumble with my keys, finally finding them and sliding them into the lock.

Dan is sitting in front of the TV playing one of those modern warfare games where you're basically in Afghanistan but with zombies. Sue lays on the couch opposite Dan and gets up to come and greet me. I roll my eyes at Dan and go back towards my bedroom. Sue follows but Dan doesn't even look away from the screen to acknowledge me.

I kick my door open and throw my bag down onto my bed. As I do, my phone starts to ring. I dig into my purse, feeling for it. I grab it and look at the number.

UNKNOWN

Normally I wouldn't answer a call from someone whose number doesn't show up, but something in me urges me to accept the call, so I do.

"Hello?"

"You look good in that light blue sweater," says a husky male voice.

Chilled, I look down at my chest, seeing the little black dots of running mascara that stained my light bluish grey sweater.

"Who is this?" I demand.

"You're Natasha, right?" the voice asks. "I liked your pictures. You think you could pose for me sometime?"

"Fuck off," I mutter, my heart racing.

"I wouldn't be a bitch if I were you," the guy growls. "I know where you live."

I think of the car that was parked out front of the house when I pulled up. It makes my stomach drop through the floor.

"Now, when can I see you again?" he asks, suddenly sounding as sweet as he can possibly be. I hang up the phone and drop it on my bed, running my hands through my hair.

Fuck.

I think of my address, phone number, and e-mail address that were posted alongside the nude photos of me. I cringe. Groaning, I sit down on the bed and cradle my head in my hands. Sue comes to nuzzle me and I accept his affection eagerly, being glad for the small comfort that he affords me.

I can't imagine how this day could possibly get any worse.

CHAPTER 14

Nashville Dec. 2016

Just as I'm wondering how the day could get worse, Dan barges into the room.

"Do you know how to knock?" I bark, annoyed to even have to look at him.

"Tash, I need to tell you something," he says.

"Christ, what is it?" I ask, groaning my response and throwing my body back onto the bed.

"I know you didn't want to do it, so I did it for you. I called the police. They're on their way over here right now. I was waiting for you to get home to do it," he blurts out.

I'm stunned into silence. My heart hammers in my chest.

"You what?" I ask, staring up at the ceiling, my vision tunneling from a mixture of pure anger and fear.

"I called the cops," Dan repeats. "I had to."

"You didn't have to do anything," I remind him, sitting up on the bed. "What the fuck is wrong with you? You think this is your battle? I don't need the cops. I want you to call them right now and tell them to fuck off."

He looks shocked. He holds his hands up. Sue sits beside me, his large head almost at the same height as my own. He whines, hating the discord between the two of us.

"Tash, I know it's hard and I know that Alex scares you," he says.

"Scares me?" I ask with a hoarse laugh. "Dan, you have no fucking clue what the fuck you're getting yourself into. Trust me." The cops don't need to be involved. Dan doesn't need to be involved. I want to throw something at him, shatter a vase across his forehead, knock him unconscious and drag him out back and bury him alive. I'm furious.

"Tash, I—"

"You know nothing," I hiss. Tears well in my eyes.

Tash—" he begins but there's a knock at the door. My eyes widen, the reality of the fact that I'm about to have to explain all of this away to a police officer dawns on me.

I stand up from the bed.

"I'll get it," I say calmly. I smooth my hair and my clothes and walk past Dan into the front hall. I take a deep breath and open the front door. Sue barks loudly. His growl is deep and threatening. I never tell anyone that he has no bite—it's all bark. They don't need to know that.

"Good evening, miss," says an officer with a thick moustache. He's alone.

"Hi, officer," I say with my sweetest smile. "I'm sorry that my friend called you, but I don't need any assistance," I go on. Sue growls and the officer looks down at him. I don't bother to reassure him that Sue is a friendly hound.

The officer looks at me skeptically.

"He's just concerned about me," I say.

Dan pops around the corner.

"Hello, sir," he says, pushing past me and opening the door further for the officer. "Come in."

Annoyed, I step aside as the burly police officer walks through our foyer into the living room. Dan shows him a seat on the couch and asks if he can get him anything. The officer declines and Dan begins speaking to him. Sue approaches the officer who holds out his hand to him. Sue gratefully takes that as an invitation and to my chagrin begins to wag his tail.

"She's just afraid," Dan says. "You get that a lot in these cases, I'm sure," he goes on.

"We do," the officer says. "But if she's not willing to press charges, there's nothing I can do." He looks from me to Dan and back again at me. He begins to pet Sue.

"There's nothing to press charges about," I say with a smile.

"Her ex-fiancé posted a slew of naked pictures of her on this dark website and he's sending it out to people like roses on Valentine's Day," Dan blurts out.

"Were the pictures taken against your will?" the officer asks me.

Suddenly confronted with the facts, I stammer.

"N-no," I say.

"Well, I hate to tell you this, but in Tennessee, there aren't any laws against revenge porn. Did he take the pictures here?" he asks.

"No. California," I say, feeling relieved that there isn't anything the cop can do even if he wants to.

"The best thing I could tell you to do is contact the F.B.I. and let them know about the website. I'm sure they already do, but you could add your name to the host of other girls that have become victims to it," he says, looking from Dan to me and back at Dan as though he's talking to my father and I won't remember all his instructions.

"This has been most enlightening," I say. "But I think we're done."

The police officer stands.

"Are you sure there's nothing else I can do for you?" he asks.

"I'm sure," I say and walk him to the front door. I step outside to see him to his car.

"Miss," he says, turning around. "I don't know the details of your situation, but I just want to tell you that I see a lot of girls back out of pressing charges for harassment and stalking and what not. Sometimes those girls end up on a slab in the M.E.'s office," he says.

I steel my resolve to not ask for help.

"I just don't want to see that happen to you. I'm going to ask you this once: do you feel like you are in danger?"

I stare at him for a moment and cross my arms over my chest. I feel like I'm in the most danger I've been in in my entire life, but I just smile.

"No," I say.

He turns and walks to his car. I wave as he backs out of the driveway.

Before I go back inside, I pull out my phone. I go to my contacts and find Alex's name. I tap it. I never deleted his number. I think I didn't want to be caught unaware if he ever called. Now I scroll to the bottom of the contact page and I touch the button that reads UNBLOCK THIS CALLER.

I go to create a new message. I type it out and hit send.
You've got my attention.

I slam the door behind me as I storm back into the house. My pulse is racing, my face hot at the thought that Alex just got a message from me. At the thought that he might send me one back soon. But I gather my wits and confront Dan.

"Seriously?" I ask him as he paces by the couch.

He's silent, clearly pondering something.

"I can't believe that there's nothing he can do," he says more to himself than to me.

"I'm glad," I say under my breath.

I march past him, leaving him to his thoughts and go into my bedroom, slamming that door, too. I slide down the door and collapse in a heap. My phone dings in my pocket. It's surely Alex messaging me back. I gird my loins, unsure of how I feel about our newfound contact with one another. I put so much of that away. It's painful to dig it back out and open it up. Terrifying, too.

I pull my phone out and hit the home button.

I have a Facebook message.

From Zach O'Halloran.

I haven't heard from him since I left Los Angeles. He never reached out to me and I haven't tried to reach him, either. I feel like I'm being punched in the gut, like all the air has been vacuumed out of my lungs. I stare at his name until my phone goes dark. I unlock it and go to my messenger app. I open the one with his name on it.

Tash,

I know we haven't talked in a long time, but I got something in my e-mail this morning that I thought you might need to be aware of. I hope you're well. Los Angeles isn't the same without you.

All my best,

Zach

His words are like an uppercut to my abdomen.

Reading them, knowing that he typed them out just moments before and that he's sitting at the other end of this conversation just a few keystrokes away makes my face flush with heat. My pulse picks up speed as I try to think of the appropriate response. In the message he sent the link to Blue Heroin. Instead of opening the link, I close the entire message.

Out of nervous habit, I open apps and checked my text messages over and over. I scroll through Facebook, somehow unable to go back to Zach's message for quite some time. It's like if I leave it undisturbed, I can keep in my mind the ideas that I have about him and I. That we're just two people who hadn't got the timing right.

Zach's words are so kind. He wants nothing from me. He doesn't even expect a response, that much is clear with his use of *I hope you're well.* I don't have to respond to him and further complicate my life. But before I can talk myself out of it, I'm hammering out a message back.

Zach,

I'm sorry you got the pictures. My roommate got them this morning. We're trying to deal with it.

My fingers pause above the keyboard. I almost hit send, and then,

How are you?

I can't help myself. I want to know. I want to do something to keep the conversation going. Anything to not be alone with the deafening chorus of questions in my mind that mostly center around what Alex will do next.

I stand up and change into my pajamas. I go into the bathroom and wash my face, hearing Dan cussing at the TV screen as he plays Call of Duty with his friends. I shake my head and roll my eyes. He means well, but he doesn't understand what he almost did.

I go back in my room and shut the door. I grab my phone and crawl into bed as it goes off again.

I'm doing really well! The podcast has really taken off. Eric and I are about to do a few shows where we're recording everything live. It seems to have a pretty good fan base. We've been in talks with one of the networks out here to start a TV show. How are you doing?

I smile reading his message. I'm glad that he's doing well. I respond.

I'm doing well, too. Teaching jiu-jitsu these days, of all things. Going to school for my master's degree. I'm ashamed to say I haven't listened to the podcast, but I will. I need something to take my mind off everything that's going on right now.

In a few moments, he writes back.

Beware of foul language and inappropriate commentary from Eric if you listen to the podcast. He's pretty obnoxious, even by my standards.

Eric is Zach's best friend and his cohost on the podcast. I met him once before, at one of Zach's shows, but never really got to know him.

We go on, messaging back and forth until my eyes become strained from staring at my phone screen. I can hear Dan puttering around the in the kitchen and it comforts me to know that he's up. I want to go and tell him about the phone call that I got, but I don't want a lecture on how I should let the police get involved. The idea that someone could be outside the house right now disturbs me. I don't feel safe. Talking to Zach creates an illusion of safety, though. I can wrap myself in his words and fall asleep peacefully, but I don't want to. I want to keep talking to him.

I plug my phone in to charge as the battery drains. I

listen to the sounds of the house settling in for the night: the dishwasher running, the washing machine going, and the whine of the heater coming on. Sue groans after he jumps onto the bed, making the springs moan under his weight. He walks in a circle and lays down, taking up as much space as a man would in my bed. After he settles down, the house is quiet. The silence only allows the thoughts I've been holding at bay to creep up on me. I grab my phone when it dings again and keep talking to Zach.

The next morning when I wake, my phone is in the palm of my hand.

CHAPTER 15

Los Angeles Nov. 2013

I sat in my office, knowing that in a few moments, I'd be doing what would technically considered stalking. I preferred to think of it as reconnaissance. I was sure that Amy had broken into the museum. I was also sure that I was going to follow her tonight.

Everyone else had gone home except my boss, Robert. He was walking from office to office, tacking up calendars for the coming month. The museum had lots of events coming up meant to attract tourist attention and we were usually pretty successful at it, though it seemed like interest waned a little more each year. It seemed like kids would rather go to Universal or see where their favorite movie stars lived than see the history of the earth. It was disheartening for all of us. Any time a child came through the museum, we were ecstatic. An interest in something like paleontology had to be cultivated early. Those kids would love science for the rest of their lives. That's how it had been for me, at least.

Sitting at my desk, holding my purse, I thought about my dad. I thought about him when I was a little girl and he took me to Utah. He'd gotten a new job in the oil industry and suddenly, we'd had enough money to take a trip.

We went to Vernal, and we saw Dinosaur National Monument. From that moment forward, I was hooked. He'd let me watch Jurassic Park when I was only seven, sitting on his lap in the movie theater, both terrified and entranced by the animatronic creatures I was witnessing. Even at that age, I knew they weren't real, but it amazed me that someone knew what dinosaurs had looked like. I didn't realize a lot of it was just guesswork. I didn't realize that most of being an adult was just making your best guess.

I watched the clock on the wall as the minutes ticked by at an excruciatingly slow pace. I needed to wait until close to six. That's when Alex usually left the office, and I knew Amy wouldn't leave a second before he did.

Everyone in my office had gone already. Robert had stayed a little late, but it was easy enough to make him think I was staying late to work. I'd had a lot going on since we started our latest bit of research into mammoth behavior. It was totally believable that I'd be working late. I sat in an empty building filled only with the ghosts of my past and the bones of my mammalian ancestors.

I got up from my desk and grabbed my purse. It was 5:45.

I walked to the front desk of the museum. Only the track lighting illuminated the displays and the path that would lead me out to the Tar Pits and eventually to my car. I hated to admit it, but somehow, museums still managed to creep me out in the dark of night.

I exited the building and instinctively turned to check and see if the door had locked. It was an old habit, ingrained in me by my father who taught me to always check to make sure the door was locked when I left work.

When I could feel that it was, I made my way up the ramp that led into the lower level of the museum. I walked out and looked at the Tar Pits. The statue of the mammoth family being torn apart by the Tar Pits seemed especially dark in the setting sun. Their hulking shadows stretched on from their silhouettes.

As the mammoth statue stood struggling for its life in a timeless fight, I walked out to my car, concerned only with more modern things, like where my fiance's secretary went when she got off work. I wanted to know everything I could about Amy. I didn't want her to have the upper hand. So many times recently it seemed like Alex had the upper hand and I hated it. I felt like I'd been duped by them. I hated feeling like a fool. The Amy thing was just one more tick in the box of times that Alex had done exactly what I'd asked him not to without any concern for my feelings. I shouldn't have been surprised when he hired her.

That felt like the story of our life together. Him making big decisions and then telling me about it as an afterthought. He'd done it with the last car he'd bought. Our third car. An unnecessary purchase, but because he was the breadwinner, which he frequently reminded me of, it wasn't really my place to say whether we could afford the car. He also liked to remind me that my car was in his name.

It wasn't like I didn't get exactly what I wanted, and I knew that for some women that would have been enough. Alex provided for me beyond my wildest dreams. More than my parents ever could have. I had the best of everything, the newest everything, the most upgraded version of everything. But that didn't matter to me. At first, it had been appealing. The idea of not having to work for the rest of my life and afford whatever I wanted was intoxicating. Any time I slipped into the frivolous notion that it was our money, he made sure that I knew who had earned the majority of it. Even though my own money was mine to spend however I saw fit, I socked a lot of it away in an account that Alex knew nothing about. And when I got a raise at the museum, I didn't tell him.

Me working was an annoyance to him. He didn't understand why I didn't just quit and spend my days relaxing on the beach or living a life that most girls would dream of. I couldn't imagine giving up any more of my freedom than I already had for him. I felt like my heart was trapped in a cage, one much too small at that. I didn't want to give up my last bastion of freedom, the paycheck that I earned from the museum.

Every time that I walked the path that led to the parking lot at the Tar Pits, these thoughts danced in my mind. I thought about getting in my car and driving until the wheels fell off.

I got into my Audi, started it up, and drove. I didn't connect my music like I normally did. When Alex was in the car with me, I never connected the phone.

"Do you really like this shit?" he'd asked me once. It had been enough to prevent me from subjecting him to the kind of country that I liked: Willie Nelson, George Jones, Johnny Cash.

Alex preferred the newer country that had that weird pop sound that Nashville was so in love with at the moment. His favorite, though, was Christian rock, which blew my mind. I would never forget when I first met him. Everything about him screamed sophistication and then he told me he couldn't hang out too late on Saturday night because he didn't want to be late for church. I'd barked out a laugh, sure that he was joking but he wasn't.

We had since stopped going to church. He claimed that

he couldn't find a church that he liked in Los Angeles, but I knew that it had to do with me and my non-religious raising. I hated church and never wanted to go, feeling like a fraud every time I stepped through the doors. I wasn't entirely sure how he managed to keep from bursting into flame when he passed the threshold of a church. But me not going with him was a personal failure to him.

Tonight, I didn't have my music on for an entirely different reason. Although sometimes I felt like Alex knew when I was enjoying myself. I felt like he resented me for the times that I enjoyed myself alone. Tonight, I wasn't concerned with enjoying myself. I wanted all my focus to be on the mission at hand. I didn't want to miss a move that Amy made. I drove in silence, my only company the whirring of the engine.

I found the parking garage in downtown L.A. that was across the street from Alex's law firm. I fortuitously found a parking on the street and killed the engine.

I could see into the law firm's windows. Alex's office was on the second floor, and I could see into it. He moved to get his jacket; he was getting ready to leave. He ran a hand through his hair and looked into the full-length mirror that stood by the window. I cringed a little at his primping. He was always so concerned with his appearance. My dad had compared him to a peacock once, which garnered a snort of derision from Dan. For a moment I became suddenly self-conscious, aware that if I could see Alex, he could see me. I shrunk into my seat as though somehow that would protect me from his gaze.

As he made himself ready for the trip home, I saw a figure darken the doorway. It was Amy.

He turned when he could feel her presence behind him. I couldn't make out their facial expressions, but I could see him smiling at her. I watched, lapping up every moment like a racehorse dying of thirst after putting on a huge burst of speed, winning the race.

She stepped into the room and leaned on his desk. They were talking. She turned and sat on the desk so casually, something I'd done once, and he'd ordered me to get my ass off of it and promptly reminded me that it cost 11,000 dollars.

Instead of reproaching her, he walked around and wrapped her legs around his waist.

My heart sank in my chest.

I'd known on some level, but to see it right in front of me was an affront.

I watched as she wrapped her arms loosely around his neck. He leaned in and kissed her. She kissed him back fervently. He reached for her panties and slid them off her. He unbuckled his pants. They moved together as things grew more and more heated.

Finally, he pulled away from her having got what he needed.

That was him, always in control, always getting his way. Never letting anyone else get the upper hand.

I wondered how furious he would be at me for spying on him. The thought that he was cheating was secondary. It didn't enter my mind that I was the one with the right to be furious. When had I become so broken?

Tears leaked silently out of my eyes, rolling one after another down my cheeks and wetting my shirt sleeve. I didn't wipe my face, afraid that I'd get mascara on the white blouse, knowing that I wasn't the one who'd paid for it and if he ever saw the stains, I'd never hear the end of it.

In that moment, I knew that I was stuck.

I was trapped.

I knew that because of this and so much else, I wasn't free anymore.

And I knew that I wanted to leave L.A. and never look back.

I sat immobilized in my car forever. My chest ached with the sobs that I fought, and I kept myself from wiping my tears on my sleeve. I found some napkins in the center console. If Alex knew that I ever got fast food in the car, he'd be furious. I wiped my eyes, looking down at the brown recycled paper and seeing streaks of black mascara. I sniffled, the sound weak to my ears. I hated it.

I never wanted to feel weak again.

I contemplated going home to Alex, but the idea of facing him after what I'd just seen made my stomach twist into a violent knot. As I was tossing the idea around, I saw Amy exiting the building. She walked across the street to the parking garage that housed the cars of the lawyers who worked at his firm. I knew then that I was going to go through with my plan and follow her.

The tears stopped though my eyes stung and ached with their remnants. I watched Amy as she scaled the incline of the ramp that led into the garage. I watched her disappear and I waited for her to return in a car.

In about five minutes, a silver Toyota pulled out of the parking garage. Sure that it was her, I shifted into drive and followed at a safe distance. I watched her turn onto West Temple Street. We turned on Broadway and got onto the Hollywood Freeway. We passed Chinatown and went further into Hollywood. She exited on Sunset Boulevard, and I followed her, letting a car inch in between us on the off ramp, hoping it would keep her from looking in her rearview mirror and discovering that she had a tail.

On Sunset she went past the Palladium, and I saw the Roosevelt to our North. We followed the curve that wound around the Bird Streets and Graystone Mansion but stopped short when she found a parking space on Sunset. I passed her car and made a U-turn the first chance I got. I parked on the opposite side of the street and ran to catch up with her, following in a parallel line, spying her across the street. She stopped at the Comedy Store. There was a line out front, and she went to the head of it. She spoke animatedly to the bouncer, who kept telling her no. Finally, she got into her purse and gave him some money. He looked annoyed but took it and let her cut in front of everyone and go into the club.

Walking down the sidewalk, the smells from the restaurants and the laughter of patrons trickled out. I glanced to my left and saw a couple, both engrossed in their phones. The girl looked up and saw me. I looked away. I made my way to the first pedestrian crossing that I could find and went over towards the Comedy Store. The air was cool this evening and many of the people wrapped themselves in jackets. They'd never felt the bite of a true American winter.

I took my place at the end of the line, carefully scanning the faces, making sure that she hadn't somehow slipped back outside. I wondered why she'd wanted to get in so quickly. There wasn't anyone famous on the marquee tonight. I didn't recognize the names at all.

Nighttime in Los Angeles was a sight. People moved up and down the sidewalk like ants, making the paths undulate and come to life. There were plenty of people, but unlike

New York City, it never seemed like there were too many of them.

The line slowly began creeping forward. I shuffled my feet just like the people in front of me and the people who had come after me that stood in line. When I finally got to the door, a huge bouncer with a face like a walrus greeted me with a grunt. I handed him my ID without a word, and he ushered me inside where it seemed like the club was alive with people. The small line on the sidewalk wasn't indicative of the amount of people that teemed inside.

My eyes darted around the room, hungry for the sight of her. I wanted to find her and rip her throat out. The instinct to hunt her down like an animal ached inside my gut as though I was overcome by desire. I didn't see her. So instead of stalking the room like a lion around a herd of gazelle, I went to the bar where there was a small line. Most people had taken their seats at tables. Some were marked as reserved close to the front.

I got behind two guys that seemed like douchebags. They both wore too-tight polo shirts and had perfectly coiffed, sun-streaked hair. They were both freshly tanned and their muscles bulged like they'd just stepped out of the gym. I had no doubt that was exactly where they'd just come from.

"I've heard he's pretty funny, man," said the shorter of the two.

"Eh, everyone thinks their friend is funny," said the taller of the two with the darker complexion.

"Whatever, man," said the blonde. "At least Eric scored us a seat at the front. Plus, free alcohol."

"Plus the free alcohol," the brunette agreed.

I listened to their conversation, always intrigued by what strangers were talking about. Sometimes it was entertaining, other times shocking. Sometimes it was boring. They were a disappointment.

This is just the sort of place that I would have liked to have come with Alex when things were good.

Alex.

The thought of him stung like salt in a fresh wound. I felt like he had ripped my heart out of my chest, shit on it, and used it to paint the wall in his office. As I thought about that, the line moved forward, and I lost track of the conversation going on in front of me. The chaos of people moving beside and behind me swept me away in thought. The line moved ever forward and finally I was next in line to get a drink. I felt an impact against my right shoulder and a rush of cold liquid running down my right arm.

"Oh my God!" I cried, startled by the sensation.

"Holy shit! I'm so sorry!" said a guy and I looked up to meet his brown eyes. He had shaggy brown hair that fell just around his shoulders. It was graying seemingly prematurely at the temples and he had a beard that wasn't incredibly finely trimmed. He stood at least eight inches taller than me, a good two inches taller than Alex.

The two guys in front of me turned around.

"Zach!" said the blonde, reaching forward and extending a hand to the guy who had spilled his drink all over me. I shook my arm, shaking the beer from my fingertips. The stench of yeast flooded my nostrils, and I thought about how pissed Alex would be that I got a drink on my blouse. I wanted to peel it off, get the smell off me and just wear the camisole that I had on underneath it.

"Eric's friends?" the bearded beer-spiller asked the two douches in front of me.

"Yeah, man. Can't wait to see you perform," said the blonde. The brunette looked a lot less excited. The beer-spiller shifted his focus back to me. He didn't seem all too happy to be talking to the two douchelords.

"Thanks. Hey, let me get this girl a towel," he said to the two guys. They looked at me and looked at him knowingly. I rolled my eyes at their unspoken statement. It was like he had claimed me, and I didn't even know his full name. Only his first and that he was a comedian. So far, he wasn't very funny.

"Hey, I'm so sorry," he said to me as I watched the other two guys take their drinks and step away from the bar. Zach stepped up and asked the bartender for a towel. "And what do you want to drink? Let me get it," he said.

"No. That's not necessary," I said.

"It is necessary," he insisted.

I looked around. I'd been temporarily distracted from the purpose of my little foray and searched for Amy. I didn't spot her still. The thought occurred to me that it would piss Alex off royally to know that another man was buying me a drink.

"Sure. Fine. Whatever," I said, echoing my television heroine, Dana Scully.

"*X-Files* fan?" he asked, arching an eyebrow.

I was shocked that he got the reference, and a smile tried to creep up the corners of my mouth.

"What can I get you?" he asked and pointed at me, tilting his head down and raising his eyebrows.

I looked from him to the mildly annoyed bartender.

"Bloody Mary," I said. Oh, fucking well if I spilled some on my sweater. I already had beer all over it.

Zach ordered it and got himself another beer. He turned to me with our drinks and put a hand on the small of my back, more familiar with me than I thought was appropriate, but it felt nice. It probably had to do with having just watched my fiancé cheat on me. It felt good to think that maybe in another life I could have flirted with Zach and even gone home with him. It felt good to know that someone found me attractive.

He stopped somewhere in the back of the club, behind all the tables and chairs. People walked to and fro around us.

"Look, let me get your shirt dry cleaned," he said.

"I really don't need you to. I can have it done myself," I said stiffly.

"I'm sure you can, but it's my fault," he said. "I have a shirt in the back I can get for you. Let me at least do that much. I feel awful and I'm pretty sure that shirt is more expensive than my entire outfit."

I chuckled a little at that. He wasn't wrong. He was wearing faded jeans, a black t-shirt and a heather gray hoodie with white shoe strings coming out of the hood. He looked good. Something about him stirred up something inside of me, even if I wasn't willing to admit it. He wasn't fancy like Alex, and I enjoyed that most of all.

"Okay," I acquiesced. "What do I need to do to get a t-shirt?"

He tilted his head slightly and looked right in my eyes. He didn't shift his gaze down at my chest, something that I was accustomed to.

"Stay for the show and let me buy you a cup of coffee afterwards," he said.

And then, as though it was an instinct I'd been waiting to act on all along, I slid my left hand into my pants pocket, hiding my ring. I wondered if it came so easily to Alex as it had to me. I wondered if the instinct to cheat was in all of us, just waiting for the right situation, the right set of circumstances, the right amount of dissatisfaction. I wondered if I was really capable of that.

I thought about my capabilities only for a split second before I nodded my head wordlessly. A huge grin broke out across Zach's face.

"I've got a reserved table at the front if you want a seat," he said.

I looked towards the front, scanning the crowd for Amy once more and not seeing her. I thought about how prominent I would be sitting up front. I thought about her seeing me, telling Alex where I was, saying that she saw me leave with some guy. The thought of it made me bold. I wanted all those things. I wanted Alex to be so angry that he showed his emotions instead of keeping them locked away from me like he did his precious weapons collection. I wanted him to feel something, anything at all, towards me. I wanted his fire and his passion back that seemed to have been extinguished in the last year. I wanted what he had with Amy in his office tonight and I didn't care how I had to go about getting it. I nodded my head and smiled sweetly.

"That would be lovely," I said.

He was funny.

"I went to this restaurant in Cleveland that had a buffet it was famous for. They were known for their chili and it was all I wanted to try the whole time I was there," he said, running a hand through his shiny, dark brown hair. He had reached the end of his set and people had laughed. Some so hard that they were crying, like the girl to my right. "I went up to the buffet and there was a woman behind me. There was about one scoop of chili left and they were closing pretty soon. I asked the cook about it and he said, 'Oh yeah. That's all we've got for the rest of the night,' so I grabbed the spoon and started to scoop it up when the woman behind me tapped me on the shoulder.

"'I wouldn't get that if I were you,' she said.

"'Why?' I asked.

"'I come here all the time, and that stuff will make you sicker than a dog,' she said.

"I thought about it for a minute and decided not to get the chili. I had a show that night and the last thing I needed was to be sick. I was sad, a little bummed, but I went on to the rest of the buffet and loaded up on other stuff that looked pretty good—not as good as the chili—but pretty good.

"So, then I'm getting ready to pay and the woman passes me on the way to the cashier. She pays for her food and turns to walk to a table, and I look at her tray. And there, in a neat little scoop, I shit you not, is the last of the chili. And I look at the woman like 'What the fuck, dude?' and she looks at me, caught red-handed, and in her sweetest grandma voice she says, 'What? I wanted to see if it was as good as they said it is!'"

The crowd erupted into laughter and Zach raised a hand.

"You guys have been great. Thank you!" he said, putting the microphone back on the stand. He walked off stage and the crowd stood. I stood with them. I cheered and whistled, my second Bloody Mary helping me out in feeling celebratory. There were a few other people at my table that I didn't know but that seemed to know Zach or Eric, who was sitting at the table.

Still, I hadn't seen Amy.

The crowd began to go up for more drinks and I worked

my way back to the bar when I saw Zach coming out from backstage. Just as he walked out of the backstage door, I saw a woman with flame red hair stop him.

Amy.

She looked furious.

She was waving her arms, gesticulating wildly, enunciating every word with a sharp poke into his chest or a shove. He grabbed her by the shoulders, trying to calm her down. She fought him off like a tiger, caged and cornered. She shouted at the security guard who came to Zach's aid.

He grabbed her by the arm and started to haul her out against her will. They were headed my direction. I looked around for somewhere to step but there were people blocking every possible route that I could have taken.

Amy and the security guard came past me and she locked eyes on me, a heat-seeking missile having found a target. She looked like she wanted to kill, and I would have been as good a victim as any. For a brief moment, her anger faded, and she seemed shocked to see me there. She craned her head around to look at me as the security guard dragged her out of the club.

"My ex," Zach said, stepping up beside me as I watched Amy's puff of curly red hair disappear out the door.

"I'm sorry," I said, my statement more loaded than he realized. What a coincidence.

"Let me get you that t-shirt," he said. "Come with me. You can wash up backstage."

He reached out a hand and I looked at it for a moment. It was an invitation. Maybe just backstage but maybe to something else entirely, I wasn't sure, but something told me to take that hand stretched out towards me and never look back. I wanted to go with him backstage and to wherever he was going after that. I never wanted to see Alex or Amy ever again. I wanted to be so far from where I was.

Zach took great strides and I almost stumbled trying to keep up with him in my pumps. I scampered along, taking more steps than him to keep the same pace. He opened the door and ushered me down a long hallway where a bathroom lay to my left.

"I'll be right back with a t-shirt," he said.

I walked inside and shut the door, locking it behind me. I looked in the mirror. My cheeks were flushed from the alcohol and my eyes were a little bloodshot from crying. I wondered if he could tell that looking at me in the dim club lighting.

I also wondered if I cared.

I washed my face with the hand soap, scrubbing off all the remnants of my makeup. I dried my face with a rough paper towel that scratched my face as it absorbed the residual water. I looked in the mirror again, seeing myself almost as though for the first time. I looked so tired. I was so stressed. I was so unhappy.

Zach knocked on the door.

"I've got a shirt for you," he said, his voice muffled by the thin piece of wood between us.

I unlocked the door and opened it.

"A small and a medium. I wasn't sure which size you'd want," he said, offering them up.

"Thank you," I said, grabbing the medium in his left hand.

"I'll be right here," he said.

I shut the door and unfurled the t-shirt. It had his face and Eric's face on it, but they were cartoons. It looked like Looney Tunes and it said, "That's bullshit, folks!" I surmised that it was their catchphrase from the podcast. I pulled my sweater over my head and sniffed it, inhaling the scent of beer. I stuffed it into my purse and threw on the t-shirt and stepped out of the bathroom.

"Hey, it looks great on you," he said with a huge smile, sitting in a chair directly across from the bathroom.

I twirled like I was doing a fashion show.

"It certainly smells better than my sweater," I said.

"God, I'm so sorry about that," he said. "Let me have it."

I pulled it out of my bag and gave it to him. He rolled it around in his hands, admiring the place where the beer had soaked in.

"I'll take it to the cleaners tomorrow," he said. "Now," he stood. "Coffee?"

My heart raced in my chest. What was I doing? Amy had just seen me and now I was going to have coffee with a strange man. I had just watched my fiancé cheat on me and my moral compass was spinning out of control, so far away from true north that I couldn't have fought my way out of a wet paper sack.

"Yeah," I murmured, the blood pounding my ears so loudly that I could barely hear myself speaking.

Zach smiled and jerked his head, motioning for me to follow him. I did. We walked down the hallway and out into the comedy club where most of the people had begun to socialize at the bar. We walked past them and the tables. Zach took me out the back door.

"I can drive," he said.

"That's not necessary," I countered.

In the back parking lot, we were at an impasse. I could either get in the car with this complete stranger against my better judgment, or I could just call it all off and go home and have my moral superiority to Alex to keep me warm tonight.

I wasn't sure if it was what I had witnessed earlier in the evening or if it was the alcohol running through my veins, but a grin broke out on my face. Zach smiled and led me to a Challenger SRT Hellcat, and I took it in when I saw it. It was the car of my dreams. It was red with black racing stripes, and it looked like a beast.

"Oh shit," I said as we came up on it. "This is yours?"

"Yeah," he said, a big grin breaking out on his face. "Wait 'til you hear her."

He opened the door, got in, and started her up. The exhaust was modified and the V8 purred loudly through it. It was throaty and threatening, everything that an Audi wasn't.

"I love it," I said, clapping my hands together, feeling like a kid on Christmas morning at the thought of getting to go for a ride in the Hellcat.

"Just wait," he said, leaning over the console and opening the passenger side of the car. "Get in."

I hurried around and hopped into the bucket racing seat. I buckled my seatbelt and took in the interior of the car: the dash glowed white into Zach's face as he shut the door. There was a large display that showed racing statistics as well as what was playing via Bluetooth. He shifted into gear and we were off.

The exhaust vibrated the cabin, sending a shock wave through me. I could feel my heart begin to beat faster in anticipation of its abilities.

On LaBrea, he raced a Mustang and left him in his dust. He did a burnout, and I laughed, high and nervous, knowing that we were only a hair's breadth away from being caught by the cops. But it was exhilarating. I thought about being arrested. I thought about Alex finding out that I was with Zach—a stranger. It was intoxicating.

Speeding through the hills, hugging every curve, listening to the whine and roar of the engine and exhaust—all of it was intoxicating. I felt like I was in high school again. The weight of the last year lifted off me like the Jaws of Life were prying me from a fiery crash. Zach smiled and I melted into the moment. All that mattered was now and I was fully present and ready for whatever was going to happen next.

We drove past the homes of several movie stars and cruised around Hollywood. Something caught my eye that I'd never noticed before. On the north side of Hollywood Boulevard there was a huge skull mural with hundreds of roses. Above the painting were the words MUSEUM OF DEATH.

"Hey, what's that?" I asked.

"The Museum of Death. Ever been there?" he asked.

"I haven't, that's why I asked."

"Want to go?" he asked, raising an eyebrow and smirking so delightfully that I felt my stomach jump.

"Are they open right now?" I asked, looking back in the side mirror at a group of people that were exiting the building.

"I think they stay open pretty late," Zach said, turning at the next light to make a circle around the block.

"Yeah, I want to go," I said, feeling more adventurous than I thought I had it in me to feel anymore.

He turned at the next light and made a circle around the block coming back to the museum where he pulled in and parked. We got out and walked around to the front where several tourists were getting ready to take a picture in front of the museum. It looked like the matriarch was going to sacrifice being in the picture in order to get a good one. It reminded me of my own mom.

"I can take that for you," I offered, catching her off guard. She jumped and then laughed.

"That would be wonderful," she said with a southern accent.

"Where are you from?" I asked, taking the cell phone from her as she backed up to the museum front.

"Georgia," she said.

"Nashville," I said in response. It wasn't often that I encountered another southern belle in the City of Angels. I smiled at her and her family, counted to three and snapped the picture. I handed her the phone and she smiled, thanking me.

"I figured it had to be Nashville or somewhere down there," Zach said, his thick east coast accent coming out.

"You got something against us?" I said, turning up my accent to an eleven and flipping my hair over my shoulder.

"Nothing at all against *y'all,* ma'am," Zach said, trying his best to imitate a southern drawl and failing miserably.

"Stick to the Yankee accent, sir," I said with a smirk as he opened the wrought iron gate that lead into the entrance of the museum.

We stepped up to the cash register and I was greeted with lapel pins of Marshall Applewhite. I picked one up and examined it.

Before I could stop him, Zach paid for the tickets.

"You shouldn't have done that," I said, feeling guilty. The whimsy of the moment we shared outside was gone. He had no idea that I was engaged. My tone was more serious than it had been the rest of the evening when I'd tried to refuse his kindness. I didn't know what he thought was going to come of this, but I didn't want to hurt him.

"Let's go," he said with a gleeful smile that didn't match the macabre subject matter of our location. We entered a room that was decked out with the art of various serial killers. I examined the shoes of John Wayne Gacy that he would wear when he dressed as Pogo the Clown. It was chilling to see the paintings and then read the headlines about the men and women who painted them.

We stopped in the next room, full of mourning jewelry and antiques from the Victorian era. Another room held all that was needed to embalm a body and featured a video playing that showed one how to set the jaw of a dead person.

I watched in both fascination and horror. The corpse lay on the table, cold I was sure, and the man narrating the video spoke so calmly as the hands on the screen slipped a needle up through the gums of the cadaver and pulled it back down on the other side, securing the mouth with the thread. I thought of the missing girl, Samantha Logan.

"Appetizing, right?" Zach said over my shoulder. I turned and looked up at him, wanting to banish an unpleasantness from my mind. In the dim lighting of the room, his stubble seemed to glow on his face, and I wanted to reach out and touch it. I wanted to feel his skin beneath my fingers. I just wanted to touch another human being that wasn't repulsed by the sight of me. There was something pure about Zach. He wasn't tainted with darkness. I pictured my touch like Midas's, only mine brought grief instead of gold. I didn't want to burden him with that.

We walked into a room that featured nothing but a huge display of the Black Dahlia, the most infamous of all the Los Angeles crime scenes. The pictures were hung high and large across the wall. There she was, severed in half and left to rot in that field only to be found by a mother walking with her children. I tried to imagine the woman's horror upon discovering something so awful. I couldn't. Walking with her children, she had to have seen the girl's hair. She had to have wondered what she was seeing, surely unable to make sense of something like that. She probably walked closer and closer until she could make out that it was a naked woman, severed in half and dead. I shuddered and a cold chill took me over.

The next part of the museum was a hallway with car accident photos. Then there was a display about Heaven's Gate. There was Marshall Applewhite spewing his insanity on a small color television while a mannequin lay in a bunk bed behind him wearing the Heaven's Gate Away Team windbreaker.

"This place is something else, huh?" Zach asked quietly as we passed another couple in the gallery of suicide photos.

"Something else," I repeated, not really sure what else to say.

I'd always loved things that were dark. I'd gravitated towards them. Perhaps that's how I wound up choosing Alex. His darkness. Maybe it was that I thought I could bring some light to him. Maybe in some other life I could have, but not now. Now that was impossible.

As I looked at the pictures of the people who had taken their own lives, I wondered if Alex could do something like that. He was too keen on himself, I thought.

I looked over at Zach who was examining the pictures of a self-inflicted gunshot wound to the head via shotgun. The guy's brain was plastered on the wall behind him. His jaw was entirely gone along with part of one side of his face.

I stepped closer. I looked more at Zach than the remnants of the man in the black and white photograph. His eyes were locked on the man in wild concentration like I'd never seen before. I imagined him looking at me that way. I wondered if Zach could relate to the man the way that I was.

Finally, the silence was too much. I broke it.

"What do you see?" I asked him.

He looked at me, his eyes sad.

"I see a man who gave up," he said. "I see a family torn apart." He looked back at the photograph and spoke candidly, as though I wasn't there. "I see desperation and pain and loneliness that couldn't be cured. I see myself and I see you."

He was silent for a moment and then he looked at me.

"I saw your engagement ring," he finally said.

My stomach flipped, nausea overtaking me. My cheeks flushed hot with embarrassment. The gravity of the situation pulled me back down to earth and out of the high I'd been riding on since we got into his too-fast car and drove through the hills. The jig was up, as they say.

"Why didn't you tell me that?" he asked.

He wasn't angry and that surprised me.

"I'm sorry," I said. It was all I knew to say. I was so used to apologizing to Alex for everything.

"Don't be sorry," Zach said softly with a sad smile. "I just wonder why you felt like you had to lie about it. I wonder what you thought my intentions were when I asked you to get coffee."

I blushed at his directness.

"I thought... You know what I thought," I said, looking away.

"Hey," he said, and he touched my face, bringing it back to face him. I felt the electricity of his touch run through me and I wished so strongly that I wasn't engaged. "That wasn't my intention. I'm sorry if that's what you thought. It wasn't like that."

"What was it like?" I asked.

"When I saw you, you looked sad. And I know what it feels like to be so sad that you say something other than the truth," he said.

I looked at him and felt my lips curve involuntarily into a smile. For a moment, the hollowness that I'd felt when I'd seen Alex with Amy in his arms left me. I felt full of something that I couldn't identify. It was strange and familiar at once.

"You still want some coffee?" he asked.

"Yeah," I said. "If you're not opposed to that."

"I'm never opposed to making a new friend," he said with a smile that hit me dead in the stomach.

Zach took my hand, and we walked out of the museum together into the cool night air of Los Angeles.

"So, what do you do, Tash?" he asked me as he sipped a cup of coffee at a late night café that we found in Hollywood. Tourists bustled in and out wearing the shirts they'd bought on the Walk of Fame.

"I'm a paleontologist," I said. "At the Tar Pits Museum."

"No shit?" he asked, delighted. It wasn't often that I got that reaction when discussing my job.

"*Jurassic Park* fan?" I asked with a smirk, stirring my latte.

"You have no idea," he said and turned sideways in the booth. He pulled up his shirt. On his ribcage was a detailed photorealistic tattoo of two velociraptors in the kitchen of the Visitor's Center on Isla Nublar. One of them stood on the counter while the other followed close behind on the floor.

"Wow," I said. "That's really good."

"Thanks," he said.

"You have any more tattoos?" I asked, always curious about what people chose to have inked into their flesh forever. I had always wanted one. Alex detested them. He thought they made someone look cheap. Just the way he felt my nickname made me sound. Tash. It sounds like a stripper's stage name, he'd once said.

"I have another on my ribcage on the other side. It's kinda douchey. It's just my last name," he said, brushing the hair out of his face and running his hand through it. It looked incredibly soft.

"What's your last name?" I asked, curious to know more about my new friend.

"O'Halloran," he said with a wiggle of his eyebrows. In an Irish accent he added, "Irish as they come, lassie."

I couldn't help it. I liked him. I wanted to be his friend and if it were another life, maybe even more than that. I wanted to tell him everything. I wanted to care about him and for him to care about me. I wanted to be so far away from the life that I was living that it faded into the horizon, a dot in the grand map of my life.

We chatted for a little while longer. Zach told me about the podcast he ran with his friend, another comedian named Eric, and how they were gaining some traction with it in New York, where a lot of their fan base was located. I asked him what it was like to be a comedian and if he knew anyone famous. He didn't, he said. We laughed about it. He asked me more about my job and told me about his passion for dinosaurs and how he'd gone on a volunteer dig in Montana one summer.

When we were finished with our coffee, I didn't want to leave. Alex would soon be wondering why it had taken me so long to get home from the dinner I'd told him I was having with Melinda. We drove back through the hills, and I asked him to gun it a couple of times. He obliged and I shrieked in delight. The car was an intoxicating beast all of its own accord.

Back at the club, he dropped me off.

"I had fun, Tash," he said as I opened the door of his car.

"I did, too," I said, not lying in the slightest.

"It wasn't my intent," he began, looking away out the windshield. "But I can't help that wish you were single."

I felt a pang in my chest. I realized in that instant that I, too, wished that I was single. And that's when I knew that I had to go.

"I've got to go," I said hurriedly, sadly.

"I'm sorry," he said. "That was too much."

"No, it's fine," I said, unable to meet his eyes. Unable to tell him that it wasn't too much, that it was exactly what I wanted to hear him say. What I'd wanted to hear him say all night. I knew then that if I stayed one instant longer, I'd kiss him, and it would all be over. The life I'd built with Alex would topple like the fragile row of dominos that it was. A fake castle, built of cards.

I had to at least try with Alex. After everything, I had to give him another chance.

"Good night," he said.

"Good night," I replied, quickly shutting the door. I walked around the building and across the street, down the sidewalk and arrived at my car. It was humble in comparison to the Hellcat and I was a little sad that it would be taking me home tonight.

As I got in, I heard the roar of a V8 engine coming

around the corner. He revved it as he went by, and I smiled wildly.

CHAPTER 16

Los Angeles Nov. 2013

Things were dull at the museum. We were at a stand-still on the mammoth behavior research due to financial issues. We had been doing fundraising for it, but the money wasn't there at the moment. Alex didn't like the extra time that I was spending at work, but I didn't feel incredibly guilty about it in light of recent events. Besides, being alone with him in the apartment was suffocating.

Melinda was knee deep in writing a presentation for the kids that visited the museum. It had to do with a person dressing up as a sabre-toothed tiger and I still wasn't entirely clear on the logistics of it. I walked out of my office and into hers.

"What's up?" she said as I hovered in the doorway.

"Nothing. That's the problem," I groaned.

She looked up from her computer.

"Sit," she said.

"I've been sitting all day. I want to get my hands dirty," I said.

"I know," she mimicked my groan. She stretched her

hands above her head and arched her back, extending her spine like a cat.

I looked out the window and saw a couple with their little girl walking towards the tar pits. I wondered if it was her first time going somewhere like this. I wondered if her parents told her anything about the mammals that lived after the dinosaurs were gone. Fostering a love of science in a child was important, but what was imperative was fostering curiosity and a love of learning.

"Hello?" Melinda said, waving a hand as though I was across a stadium from her at a concert.

"What?" I asked.

"I asked how your weekend was," she said. "I'm sorry I couldn't go to dinner with you. Did you go anyway?"

"Oh," I said, thinking about Friday night. I thought about the way the Hellcat ripped off the pavement at the green lights and I thought about Zach's crisp laughter in the cool evening air. It echoed in my mind whenever I got quiet. An image of Alex and Amy danced in the background, a demon on my shoulder, telling me to do things I normally wouldn't think of. "It was great," I only half-lied. "How was yours?" I asked, trying to change the trajectory of the conversation.

"Too fast," she said, rubbing her eyes.

"Have a date?" I asked, wiggling my eyebrows suggestively. Melinda was always dating someone new. I lived vicariously through her. I had gotten with Alex so early that I had missed out on most of the dating scene. She always assured me that I was the lucky one—that I hadn't missed anything. Sometimes I doubted her. Since Friday night, especially.

"I did," she said and seemed to force a smile.

"Not great?" I asked.

"Not great to say the least. He brought a sugar glider with him."

"But that's so cool!" I cried.

"Tash," she said. 'Try to imagine a guy ordering a plate at El Coyote with a tiny marsupial poking out of his dress shirt. Not cute."

"I would think that was cute."

"Of course you would. And that's probably why you're engaged and I'm single."

I balked at the comment. It stung. I wondered what she meant by it.

"That's not what I meant," Melinda said. "Alex is great."

I smiled. Everyone thought Alex was wonderful and why wouldn't they? On the outside, everything about him was sheer perfection. He was athletic, he was smart, he acted nice to strangers, and to top it all off, he was loaded. Wasn't that what every woman wanted? I had thought so when I was twenty-one.

There was a knock on the door beside me.

"Tash," Robert said. "You've got a visitor."

I knew it was Alex. I didn't want to see him just now. I hated it when he came to the museum. Everyone fawned over him and I heard about how great he was for the next day or two. Usually, he brought me something and they thought I was the luckiest girl alive.

"I'll talk to you later," I said as I turned and left Melinda's office. I walked briskly to the front of the museum, girding my loins for a conversation with my fiancé. It was like playing chess with someone who was always two moves ahead of you.

I continued around the corner and walked to the front desk, looking for Alex, but I didn't see him. Instead, I saw a

head of black shaggy hair that fell about shoulder length on a guy who was a little taller than Alex.

It was Zach.

My stomach lurched.

I racked my brain for a reason that he would show up here and came up short. I almost stopped in my tracks but forced my feet to find themselves and keep moving.

I walked up to the desk, my eyes wide and my heart pounding my ears. I hated the effect he had on me.

Zach turned just as I walked up, and a smile cracked across the slight beard that covered the lower half of his face.

"Hey," he said more softly than I think he meant to.

"Hey," I said more softly than I know I meant to.

I smiled.

I glanced over at the receptionist. She looked from Zach to me and back again. Her eyes told the tale of how amused she was by the situation. She knew Alex and she knew this guy wasn't Alex. I watched her put the puzzle together in her mind.

It was uncomfortable, but Zach's presence was such that I didn't care. I was so glad to see him again. I couldn't deny that.

"I brought you this," he said, holding out a plastic bag.

I looked down at it, confused. I took it and opened it, seeing my white blouse. I pulled it out and unfurled it. The stains from the beer were gone and it smelled fresh.

"Thanks," I said with a big smile. My relief was in the fact that Alex wouldn't find out that something had been spilled on it. I couldn't stomach the thought of him blowing up on me and railing about money when he had more than enough of it.

Zach looked different under the warm lighting of the

museum. Not illuminated by neon signs and streetlights or the fluorescents in the café, I could see small lines around his eyes indicating he'd spent a good deal of his life laughing. Or perhaps it was crying, his handsome face contorted with pain.

"No problem," Zach said. "I was wondering if maybe—"

As the words came out of his mouth, one of the doors leading into the museum flew open and a gust of air slammed it shut. I looked over and jumped, startled. What got me was who came through that door. It was Alex.

Papers flew out of his briefcase as it slammed into the doorframe. His tie fluttered as he stormed in. He looked like a mess. I couldn't help but wonder if he had been canoodling with Amy. But despite his frazzled appearance, he was sporting a winning smile. My face must have been puzzled. A mixture of horror and curiosity. I had landed myself in a sticky situation that it would be challenging to get out of, to say the least.

"Natasha!" he shouted, loud enough that patrons of the museum turned, startled by his boisterousness.

I looked around and stepped towards him, away from Zach.

"Hey," I said, sounding much less excited than he was.

"I have good news," he said. "I want to go to dinner tonight. Let's leave right now and get ready. I want to go to Providence."

The fancy restaurant was where we did a lot of our celebrating when Alex won cases or small victories at work. I looked back at Zach and then turned to face Alex again. His eyes had followed mine and landed on the rescuer of my blouse.

I looked between them. They took each other in. They sized each other up.

"Am I interrupting something?" Alex asked, backing away from me a step, pulling away the hand the touched my arm. It was his most utilized weapon, pulling away. He did it physically and emotionally, and every time I felt like a child being pried mercilessly from its mother, forced into the halls of a grade school for the first time. Except in this version, the mother laughed at the child's pain.

"No. Not at all," I said, waving a casual hand at Zach. "This is—" I paused. How was I going to do this? Introduce the man I was going to marry to the man I'd spent Friday night flirting with and driving around the Hollywood Hills in his fancy car? I felt like a hypocrite, mad at Alex for what he'd done with Amy. But it wasn't the same.

"Who are you?" Alex asked, stepping past me towards Zach.

They were almost of equal height with Alex falling a few inches shorter than Zach. Alex looked up at him like he was something unpleasant that he'd picked off the bottom of his shoe and was holding up into the light to get a better look at.

"Zach O'Halloran," Zach said without hesitation. His New York accent making him sound tough. "Who are you?"

"Alexander Roth," he said, sounding so proud of his name that it made me cringe. "Tash's fiancé and Senator Jim Roth's son." I double cringed when he name dropped his dead father for emphasis on his importance.

Zach confusion over the situation evaporated like water on a desert highway outside of Las Vegas in 120 degree heat. It was replaced with what looked like hurt. I wanted to jump between them. I wanted to save Zach from whatever Alex would hurl at him.

"I see," Zach said. He looked at me with a smile pressed tightly between his lips he nodded, taking his leave. He walked past me and toward the door. My eyes followed him, and I turned my head, watching him exit.

"Who the fuck was that?" Alex asked, louder than he would normally drop the f-bomb in polite company. I startled slightly and he grabbed my arm hard enough for me to wince and jerk away from him.

"A friend," I said, rubbing my bicep where his nails had begun to dig in through the fabric of my shirt.

"Bullshit," Alex whispered dangerously.

He raised a finger to my face and pointed at me like a dog that couldn't quite get the hang of pissing outdoors. I pulled my head back, straining my neck to get away from his gesticulation.

"We'll talk about this later. You need to get your things. We're going home," he said. "Now."

I felt like a child being scolded. I felt like I'd been caught red-handed at a crime that I hadn't committed. Hadn't I been the one to catch him? My memories of Friday night clouded. Should I have been so surprised after everything this year?

He dropped his finger and rage boiled in his eyes. I wondered why they hadn't popped out of his skull yet. His property might have been touched by someone without his permission, and it was more than he could stomach. I wanted to ask him how it felt.

Instead, I turned and caught Robert's eye. He looked away quickly and continued his conversation with the receptionist. Everyone had been watching and now their eyes scattered like cockroaches when the light comes on.

Almost a week passed without mention of the run in Alex had with Zach at the museum. I hadn't seen or heard from Zach in that time, though I had looked him up on Facebook. He was single. There was no evidence of a girl in any of the pictures I was able to access of him. If he had a girlfriend, it wasn't apparent on his social media presence.

Alex and I passed like two ships in the night. We were no longer headed towards the same destination. Our relationship had transformed in the last year into something that I no longer recognized. Finally, that Thursday evening, he hit his boiling point.

"Why don't we have groceries?" he barked from the kitchen. I sat on the loveseat watching reruns of *The Walking Dead*, my favorite show and Alex's most hated. He couldn't stand that I liked the violence. He said it was unladylike. Why couldn't I just watch *Grey's Anatomy* like Amy did? It only steeled my resolve that I'd never stop watching Rick Grimes take out the living and the undead.

"I'm supposed to go pick them up tomorrow. I ordered them this afternoon," I said, annoyed at him. I'd told him yesterday that I'd order groceries today.

He slammed the pantry door and stormed into the living room.

"It would be nice if you did anything to keep this place running," he said viciously.

I turned to face him.

"Well, Alex, there are a lot of things that would make our lives nicer. Many of which you could do, but I don't see any of that happening any time soon," I said.

He ran his hands through his hair.

"I know you're cheating on me," he said nervously. I didn't ever see him that way.

I looked at him.

"Projecting much?" I asked, looking back at the TV, uninterested in having this argument.

"What?" he asked, incredulous.

"You and Amy!" I shouted, losing my cool, turning to face him, on my knees on the couch. "I know you're fucking her. I should have known a long time ago."

"I can't believe you'd think that," Alex said, his ability to lie so convincingly was frightening. If I hadn't witnessed him doing it with my own eyes, he might have snowed me.

"Don't lie to me," I said.

"Lie? What about you? Where were you last Friday?" he barked.

"I was with Melinda!" I lied.

I wondered once again, for the second time in less than a week, when we had become so broken. But I knew when it had happened. I knew the exact moment. I knew when I had become someone that I wasn't in order to please Alex. But I was sick of it.

"No you weren't, you whore," he spat.

The words stung. I got to my feet.

"I saw you with her," I hissed. Ready to unleash on him. "I saw you with Amy. I saw you fuck her in your office."

He looked baffled.

"You know and I know that you're fucking her. Why don't you just ask her to move on in with us?" I screamed. "Wouldn't that be just what you wanted all along?"

I shoved past him and put my shoes on. I grabbed my purse.

"Where are you going?" he asked.

"Wouldn't you like to know."

I slammed the door behind me, feeling for the first time in ages that I'd won one small battle.

CHAPTER 17

Los Angeles Dec. 2013

"And now, back to you, Connie," said the weatherman with a big grin. The camera focused on a petite blonde sitting behind a news desk. With a serious face, she reported.

"Tonight we have learned that the jawbone found on El Matador Beach outside of Los Angeles belongs to the missing girl, Samantha Logan. Dental records were found to be a match. Samantha was missing for more than three months before the discovery of the jawbone was made by a couple on their honeymoon. Our thoughts are with her family this evening."

The feed cut to a shot of a vigil at El Matador Beach. People held candles. The gathering was small but those who were there were struck by the tragedy. I felt a knot in my gut at learning that the dental records had been a match. I wondered how her friends felt. I didn't know her that well, but I knew that she wasn't close with either of her parents. I wondered if they were even in the crowd. I recognized some of the people from the Sanctuary.

"We should be there," Alex said.

"We didn't know her that well," I said. "People would think it was weird."

Alex was silent. He didn't argue with me. I thought about how awkward it would be to interact with everyone on the eve that their friend had been discovered dead and not missing. I felt for them. I'm sure that all of them wanted justice for Samantha and I didn't blame them. I wanted it for her, too.

My chest tightened. I grabbed my phone, looking for comfort and not finding it in Alex, I opened Facebook. I found Zach's page and sent him a message.

Can you meet me tonight?

It was only moments before he responded.

When and where?

I felt relief flood me just at reading his words. I needed his warmth and his kindness. I needed to see him smiling, unaware of the tragedy that had befallen the little community at the Sanctuary.

I told him where to meet me and I got up from the couch.

"I'm going for a walk," I told Alex.

"What? Right now?" he said.

"I need to clear my head," I said evenly, indicating that he wasn't welcome.

He said nothing and went back to watching the news, which now featured a story about a kid on a soccer team that had cancer. They were fundraising for his treatment.

"If you want to do something good for the world, you could donate to that boy," I said, my voice lamely attempting to hide the viciousness behind it. Alex didn't flinch.

I grabbed my things and headed out the door.

I waited in my car at El Matador Beach. I watched as the vigil broke up and the people began to go to their cars. I told Zach to meet me there in an hour. Thirty minutes had passed. As there were less and less people, I got out of my car.

I slung my purse into the back seat and locked the doors, shoving my cell phone and my keys deep into my pants pocket.

I walked down towards the beach. I kicked off my flip flops and let the cool sand push up between my toes, like daisies growing and forcing their way through a corpse buried in the soil of a cemetery. I carried my shoes in my hand and walked down towards the water.

Giant rocks protruded from the sand, coming up out of it like the stained teeth of some ancient monster. The beach was wild. Nature was brutal. I imagined Sam's body floating in the water long enough to be consumed by sharks and fish and whatever else lurked in the waters. I imagined them picking her bones clean until her jaw washed up on the shore. My stomach rolled.

I strolled down the beach, the sun setting in the distance, coloring the water a beautiful orange and pink, fading into the darkest purple that could swallow you whole, never to be seen or heard from again.

I wondered what the theory was on how she got there. Was she dumped? Did she drown? Had she come to the beach of her own free will? Was there a strange man that they were investigating? I didn't know and it gave me anxiety to wonder about their speculations.

"Hey," came a familiar voice over the crash of the waves

against the rocks and the shore. I turned in the ankle-deep water to see Zach, his own shoes in hand.

"Hey," I said softly.

I hadn't seen him since the day at the museum when Alex had gotten furious. I had missed him. I'd missed his smile and the warmth that radiated out from it. The cold of my apartment was getting to me. I felt it in my bones. I felt Alex's cold touch at every corner. I felt his grip extending into the most private reaches of my life where I never thought anyone could own me, and yet, Alex did.

Zach ran a hand through his hair as the wind whipped it around his face. He tried to tame it, get it out of his eyes, but the wind had other plans. He held it back with one hand. My hair, in a ponytail, was a little tamer.

I smiled at him, wanting to keep his face exposed.

"Need a ponytail holder?" I asked him.

"Yeah, I could use one," he said.

I slid one off my wrist and handed it to him. He put his hair up into a tiny ponytail. He picked his shoes back up and we began to walk.

"What did you want to see me for, Tash?" he finally asked after the silence between us became so heavy that it was like a weight on my chest.

"I don't know," I said. I wasn't entirely convinced by my answer, and he wasn't either.

"You do know," he said, stopping me. He turned to me and took my free hand with his. "You're unhappy," he said. "I know that when I see it. Hell, I should," he laughed bitterly. "Why don't you leave him? Why do you stay?"

I choked back tears. He had no idea how badly I wanted to.

"I can't," I said, sure that he'd never understand.

"Yes, you can," he said. "No matter what you think holds you to him, it doesn't."

He had no idea. He didn't know that Alex knew me in a way that he didn't. Alex had seen my darkness and embraced it. I didn't know that anyone else could ever do the same. Including, and most importantly, me.

"You don't understand," I said, and I smiled sadly. "And I don't expect you to."

"Why did you ask me to come here then?"

"I just needed to see you," I said, growing exasperated. I didn't want the questions. I wanted his presence. I needed to be with him.

He was silent.

"I needed to see you, too," he said at last.

We began to walk again, further and further from our cars.

"Why?" I asked, curious.

"I can't stop thinking about that night a few weeks ago. Driving around with you. The museum. Coffee. It just felt better than anything I've done in a long time," he said. "In spite of our circumstances," he took my hand and rubbed my ring. I pulled it away from him.

"We shouldn't be here," I said, almost breathless, sure that if I spent one more moment with him, I would cross a line that I couldn't come back from and Alex and I would truly be done.

"We should," he said, turning to face me again. My back to the water, the sun crashing into the ocean illuminated his face in pink and orange light, stray hairs danced across his face as he wrapped his arms around my waist and pulled me to him.

His eyes traced the surface of my face like tiny hands. I

felt them roll over my lips. His parted slightly. He leaned down towards me and pressed his to mine.

His tongue parted my them gently, gliding over them like liquid silk. I opened my mouth, eager for his kiss. It was a kiss as powerful as the waves crashing around us against the rocks that jutted from the sand. I wrapped my arms around his neck and swayed in his arms.

He pulled away from me, his eyes dilated wide like an animal's. He panted. I placed a hand on his chest as I laid my head against it.

"Let's go," he said, taking my hand.

I followed without a word of protest.

Zach dropped his keys on the washing machine, and they fell with a clang. He turned to me and pulled me close to him. With great need, he pressed his lips to mine, his beard scratching my face. I didn't care. He parted my lips with his tongue and nibbled lightly on the bottom one. I emitted a noise of wanting and felt my tummy tighten with his embrace.

He kissed my cheek, and his whiskers tickled my throat as he sucked lightly on my skin. His lips went to my shoulder and down my arm. He brought my hand to his lips and kissed it. I stared at him, struck by his handsomeness. He interlocked our fingers with one hand and with the other pulled me back to him. He pressed his mouth to mine and a heat-seeking missile could have been derailed from its course had it sensed what passed between us.

He backed me out of the laundry room and slid his hands down my back to the tail of my shirt. He worked it up, over my head and threw it to the side as we entered the living room. My legs hit the couch, and he turned me around, switching places with me. My hands worked his shirt over his head, revealing his muscular arms and chest, not waxed to perfection like Alex's. I pushed him down on the couch, straddling my legs over his waist. He strained against his jeans and when my groin contacted his, he closed his eyes and drew in a breath. He groaned and opened them to face me, his eyes hungry.

With both hands he took my face. He stroked my cheek lightly with his thumb and pulled me into him, kissing me once more. I found my hips grinding against his, eliciting primal noises from both of us.

His hands moved to my hips, holding on with a grip so masculine that I sighed, my breath ragged and becoming more so. My heart thudded in my chest like a bird in a cage, ready to fly away at the first opportunity. He dug his fingers in, and I moaned, pressing down until the jeans that separated us became too much.

He flipped me onto my back on the couch and kneeled between my thighs. Expertly, he unbuttoned my jeans and slid them from my hips, exposing them to the cool air of the living room. He placed a hand on my belly, using his other one to free himself of the confines of his Levi's.

He wore black boxer briefs that silhouetted his ass perfectly. He was hard, showing through the fabric and I longed to touch him. I reached out a hand and he took it, gently guiding it back to its place at my side.

"You first," he said, his voice husky.

The hand on my stomach traced a trail down my abdomen and to the edge of my panties. I sucked in a jagged breath when his hand found the heat between my legs. With deft skill, his fingers moved the fabric aside. Instead of the rough penetration I was accustomed to with Alex, Zach ran a lazy stroke against me, causing me to grab the pillow behind my head and arch my back. He found the most sensitive part of me with his mouth and gently traced circles around it with his tongue. I sighed at that first contact and bit my own arm as the pleasure grew.

My phone dinged on the floor, having fallen from my pocket. Out of my peripheral vision, I saw it and looked at it dead on. It was a text message, and I could make out Alex's name with the heart emoji next to it.

That damned emoji.

I'd saved his number that way when I'd had my first iPhone so many years ago. The heat of the moment was sucked away as though by an undertow. I felt Alex's coldness descending on the room like a wet blanket. I scooted away from Zach.

"No," I barely managed.

Zach stopped and looked at me confused.

"What's wrong?" he asked, resting his hand on my thigh.

"We can't do this," I said to him, shaking my head, tears stinging my eyes. Even if Alex had done it and I was justified, I wasn't Alex and I couldn't.

Zach breathed a ragged breath of resignation.

"Tash," he started, running a hand through his hair.

"Don't," I said.

"Let me take you back to your car," he said.

"No," I said. "I can get a taxi," I said, righting myself and grabbing my clothes. I threw them on. Sitting on the couch without his shirt, Zach rubbed his face.

"Let me at least take you back to your car," he said.

"It's not necessary," I said, my tone taking on a professional and cold edge. "I can take care of myself."

"Are you sure about that?" Zach asked, his question pointed.

I looked at him, sitting there in the moonlight. He was gorgeous.

I could never see him again.

"Please don't do this," I said.

Zach stood from the couch and walked towards me. He took my arm.

"Tash," he said, barely a whisper. He brushed the hair that had fallen from my ponytail back behind my ear.

I turned my face away from his hand, away from the warmth of his touch. I didn't deserve someone like Zach. I deserved Alex. I had made my bed, and I needed to lie in it.

"You don't want to be with me, Zach," I said.

"You don't know what I want."

"I'm not like you," I said. "Don't contact me."

As I said it, there were tears in my eyes. I went to the front door, unlocked it and opened it. I slammed it behind me. I ran down the steps and onto the sidewalk. I raced down the street, as fast and as far as I could get from Zach.

CHAPTER 18

Nashville Dec. 2016

The next morning when I wake up, my head pounds uncontrollably the way it does when you spend hours crying. My nose is stopped up and my sinuses feel like they might explode at any moment. I would think it was allergies but it's the dead of winter in Tennessee. It doesn't seem likely. What's more probable is that I'm stressed out enough to be feeling the physical effects of it.

I swing my feet out of bed and when they hit the floor, the magnitude of everything hits me. I remember the pictures that Alex posted. I remember his e-mail, *Ha. Ha. Ha.* And I remember the cop coming to the house. I remember the phone call and I remember texting Alex. Sue groans at the thought of having to get up for the day and I look back at him, jealous that all he needs to do today is be a dog. He looks at me with his wet brown eyes that seem to be the size of saucers.

"Don't look at me like that. You make it impossible," I say, leaning back to stroke his oversized head.

He sighs contentedly and I sigh discontentedly and

throw myself back on the bed. When I crawl back out, I grab my phone that's on the nightstand. I press the home button and it illuminates the screen, showing that I have a new text message.

Alex.

Seeing his name there with the little heart emoji still beside it chills me. I didn't want to ever talk to him again after I left Los Angeles. I don't feel like I have much of a choice, though. I open the message.

I miss you.

That's all.

I feel my blood pressure skyrocket. How dare he? He misses me? It makes my stomach turn. I begin to hammer out a response.

FUCK YOU.

I think better of it and deleted it. Instead, I let the message sit, unanswered.

I cradle my head in my hands and rock slightly back and forth. A stance that I saw Alex assume once before in dire circumstances. I think I'm going to be sick.

"Tough morning?" Dan asks from the doorway. I whip my head up and see him standing there, his silhouette all I can make out with the light from the hallway behind him.

"You could say that," I snap. I'm not as angry at him as I was. I know why he'd done what he did. How could he know what the ramifications of it could be? He isn't the bad guy here.

"It's gonna be okay, Tash," he says in his most reassuring tone. I guess most of his anger at me has evaporated in the night, too. I wonder how things will ever be okay again. Sue gets up from the bed and plods across the floor to greet Dan who stretches out a hand to rub between Sue's gigantic ears. He wags his tail in response.

"You sound pretty sure of that," I say, my voice breaking as tears fight their way to the surface. I hate how weak it sounds.

"I am pretty sure of it," he says, taking a sip of his coffee and running a hand through his bed head. His eyes are still full of sleep and he rubs them with his free hand. "It's all going to work out. He doesn't get to win," he concludes.

I don't share his certainty. I try to imagine a world in which those pictures aren't available for the world to see. I can't. That world doesn't exist anymore. My privacy is gone. My dignity has been taken by Alex and now my privacy and I have nothing to show for my troubles but heavy emotional scarring.

"What are you going to do today?" I ask Dan, unsure of how the rest of the world could keep marching on in the face of something like this.

"I'm going to work," he says.

I look away from him and sigh. Of course he's going to work. He has to. I can't expect him to put his life on hold because mine is falling apart. I need to get a grip or I'm going to lose it.

"Do you want me to stay here?" he asks cautiously.

I can tell by his tone that he does't want to but if I ask him to, he will. I don't though. I shake my head and force a smile.

"That's convincing," he says. "Why don't you and Sue come to work with me?"

Sue looks up at Dan as though he knows what he's asking. He's familiar with the words *ride* and *car* and *bye-bye*; however, he is exceptionally smart and I wouldn't put it past him to put two and two together when Dan said *Sue* and *work* in the same sentence.

"I have some private lessons that I'm supposed to teach," I say with a groan.

"Cancel them. Reschedule them. Whatever," he says.

I mull it over. The idea of being anywhere but in my own skin was appealing. Anything out of the ordinary would serve the purpose of getting me out of my head. I know that much. Going to work with Daniel is an enticing possibility. Finally, I nod my head.

"Okay," I say. "You convinced me."

Dan smiles and walks away from my doorway.

"Be ready by eight," he calls back over his shoulder.

After getting to Dan's studio, I scroll through all my apps for an hour. Finally, I put my phone down and nervously check Facebook again. I go back to the message from Zach and decide to try something. I search for his professional page and quickly find it. Zach O'Halloran. Comedian.

I go through the most recent posts and even back further until I've seen every profile picture that he's ever posted. The first one looks so much like him when we first met. His hair was shorter like it had been that night at the Comedy Store. Now, his hair is longer but his beard is a little shorter, more of a week old five o'clock shadow that gets regular trimming.

I scroll through the posts, reading each one carefully. He wrote them, I'm sure. There's something too personal about them and I know he'd want to have that kind of contact with his fans. Fans. That's crazy. When I met him, he was just getting started. But it was clear from the links that he shared and from the amount of comments that he is getting big. There's a clip of him on a show on Comedy

Central performing stand up. There are pictures of him with Bill Burr and Sal Vulcano.

I wonder if the fame has gone to his head, though I can't really imagine that. Zach is someone who is so down to earth that I don't think anything like that could ever go to his head. He's so modest and soft spoken when he isn't on the stage. Just thinking about his presence is enough to calm me down.

I scroll through his page some more and come to something interesting. There is a post for a comedy show, a podcast recording, that he's doing with Eric. It's in New Orleans the same weekend as the women's camp that Heather and I are going to be teaching there.

My stomach drops at the thought of even being in the same city as Zach. I don't want to see him. I don't want to revisit those feelings.

It's morning but I'm already exhausted. I see a link that says BUY TICKETS HERE for the show in New Orleans. Before I can even think twice about it, I click the link and am taken to a different page. Zach's website. It's so strange, him having a website. I think about how unknown he was when I met him.

I look at the tickets and use the menu to bring up the price for two of them. I dig into my purse frantically and grab the first credit card I come across. I buy them. One for me and one for Heather and then stare at the confirmation page.

"Whatcha up to?" Dan says from behind me.

I slam the laptop shut and jump, feeling like a criminal.

"Nothing," I say. Sue snaps his head up when he hears my laptop shut. He looks around as though he's been woken from a rather peaceful sleep by his less than considerate human companions.

Dan narrows his eyes. I wonder if he can smell the fact that I texted Alex the night before. I feel like all my clothes reek of him and my hair is awash with his cologne. I can practically feel Alex's touch on my skin and I go cold at the thought.

"I'm gonna go get some coffee. Do you want to go with me?" he asks, standing up and putting his jacket on. I wonder why he hadn't stopped on the way here. Maybe he's as nervous as me. I stand up.

"Yeah," I say, and try my best to sell him a smile.

After Dan and I get back to his office, I get back on Facebook. I scroll mindlessly through everyone's updates and find myself going back to Zach's page. I hover over the like button and wonder if among thousands of others, he'll get a notification that I subscribed to his updates.

I go back to our messages and read them again and again. I hover over the cursor in the field to type a message. I compose several and delete them all. Finally, I settle on one.

Hey.

My stomach drops as I send it. My heart begins to pound when I see that it's been read. I see the little typing bubble and immediately slam my laptop shut.

Dan turns around at the noise, abandoning the editing he was doing on some wedding photos. Dan had complained about having to edit the photos for one of the other photographers in the office who is on his own honeymoon in Bali. I look over my shoulder at him and smile.

"Tired of seeing everyone's bullshit," I say. I lean down and Sue cranes his head up just enough for me to reach him from the drafting stool.

"Yeah, it gets old," Dan says, leaning back in his chair and stretching his arms overhead. He turns his neck from side to side and I hear it pop, tired of hunching over Photoshop for the last few hours. I'm grateful to be out of the house, but I know at some point I'll have to be alone there. Alone with thoughts of Alex and of Zach and alone with whoever it is that has decided to park outside the house. I'm not sure which of the three upsets me the most.

"You okay?" Dan asks.

I realize that I'm staring off into space, contemplating the blank piece of wall that stretches out between two of Dan's photojournalism pictures.

"Oh, yeah," I say.

"I know it's a lot to deal with, but you know I'm here for you, right?" he asks. I'm silent and he continues. "I know how you are. You like to carry everything on your own, but you don't have to do that, Tash."

I'm silent. He sighs.

"Fine. Have it your way, tough girl," he says with a smirk.

I smirk back at him.

Dan knows me so well. When we were kids and my first dog died from Lyme Disease that she got from a tick bite, I didn't tell him. I had smiled all the way through my second-grade classes and Dan had come over after school. When he asked where Sunshine was, I broke down into tears. I didn't want to talk about it at school because I knew that I would cry. I didn't want to talk about it at all because I didn't want to look weak. I didn't want him to know that I needed anyone, and today it's no different.

I wonder how I'm going to beat this Goliath on my own. I know myself, though, and that the fight isn't over yet. An image of Alex's smiling face is burned into my frontal lobe like it's been put there with a branding iron. It almost splits my head open. I want to wipe that entitled grin off his perfect face. Hurt him the way he'd hurt me. Worse.

"It's gonna be alright," Dan says for the second time that day. He reaches a hand out to me. It's a gesture he makes when things get tough, and he knows I need him but am not ready to tell him that. It's a neutral way to give me the option for human contact. The onus is on me to take his hand and I do, as I always do. I never reject it.

He squeezes my hand in his and lets it go quickly, the brief contact enough to let me know that he's there. I know he will follow me into hell, but I don't want him to have to.

He turns back to his work, and I turn back to my closed laptop. Just as I do, my phone dings, startling me to the point that I almost pee a little like a dog that gets overly excited every time someone comes to the door.

With a shaking hand, I pick it up and look at the notification.

It's a text from Heather.

You ready for the weekend, girl?

In two days we are leaving for New Orleans. The women's seminar. I think about the tickets that I bought to the podcast recording. I decide not to tell her. I don't want to answer any questions about it right now. Those can wait. I'm sure she'll have plenty.

I am!

I type the response with much more emotion than I feel. There is no punctuation mark that indicates dread and anxiety mixed with a little excitement. I include a smiley face emoji with one eye closed and the tongue sticking out.

We text a little more about the logistics of the airport and I lock my phone, looking at the back of Dan's head. My fingers twitch on my phone, and I think about Alex. I wonder if he's patiently waiting for me to text him back. That night that I saw him bang Amy's brains out is still fresh in my memory.

Alex is the last person that I've been with. He is the last person to touch me like that. My stomach clenches and my mouth begins to water like I'm Pavlov's dog. Except the saliva accumulating behind my lips has to do with vomiting instead of a tasty treat.

I open my phone and navigate to my text messages. I hit NEW MESSAGE and begin to type Henry's name into the To field.

How about that date?

My finger doesn't hesitate as I pull the trigger. Within moments, a message comes shooting back.

Pick you up at 7?

Dan and I get home, and I go immediately to the bathroom to get ready. I pull out the makeup that I never use. Expensive products that I procured when I was a kept woman. I use the prestige brands like I know what I'm doing, muscle memory taking over my movements. They are things I learned in L.A., on days when I lazily rolled around alone in the bed, my iPad in hand, watching makeup tutorials on YouTube.

The finished product is shocking. I'm so used to going around without any makeup on, my bare face to the world that seeing myself with highly contoured cheeks and eyes makes me do a double take.

I stand, staring at my reflection in the mirror. My image is unfamiliar to me. My eyes are lined and shadow creates depth that isn't there on a normal day. I look the way I looked every day when I lived in Los Angeles. I think about the endless hours I would spend getting ready to do nothing on days when I was off work. I resented the fact that Alex preferred me with makeup, and I took it to heart.

I go out into the living room, praying that Dan is in his study or in his bedroom. I don't want to hear it from him. I don't want him to notice the makeup or the tight jeans. Explaining that I'm going on a date seems like an excruciating prospect. He will grill me, I think. There he is in the living room, playing his Xbox, a headset wrapped around his ears, shouting into it, calling someone a salty motherfucker.

He glances at me when I come around the corner and stopped, ripping the headset off. Exactly the reaction I'm trying to avoid.

"Damn!" he says.

Dan doesn't have reason to know about the strange dichotomy inside of me that wants to feel beautiful and wants, yet doesn't want any man to ever notice me again. His words are abrasive, an assault to my senses, suddenly making me aware of my body. It's painful.

"You look beautiful," he goes on. His voice is soft and friendly, he can be trusted, I try to remind myself.

"Thanks," I say, uncomfortable at the compliment but not wanting to make Dan feel like he's a predator even though the center in my brain responsible for assessing threat is telling me otherwise, like it always does.

He puts his headset back on and goes back to his game. I take a seat on the other side of the L-shaped couch that we share. I get on my phone and see that it's five until seven. I watch Dan play his game and minutes pass. At a quarter after seven, I check the time again. Henry still hasn't arrived. I check my text messages and there isn't any word from him explaining his tardiness. As I begin to get a little concerned, a text message pops up at the top of my screen.

Outside.

I get up from the couch and grab my purse.

"Don't wait up," I say to Dan. It's our signature phrase when one of us is going out. He doesn't hear me though, his head totally in the game, shouting something obscene at what I imagine are fourteen year olds.

I shut the door behind me and see Henry's Nissan Z waiting in the driveway. It's black and freshly washed. The exhaust purrs. I go to the passenger side and lean down to the open window.

"A girl can't even get the door opened for her?" I ask.

He looks surprised and leans over the console, grabs the handle and swings the door open. It's less than gentlemanly for a date, but I'll accept it. Anything to get out of the house and out of my head for a little while.

I climb in and we're off.

"Hattie B's?" Henry asks.

He knows it's one of my favorites. A specialty of Nashville is hot chicken. It's chicken that's injected with and marinated in Tabasco sauce. It'll burn your lips deliciously. It sounds like a fantastic idea.

"Always," I say with a smile.

We drive across town over by Music Row and park down the street from the restaurant. It's packed, just like usual, even though it's a weeknight. Tourists and locals alike line the street. Most of them wear casual clothes and I feel a little out of place not wearing my gi bottoms and a jiu-jitsu inspired t-shirt. Instead, I wear jeans, small heels and a strapless top. I have a light jacket over it. Henry wears a button-down black shirt and jeans that look like he had paid good money for someone to make them look like they were distressed.

We stand in line and talk about the school. We talk about our students and we maintain a safe distance from each other. Henry doesn't know everything about my past, but he knows enough. He knows that I was skittish about rolling with guys for the first year that I was at Red Triangle. He knows that it wasn't until last year that I started rolling regularly with him.

"So how's it going with Brian?" I ask him.

Brian is a student of his. He's a teenager and has been in a lot of trouble at school. For some reason, parents often think that martial arts is a replacement for the discipline that their kids aren't getting at home. They look to us to make their kids do their homework and get good grades and keep their asses out of detention. It's one of the things that made me glad I've never had kids. The thought of having a living, breathing human being that would forever link me to someone like Alex is enough to make my neck start sweating. I reach up and wipe a hand there, not used to having my hair in any style but a ponytail.

A breeze picks up with a little winter chill and I throw my hair up, tying it with a band in my purse. The air feels good on my sweaty neck. I smile nervously at Henry.

"It's going really well. He actually got his grade up to a B in chemistry this week. He was failing when he first started with me."

"That's great!" I say, forcing a smile that I don't feel.

"Yeah, he's a good kid. Like a diamond in the rough. I should know," Henry says.

I try to keep an open mind about kids like Brian. Henry had been pretty troubled when he was younger. He'd turned out okay. But I can't help but think that kids who are bullies grew up to be adults that are bullies. I imagine Alex as a teenager and shudder.

We finally get to the front of the line and get seated.

I order my usual. A hot chicken sandwich with an extra pickle. Henry orders the same. We ear and talk. We laugh. The tension between us breaks and another kind of tension begins to build. It's familiar to me and feels strange all at once. I haven't felt any chemistry with anyone since I left Los Angeles. When we finish the meal and walk back to the car, he puts his hand on the small of my back and opens the door for me. An upgrade from my treatment earlier.

As he walks around the car, I instinctively get some gum out of my purse and begin to chew it. I offer him a piece as I get in and buckle my seatbelt. He accepts. It's the international gesture for, *Hey, I know we just ate but let's definitely makeout in a little bit.*

The last person to press their lips to mine was Alex. The last person who touched me was Alex. I long for the hands that had last traced the curves of my body to be someone else's. I want the last memory of a kiss to be something other than me recoiling in horror as Alex tried to make everything normal and alright by covering my mouth with his, stifling my protests.

"You wanna watch a movie or something?" Henry asks as we drove. He sounds slightly nervous. It's something I haven't ever seen in him before. He always carries himself with great confidence, but I've also never seen him interact with a woman in any situation but one where he's an instructor.

"Yeah," I say, my gut clenching, knowing what that means and being both exhilarated by it and dreading it.

He drives us to his apartment—mostly in silence—and

when we get there, I let myself out of the car. I feel claustro-phobic. I need the fresh air. He takes my hand as we walk to his door. His palm is sweaty and mine is cold. He grips me tighter than I do him and I feel myself being pulled slightly. I tag along, letting him lead me wherever he will.

At the door, he unlocks it and we walk into the apart-ment, cold as a meat locker. It immediately reminds me of Alex's place. He always kept it cold. I don't think a vampire can live any other way, though. Alex had a big desk lamp in his study and somethings when I was at work and he was at home, I pictured him lying on the desk as if it were a rock in a snake's terrarium, warming his corpse-like flesh under the artificial lighting, maintaining the homeostasis that made him appear more human.

Inside Henry's apartment, the lights are out. He turns on the one in the kitchen and it dimly illuminates the living room. He ushers me to a seat on the couch.

"Can I get you anything to drink? I've got a lot of liquor from my days working at the bar."

I think about it for a moment and realize that I need some liquid courage.

"Vodka tonic, please. If you have it."

"I've got the vodka but not the tonic."

"You have whiskey?" I ask.

"Jack D," he says.

"That's fine. Just on the rocks with a little water."

It's how Dan taught me to drink whiskey after Alex made a comment about me shooting it. He said it wasn't aged in barrels for years for me to throw it back like a drunken sorority girl.

Henry gets the drinks and I stare awkwardly at the TV that's off. When he comes to the couch he sits down beside me, a little too close for my own comfort, and he hands me my drink. The first sip hits my lips and warms me up as it goes down.

Henry puts his drink down and makes eye contact with me as I take another more liberal sip.

He reaches out and takes the drink from me.

I watch the scene unfold in slow motion and feel myself leaving my body. He takes a hand and places it on my cheek —someone else's cheek—and pulls me in for a kiss. His lips press to mine—to the girl's lips who I'm watching—and he kisses me—her.

I watch in horror as he moves another hand to her thigh and then it snakes its way up and under her shirt. I watch as he makes a move to remove her bra and she stiffens, unable to tell him to stop, not wanting her ex-fiancé to be the last person to touch her, but not wanting this boy to touch her either.

I watch as tears begin to fill her eyes as they kiss and she lets them silently fall down her cheeks, choking back a sob, going unnoticed by the guy who can't think about anything but getting her naked.

And I watch as he pushes her onto her back and she tries to sit back up. I watch as her heart begins to beat out of her chest like a bird, cornered in a cage about to have its wings clipped. Wings that had been cut a long time ago that she'd finally begun to grow back out again.

I watch as she pushes against him and tries to pry his face from hers. I watch as she tries to tell him to stop. I watch as he holds her down and goes to unbutton her pants. I watch as she screams and kicks at him. I watch as he recoils and calls her a crazy bitch and I watch as her makeup runs down her face and she knows the drinks off the coffee table.

And I watch as she runs for the door, slams it behind her, and runs down the street, miles away from the safety of her own home.

CHAPTER 19

Los Angeles Dec. 2013

I had already slung my strappy high heels over my right shoulder by the time Alex opened the door to our house. My feet ached as I stepped from the concrete of the garage onto the cool tile of the little mud room. It was always too cold. It was dark, as usual, like a dungeon, I'd told him once. The irony wasn't lost on me tonight.

We'd been at the Sanctuary. The first party we'd attended in a while. I'd gotten him to back off of it for a time, but he grew more and more frustrated and the further we drifted apart, and the more Amy intruded, the more I thought maybe going back would be okay.

That night, we'd watched a girl getting a needle corset. She'd laid on a leather table with straps that could have been used to restrain her but weren't. She'd been topless, her nipples pointed alertly as she climbed onto the table, even though the room was warm. Her bare back was free of any tattoos and the palest shade of pink. A man wearing a leather mask had her lie down face first and had inserted hypodermic needles into her flesh after disinfecting her skin. Each needle dipped into her back and then poked back out to have its sharp end capped with a tiny piece of cork.

When he'd finished, he'd laced two alternating shades of ribbon on each row of the needles. She had stood and walked throughout the club, topless, in a trance. Her consciousness had been hijacked by the endorphins her body had released to combat the pain.

Things had been so tense at home. I hadn't been working much lately, as per his request, and nothing ever seemed to be good enough for him. He spent more time at work—with Amy—and was more distant than ever.

The previous week, we'd had a huge fight.

He'd come home and dinner wasn't there. I'd been sitting in front of the television watching a rerun of *The Walking Dead* when he had walked in. He'd slammed the door and dropped his briefcase beside the door, unusual for him. Everything had a place with him.

"What's wrong?" I asked, pausing the television.

"Is there nothing to eat?" he snapped at me, pacing into the kitchen and throwing open the refrigerator. I could hear him banging around, searching for something.

"Food's not here yet," I shouted into the kitchen. "I guess they're running late."

He laughed bitterly.

"And I guess you can't put anything together?" His voice had a razor's edge, a tone that I'd grown weary of. The barbs he caught me with almost always left me bleeding, searching for a Band-Aid that I'd yet to find. "You're worthless," he concluded under his breath.

My back stiffened in my seat. I placed my feet firmly on the floor in front of me.

"What?" I said, my tone even, knowing what he'd said.

I usually didn't cross Alex. He was mean when he was angry. And it seemed that he was meaner and meaner lately, but he'd never said anything so vicious. I had known that things were stressful for him, and I'd tried to accommodate it, but I had a breaking point.

I'd always thought that love would be enough. I'd thought that with enough of it, I could love him into healing from whatever demons plagued him.

"I said you're worthless!" he shouted, his voice full of rage.

I stood up from my seated position and marched into the kitchen, ready for a fight. I was ready for the tension that had been building over the last few months to come to a head.

He looked surprised to see me when I entered the kitchen.

"You do realize that you're the one who told me to order food, right?" I asked.

"Because you can't cook!" he barked.

He shoved past me into the living room.

"I'm leaving," he said. "Eat without me."

I had walked out of the kitchen and into the living room to see the door slam behind him as he left, taking his angry energy with him. I'd felt relief wash over me, knowing it was only temporary, that the tide of the evening would pull it away from me when he returned later.

The week afterwards was tense. I'd felt that maybe going to the Sanctuary would provide him with some sort of release or at least a distraction. Maybe he'd lighten up. When we'd been there, he'd been entranced with everything. I'd look away from whatever scene we were watching only to see him standing there, in another world, drool practically wetting the corner of his mouth like a wolf watching a herd of sheep mindlessly grazing, unaware of his presence. It had frightened me.

I took my heels into the bedroom and threw them in the bottom of my closet. One of his requirements when we got this house was that we didn't share a closet. He couldn't stand my messiness. I grabbed some pajamas pants and a loose t-shirt and changed into them, going back into the living room.

"I'm going to get some ice cream. Do you want any?" I asked.

"You know I'm trying to watch what I eat," he said, irritated. I rolled my eyes, knowing that Amy was on a new diet kick, and he was on it with her.

I walked into the kitchen and opened the freezer. My ice cream of choice was waiting for me. Ben and Jerry's Strawberry Cheesecake with actual bits of graham cracker crust mixed into the ice cream. I grabbed it and closed the freezer with my foot, turning to open the drawer that housed the big spoons. I grabbed a special one made to easily melt ice cream.

"What are you watching?" I asked him as I took a big bite of ice cream. I longed for some kind of connection with him—the connection that we'd had when we first met. I wondered where his charming smile went sometimes. I knew he still threw it around in the courtroom and probably even showed it off with Amy, but I never saw it anymore.

He shushed me. I shrugged my shoulders and rolled my eyes again after I turned around and headed to sit at the bar. I pulled out a stool and sat the ice cream in front of me. I scooted up onto the seat and splayed my elbows out across the counter as I cracked open the container and dug into it with the spoon.

The ice cream was frigid, frozen solid. The spoon cut

through it with ease. The first taste was heaven. Tart frozen strawberry chunks exploded across my tongue, electrifying my taste buds and sending a rush of dopamine straight through me. Instantly, the cares of the evening began to melt away with the ice cream in my mouth.

I began to shovel a second spoonful into my mouth and suddenly felt two icy hands on my shoulders, squeezing. I turned, startled.

Alex was always doing that—creeping around like something undead and sneaking up on me in moments where I'd begun to relax into myself like he sensed it and constantly needed to remind me of who I was now.

"So, what did you think of what we saw tonight?" he asked, brushing the hair away from my neck, landing a kiss there. The feeling of his lips on skin made it crawl, an organism all its own. Something about him was different. Lately when he touched me, I wanted to recoil from him. I wondered if it had to do with the little rendezvous I'd had with Zach. I hadn't seen him since then and tried to push him from my mind.

Alex's skin was cold like a serpent's and I imagined him coiling around me, squeezing the air right out of my lungs until I gasped for air, exhaling, and he would coil more tightly, again and again until I had no air left. I shrugged my shoulders, signaling to him that I wasn't in the mood.

"It was...interesting," I said, not wanting to state the truth that if we never went back there, I'd be ecstatic. Not because I thought there was anything morally wrong with it. It just wasn't what I wanted and I felt coerced into going and participating in something that was so far from what I really wanted.

He kissed my shoulder then, not getting the message.

"I'm really not in the mood," I said to him, more sternly than I usually would.

"You know," he whispered in my ear, his breath tickling me and making my neck twitch involuntarily. "If you and I could have a relationship like Amy wants to, you'd have to do whatever I said."

"Alex," I began. He pressed his lips to my neck and began kissing towards my mouth. "Stop!" I said, breaking away from him.

I turned to face him. His eyes were angry, just like they always seemed to be now. There was something else there, though, something that swam just below the surface that looked like it was about to breach the water.

"Maybe we should have a relationship like that," he said, grabbing my wrist harder than he normally would have.

"What are you talking about?" I asked, trying to pull away from him.

"Maybe then you wouldn't have strange guys coming to your work trying to get their dick wet," he said, jerking me by the hand and pulling me off the stool. I stumbled and almost fell, but he pulled me towards the bedroom righting me on my new path.

"Alex, stop," I said, suddenly realized that any control I'd had of the situation was an illusion.

He pulled me behind him quickly. Once inside the bedroom, he spun me around so that I was standing in front of him, my back to him, and he pressed his body against me. I could feel him hard inside his pants. I suddenly felt panicked.

"Stop, Alex," I said.

"And what if I don't? You gonna call your boyfriend?" he whispered into my ear.

Before I could respond, my heart leapt to my throat and he pushed me, face first into the comforter, bending me at the waist. I struggled to get back up, pushing against the mattress with my hands, but he stopped me and shoved my face deep into the comforter. I shouted, began to scream. The sounds were entirely muffled and when I gasped for breath, I found no air. I pushed against the bed and felt him pulling my pajama pants and my underwear down past my ass, exposing me and leaving me entirely vulnerable to what would come next.

I fought and struggled, and I could feel my heart fluttering so hard that I thought it would burst. Oxygen began to leave my brain. I could feel everything closing in on me. I heard his pants unzip, and I screamed, the sound muffled into oblivion by the lush comforter that cost him over a thousand dollars. My tears soaked into it and my cries went unheard as I felt him press himself against me, shoving himself inside.

Just as I felt myself beginning to lose consciousness, he pulled me by the hair up against him. I gasped gratefully for the air and threw my hands to my head, trying to untangle his fingers from my hair.

"You belong to me!" he growled. "No matter what you do, you always will."

I started to scream once more and his grasp on my hair loosened. He took both hands and wrapped them around my neck with crushing force. His cold reptilian hands were circle around my throat, and I felt the choke sink in. My head filled with pressure and for six seconds that stretched out infinitely, I fought as hard as I could.

And then the world went black.

I woke in darkness, disoriented. I looked to my right and saw the alarm clock. 5:34am. I looked to my left and saw Alex's back, his side rising and falling slowly with the rhythm of peaceful sleep. I looked at the ceiling as the world began to pull away from me. I watched in horror as it sucked itself away from me, readying to crash back with enough force to wipe me out.

I couldn't breathe. My heart pounded, blood pumping to my extremities, making my body temperature run hot. I felt a dull ache between my legs, and I reached a hand down to find that my pajamas had been pulled back up. I felt wetness between my legs. I looked at my hand and saw something dark on my fingers. The scent of iron filled my nose, and I exhaled as slow and controlled a breath as I possibly could. I didn't want to wake him. I wanted to disappear.

He had systematically dismantled my existence in every other way, slowly erasing my personality methodically, one comment at a time. He had weakened and cornered me, and now that I had given him everything that I had to offer, he had taken the last thing he could.

I rolled out of bed to see my slippers beside the nightstand, undisturbed, unaware that there was a calamity. I slipped them on and quietly left the bedroom, aware with every step of the pain between my legs. I went down the hallway past the living room and into the kitchen, unsure of what I sought. I looked over at the bar.

Sitting, unmoved, was the ice cream, melted off the spoon and spilled into a mess on the counter.

It was ruined.

I wept.

CHAPTER 20

Nashville Dec. 2016

I've never been a runner.

Something about the sting of lactic acid in my thighs and the burning pull of oxygen that my lungs craved turned me off of it. I've never seen the point. But tonight, leaving Henry's, I run. I run the three miles back to my house and it feels like I'm Phiddipides, running from Marathon to Athens, except I'm not about to shout *Victory!* when I arrive at my destination.

About a block from our house, I bend at the waist, a stitch making it impossible to keep going. It's plagued me for the last half mile but I've ignored it, my adrenaline storming the cockpit of my brain and taking the pilot's seat.

Taillights catch my eye up ahead.

It's the same car that was across the street the other night. I dive into the bushes by Mr. and Mrs. Robertson's trash cans. I groan as the stitch in my side intensifies and the brambles scratch up my arms and face. I peer out and watch as the car begins to make a U-turn in the cul de sac.

Headlights point my direction and the car stops in front

of my house. I watch them for a few moments, wondering what they're doing. I imagine the guy sitting there, masturbating, thinking that I'm asleep inside the house. Finally, the car begins to creep forward towards me.

I fall backwards and they flick on their brights, possibly seeing me. I freeze.

I squint and hold up a hand to shield my eyes and watch as the car inches forward.

My muscles twitch with fatigue and ache to be released from their squatted position. I want nothing more than to stand up and limp the remaining 200 feet to my house. The car comes closer and stops just in front of the Robertsons' house with me hiding in their bushes. I inhale sharply, the stitch in my side intensifying. I grab it and pinch with one hand and cover my mouth with the other. My eyes grow wide.

The car rolls down the passenger side window and a lit cigarette butt comes flying out. The window rolls back up and the car takes off down the street. I stay squatted in the bushes for a moment. Suddenly, I feel a tickle near the nape of my neck. I swat at it, coming out of the bushes and falling on my ass in the driveway.

I groan and look over at the lit cigarette butt in the street. I get up and walk over and stomp it out. I glance back up the street to make sure that no one is watching me.

I look over my shoulder the rest of the way back to the house. At the door, my keys clang more loudly than I want them to. The last thing I need is an intervention from Dan. Luckily, he's asleep. Sue, however, greets me at the door with a bark.

"*Shhh!*" I urge him. He quiets quickly, knowing the command. I listen for a second to see if Dan has woken up, but he hasn't.

I go to the bathroom and Sue follows. I shed my clothes and shower, trying to erase all traces of Henry's hands from my body. I turn the water as hot as I can stand it and stand in the shower stream, inhaling the steam and imagining his fingerprints melting off of my body and running down the drain.

Afterwards, with a towel wrapped around my head, I climb into bed with my canine companion and wrestle with the facts of what's going on in my life, the red-hot center of that cigarette butt burning a hole in my brain.

CHAPTER 21

Los Angeles Dec. 2013

After the night that Alex took everything he could from me, there was an impenetrable wall between us. He didn't try to have sex with me, and I never offered it. We didn't kiss. We didn't touch. When his hand did brush across mine, he recoiled like he had touched something dirty. I was ruined. Spoiled. And he had done it to me himself.

I knew the morning after that I would leave.

It took a couple of weeks, but I finally worked up the nerve. I had a credit card that was still tied to my parents, and I used it to buy a ticket from Los Angeles to Nashville. I didn't write a note. I didn't say goodbye. I grabbed my purse, some clothes, and left the rest.

I didn't want anything that he'd bought for me. I didn't want him to have anything he could hold over my head. I wanted a clean break. I wanted a fresh start. I wanted to go home.

The day after it happened, I'd gotten cleaned up and ready to face the harsh, cool day. I had asked Alex if he was okay.

I wanted to make sure that *he* hadn't been traumatized by what happened.

What happened.

Not what was *done*.

By him.

To me.

I stopped as I was walking into our bedroom and saw him getting ready. I felt a coolness settle in the deepest pit of my stomach, chilling me to my extremities. I watched him for a moment. He didn't know I was there. He combed his hair and coiffed it as he had always done. A ritual that I used to relish watching.

But that day was different. I just watched, unattached, and felt nothing. But something inside of me wanted to know that he was okay. I cared for him.

"Alex," I said, my voice crackling in the silence that lay between us like the expanse of a desert.

"Yeah?" he replied. His tone was normal, kind even. Patient.

"Are you okay?" I asked.

He turned and looked at me. He smiled.

"Yeah," he said. He looked peaceful. He looked like someone who had gotten a full, good night's sleep. I stared at him for a moment and then smiled. If he was at peace, I could be at peace, couldn't I?

I tried to suppress the urge I had to run from the beast that stood smiling before me.

Later, after a couple of weeks had passed and I was alone in the apartment, I couldn't fight it anymore. I packed just enough. I left everything that was in his name. My cell phone, my credit cards. All except the one that was still billed to my parents.

I opened my phone one last time to text Dan for the first time in years.

Hey.

I was cautious. I didn't know what he was going to do. I didn't know if he would tell me to fuck off, but it was only a moment before my phone lit up.

Hey. How are you?

I choked down a sob. I wasn't okay. I wasn't peaceful. I needed to be home right that minute.

I told Dan no more than I had to. I told him things hadn't worked out. I told him I was sorry and that I'd been wrong. And then I told him when my flight would be arriving. I had three hours before I needed to be at the airport.

That was all it took. He agreed to meet me in Nashville and give me a place to crash.

After I talked to him, I send another message. This one to Zach.

I hadn't seen him since that night in his house. I didn't know why I wanted to see him, only that I did.

I typed out a message asking him to meet me at the Tar Pits in thirty minutes. I wasn't sure he would come, and I didn't wait to see if he responded. I took the SIM card out of the phone and broke it. I went to the kitchen and grabbed a lighter. I set it on fire in the sink while I reset the phone, erasing all my messages and settings.

I left I on the counter and looked around one last time. I was leaving this hell hole for good. I was getting out. I would be done with Alex and I'd never have to see him again.

At the Tar Pits there was a family. A mom, dad, and two kids, probably ages five and seven. They were playing near the ultra-high fence that kept most idiots from climbing over and getting stuck in the pits. Most people think that once you fall in, you're going to sink to your death, overwhelmed by tar, but it doesn't work that way. What would happen to mammals was they would wander in and get their feet stuck in the shallow pit. They would die a slow, lingering death from starvation and exposure after that. I watched as the kids hung on the fence. I smiled at their dad as they walked past me, and I waited. Almost thirty minutes had passed. I needed to get somewhere to call a cab and get to the airport. I began to walk out of the park.

I looked down at my feet in my Nike sneakers and followed the gravel path.

"Tash!" called a voice from behind me.

I turned to see Zach jogging up the path that led out of the park. I turned and smiled without thinking that this was the last time I'd ever see him.

"Hey," I said, my voice breaking a little.

Seeing him was like salve on a wound. His kindness and warmth contrasted so sharply with Alex's coldness.

"What's going on? I texted you back, but you didn't respond," he said, coming up to me, a look of concern on his face. His eyes searched my body language for some hint of what was going on.

"I'm leaving," I blurted out, my voice quavering.

"Leaving?" he asked, his brown eyes lighter in the daylight.

"Los Angeles. Going back to Nashville," I said.

"Are you and him moving there?" Zach asked, his eyes pained but also full of compassion.

"Just me," I said. "I'm leaving him, too."

I looked down at the ground and kicked a rock that lay between us. It rolled over and tapped Zach's foot. He looked down as well and kicked it back to me.

"Why did you have me come here?" he asked, his voice suddenly pained.

I looked up and swallowed. I looked around the park. I took in the bleak day. The lack of sunshine matched the lack of hope I held for anything between us.

"I wanted to thank you," I said.

"For what?"

Tears began to spill down my face. I wiped them with my sweatshirt. My nose grew snotty and I wiped it as I spoke, a little laugh breaking out.

"You came into my life at a really dark time when I needed someone like you. You were a friend to me when you didn't have to be. You're a good person, Zach. The world is cold. Someone like you is special. I just want you to know I'll never forget you, even if I never see you again."

I was blubbering, crying until I couldn't see, and he reached out for me. Taking his hand was like grabbing a life preserver after falling overboard.

"Please don't," I whimpered, a whipped and beaten dog.

"I'm sorry," he said.

"I just wanted to tell you that before I left," I said, composing myself. "I've got to go. I've got a flight to catch."

"Let me take you to the airport," he offered.

I shook my head.

"No. I'll get a cab."

"Are you sure?"

"Yeah," I said.

I wanted to wrap my arms around him. I wanted to hug him and feel another person's warmth against my body. I wanted him to envelop me in an embrace, protecting me from what lie ahead of and behind me. I wanted all those things but my brain, hijacked by adrenaline and fear, wouldn't allow it. So instead, I stood there, stiff as the petri-fied forest.

"Bye, Zach," I muttered, turning around and taking the path that would lead me to the nearest payphone.

CHAPTER 22

Nashville Dec. 2016

Heather and I are flying from Nashville to New Orleans at 5:05pm. It's noon and I'm still packing. I'm never ready on time when it comes to traveling and if this was a road trip, it wouldn't be a big deal; however, I don't think the TSA is going to care that I need to sort through my underwear drawer to find the sports bra that doesn't give me a backache but manages to keep my boobs from bouncing painfully.

I take a break for a minute and lay down on the bed. I spread out and stretch. I pop my neck. I grab my phone and open Facebook. There are about twenty notifications in the bottom right-hand corner.

At least two hundred people have liked Heather's status that tagged me as being at the women's seminar that we're putting on in New Orleans. Most of them are jiu-jitsu friends, but Dan also liked it and I scroll through who else had bothered to look at it and express their support.

Zach O'Halloran.

The dates are published on the post. The location is

published on the post. Zach saw it and liked it and he knows without a doubt that I'm going to be in the same city as him on the same weekend. My heart beats faster.

Just as I'm thinking about deleting my entire social media presence, a message notification pops up. It's Zach.

Hey,

I saw that you're going to be in New Orleans for the weekend. Eric and I are recording a live podcast show there this weekend. I know you probably have no desire to see me, but the tickets are yours at the door if you want them.

I let the blinking cursor taunt me. I type out at least seven different messages. Part of them inviting Zach out for a drink once we get to the Big Easy and part of them telling him that the post is incorrect and that I won't be making the trip to New Orleans. I settle on the last message. The blank one.

I exit out of Facebook and shut my phone down. My head spins at the possibility of seeing him and him seeing me. My pulse races knowing that tomorrow night I'm going to be at the podcast recording and see him for the first time in three years.

My vision tunnels. If Zach saw the post, anyone can see it.

I try to breathe evenly, inhaling for four seconds and exhaling for eight. I try looking around the room and naming objects in my head. All the grounding exercises that we teach in the women's camp for dealing with anxiety, but it only mounts.

I breathe harder. I force myself to focus. Then Dan knocks on the door.

"Come in," I say, breathless and grateful for the interruption.

"Are you ready?" he asks, knowing full well that the

answer is no, having traveled numerous times with me in the past.

"Of course not," I say, gesturing around the bed at the clothes and personal hygiene items that remain to be packed.

"When's your flight?"

I tell him and he nods, knowing that I have the ability to get ready at the drop of a hat if I have to.

"You excited?" he asks, almost like a dad getting his daughter ready for her first out of town cheer competition.

"Yeah, dad," I snark good-naturedly.

"Har har," Dan fake laughs. "I'm just looking out for you. You deserve a weekend away. Get drunk. Get some strange," he says, wiggling his eyebrows.

"Yeah, we both know how likely that is," I say.

"A boy can hope."

"Yeah, well, don't get your hopes up too high there, cowboy," I say back to him, smiling now. I kick at him from the bed.

"You'll have a good time," he says.

"I hope so."

Dan turns and leaves the room, leaving me to the duty of packing my suitcase that I know will be overfilled with more gis and less hair product than I actually need. I think about the prospect of sleeping with a stranger. The only slightly strange man that I planned on seeing this weekend wasn't going to be seeing me, so that isn't a possibility. It probably couldn't be even if I wanted it to be. The night with Henry comes to mind and I shudder.

I lay back on the bed and measure my breaths. The panic that was present before Dan entered the room is gone. I'm left only with the feeling of emptiness. The last three years of my life have been devoid of any intimate relationship.

It's hard to fathom letting someone in. It reminds me of an interview that a Rolling Stone journalist did with Charles Manson. Manson asked him if he thought he was a killer. He walked up to the reporter and touched his nose. The man though he was seeing a softer side of Manson and commented. Manson replied by whispering, "If I can get close enough to touch you, I can get close enough to kill you."

That's how opening up feels. Even with Zach. When you open up to someone, you let them have the upper hand. Whoever divulges the most about themselves is most vulnerable, the weakest. One person will always love more. One person will always need more. I never want to be that person again.

That level of vulnerability isn't an option.

Even having followed that train of thought all the way to the station, I'm still looking forward to seeing Zach, even if he isn't going to see me.

CHAPTER 23

New Orleans Dec. 2016

We get to New Orleans that Thursday night. The seminar starts on Friday and goes through Sunday evening. On Thursday, I'm exhausted. We get our bags and barely make it to the hotel before falling asleep. It isn't until the next day that I bring up the podcast recording.

Despite my tiredness, I'm glad to be back in New Orleans. The city is alive with music and the smell of Cajun food. The Quarter is particularly vibrant, though not as bustling as I know it will be in the coming nights. I'm looking forward to a weekend of losing myself in strong alcoholic beverages and choke holds, hopefully not at the same time.

We are surrounded by other women, getting ourselves some salad and protein options at a buffet that Hernandez Jiu-Jitsu is putting on for the seminar guests. We go into the office with Dana, one of the women who organized the seminar.

She shoves a slice of a Clementine into her mouth, a

little bit of juice sneaks out the side of her mouth and down her chin.

"I can't thank you guys enough for coming," Dana says, chewing the small orange.

"Of course," Heather says through a mouthful of Caesar salad. Women are walking outside the office, the atrium is abuzz with conversation. Some of it concerning the techniques that we went over that morning and the rest of it a mish-mash of weekend plans, kids getting in trouble at school, and marital issues. I listen to them with one ear and to Heather and Dana with the other. I sit back and let Heather do the talking.

I enjoy the trips with Heather. I enjoy being in a city where no one knows me, particularly this weekend. I enjoy the anonymity of a crowd. It's how I first felt in Los Angeles.

I chomp on my salad and listen to them talk. Dana tells us about a woman who came to train martial arts at the school that was a rape victim. She got extensive therapy and became a motivational speaker. She's giving a speech at a women's college as we speak. She's going to be there for the rest of the seminar, though.

I try to imagine myself as a motivational speaker and feels like the likelihood of that happening was about the same as Alex being struck dead by lightning.

"You'll love her, Tash," Dana says to me with a smile. She looks like the kind of woman that's always able to look on the bright side. I wonder what happened in her past that made her seek out martial arts or if she's one of those incredibly rare and fortunate women that seeks it out before they need it.

I smile with my lips together as I chew on a crouton. Suddenly, from the atrium, I hear some chatter by the door.

"—the one in the pictures," says one woman.

"Where did you see that?" another woman asks.

"On a jiu-jitsu forum. Some guy posted the link under a thread about this weekend's seminar. I'm positive it's her."

"Jesus Christ. And she says she empowers women?" another woman snorts.

"I'd never let someone take a naked picture of me," says the first woman, clearly having to crane her neck to see the others from her moral high horse.

"Only sluts do," says one of the others.

My stomach drops. I feel my hands grow clammy and my forehead gains a sheen of sweat. I think about having to step outside and face those women. Heather is lost in conversation with Dana. I'm the only one who'd heard them.

I walk over and stand in the doorway crossing my arms. They're engrossed in their own little petty world.

"I heard she's a real bitch, too," I chime in, stepping up behind two of the women. The first, and youngest, looks at me like a bush baby with bulging eyes that might fall right off its head if it moved too quickly in one direction or the other.

"I didn't—"

"Know I was in there and could hear you," I finish for her.

"No—"

"Save it," I say, turning and dropping the rest of my lunch in the trash can. I walk back into the office.

"What's wrong?" Heather asks as Dana steps out. She smiles at the group of women that I just attempted to set straight, unaware of what's transpired.

"Nothing," I lie, putting on my best work face.

"You're a bad liar. You know that right?" Heather asks, tossing back a couple of almonds.

"I'll be glad to get the fuck out of here and get some real food," I say, glancing down at her plate, every option only designed to make its consumer healthier. Suddenly I want food that equals comfort instead of fuel. More than that, I want a drink.

"Yeah. Me too," Heather said. "This rabbit food's bullshit." She puts her plate down on the desk in the center of the room.

"I have a surprise for you," I tell Heather, thinking now is a good time to tell her about the podcast recording. I need to get my mind off those women.

"I love surprises," Heather says with a conspiratorial grin. She rubs her hands together like a cartoon villain.

"It's nothing big," I say.

"Go on," she encourages.

"There's this podcast I really like and the two guys that do it are doing a live recording here in New Orleans tonight. I bought us tickets," I say, all in one breath. I don't know why I'm anticipating judgment from her. She doesn't know anything about Zach. There's no reason she would give me a hard time. Heather and I share a lot with each other, but as with all my other relationships, I make sure that she's the one who shares more.

"Sweet," Heather says. "Are they hot?"

"What?" I respond, caught off guard.

"The two guys," she prods.

"Oh, I—" I'm not sure what to say. *Yeah, one of them is devastatingly handsome and every time I think about the way his hair felt running through my fingers, I feel like I'm on a rollercoaster.* "I don't know," I splutter.

Zach *is* hot.

"What are their names? I'll look them up and see for myself," she says.

Suddenly, I feel defensive. I freeze.

"Earth to Tash," Heather says after a couple of moments passed. I look back at her.

"Sorry, I just—"

"I get it. Sometimes these things can be too much," she says.

I nod, misunderstanding her. It takes me a full two minutes to realize that she was talking about the self-defense seminar and not the situation I'm in with Alex.

After we sits there for a few more moments, Heather stands up from her seat.

"Ready to get back after it?" she asks, putting on her game face and grabbing her plate. It's a face that inspires the courage of hundreds of women around the country every year and somehow, even as familiar as I am with it, it does the same for me. I think about staring those women down and making them as uncomfortable as possible. I nod my head.

"Let's do it," I say.

"So how did you find out about these guys?" Heather asks as we hurry along the sidewalk into the theater in downtown New Orleans where the recording is being held.

I fumble for an answer.

"I heard about them when I was in Los Angeles," I say, not entirely lying.

"I hope they're hot," Heather says, only halfway joking. I know if it were up to her, we would be hooking up with them in their hotel room. The thought gives me hives.

"Come on," I urge, hurrying up my stride on the pavement, eager to get in and find our seats.

We get to the entrance and there is a line. It's about ten minutes before they're going to start seating people. My stomach feels like it might fly away and take me with it. In just a few moments I'm going to see the one person I've been trying not to think about for the last three years.

In line, we're behind two younger girls, probably twenty-two or twenty-three. They're jabbering on about Eric and Zach.

"What if he comes out and talks to us?" wonders the taller of the two.

"Oh my God. I'll die," says the other.

"I heard that he comes down into the audience before the show to sign autographs."

"Holy shit. What if that's true?"

What if it is true? I feel my stomach that was rocketing towards the heavens plummet back to earth. The last thing I want is for Zach to notice me in the crowd. Maybe they're talking about Eric. He's the one who always seemed to love the attention. A girl can hope.

The line begins to move and Heather has grown silent. She's looking at the promotional posters around us for the event. Finally, she speaks as we gave the doorman our tickets and enter the theater.

"They are hot!" she declares. "Why didn't you tell me?"

I chuckle nervously. I know why I didn't tell Heather and I hate to admit it to myself. The idea of thinking about anyone sexually since Alex makes me physically ill, but there are times when I think about Zach that it doesn't. I don't want to speak any of that out loud. I don't want to voice my thoughts about his attractiveness.

We go through the atrium of the theater and immediately go to our seats. I can't get there fast enough. At the same time, I dread the thought of either Zach or Eric coming out into the crowd, but I hope it will be Eric if it has to be one of them.

Even though I tell myself that, a tiny part of me hopes that it won't be. That tiny part hopes it'll be Zach who comes out to sign autographs.

The two younger girls are seated in front of us. They chatter on endlessly about their crushes on each of the guys. They joke about getting to go backstage and how bad they want to meet them, insinuating more. I know they're only partially joking and it makes me feel a little ill. I wonder if this is how the wives of rock stars feel when they wander through the crowd at their husbands' shows.

It grows closer to time. There are about ten minutes left before the curtain will go up. That's when the crowd to our left starts to hoot and holler. My stomach lurches.

I look over and there he is.

My heart flutters around in my chest, trying to escape.

I look down at my feet and then clasp my hands together. They're coming our way. I turn away from Heather, who is on my left and looks around aimlessly at the seats beside and behind us where the people are standing or at least looking in the direction of the guys.

"Hey, they're coming over here!" Heather says, jabbing me with her elbow. "I want to meet them! Don't you want to meet them?"

I pretended not to feel or hear her. I want to disappear. I want to melt into the fabric of my seat. This wasn't about Zach seeing me or knowing that I'm here in New Orleans. It was about me seeing him. Just being close to him without hurting him. Just knowing that good like him still exists in the world.

I hear Zach's voice at the end of the row and it's like being hit by a wrecking ball. It goes right through my chest, deep into the darkest parts of me, illuminating my secrets and making me so aware of all that's missing from my life.

"Zach!" shouts one of them.

"Hey!" I hear him shout to them. They push their way towards the end of the row and I can see in my peripheral vision that they're getting an autograph. To my left, Heather stands up and is not sitting back down as Zach and Eric meander closer to the front and left where the backstage door is. I breathe a heavy sigh of relief.

"What the hell is up with you? I thought you loved these guys," she says, sitting down.

I don't respond. I don't know what to say without saying everything.

"Oh my God," she says. "You know them. Like know them know them."

I only nod my head.

Heather puts an arm around me.

"Which one? You knew one of them when you were in L.A., didn't you?" she asks.

"Zach," I say. "I met him right before I had to leave."

"Are you—" she begins and hesitates. "Are you like, in love with him or some corny ass shit like that?"

"Oh! God no!" I almost shout, laughing nervously.

The lights begin to dim, and the show starts. Heather releases me from her embrace and the curtain rise. The audience stands and the guys take center stage where two bar stools and a table with two glasses of what looked like whiskey are waiting on them.

Zach raises a hand and Eric does the same. They wave at the crowd and look around. For a moment, Zach's eyes settle on our row and my body tenses. His eyes feel like they've found mine. It's too far away, I think. Surely. And with the bright lights in his face, he can't make out who's here. Right? He covers his forehead with his hand, blocking out the spotlights. For a moment, the smile on his face falters.

"Hello, hello, hello!" Eric says, the same way he begins all of their podcasts. "I'm Eric Anderson," he says and looked at Zach who is looking my way.

Eric clears his throat.

Zach looks over at him, bewildered, somehow looking like he forgot where he is.

"And I'm Zach O'Halloran," he says.

The crowd goes nuts.

After about thirty seconds of straight applause, everyone sits down, including me and Heather. I silently pray that they won't have any moments where they call for someone in the audience.

They start the evening by talking about some of the latest movies to come out of Hollywood. Then their focus shifts to relationships. There are some jokes and Eric tells a couple of funny stories about his romantic life. The audience laughs uproariously at his terrible luck.

The time comes for Zach to share. He pauses. This is normally where he shines as the brighter star of the two of them. His insights into relationships and his comedic way of bringing them to light are his forte.

"You know," he begins. "I haven't really dated anyone in three years."

The audience makes a collective sad noise.

"I know. Shocking right?" he jokes. "Someone as devastatingly handsome as me hasn't dated anyone in three years. Tragic. Stop the presses." Everyone laughs. "I met a girl about three years ago when my last serious relationship had fallen apart. I thought she was it, man," Zach says and Eric just covers his face with his hand.

I wonder why I've never listened to the podcast. I think about all the hours that I could have spent surrounding myself with Zach's Yankee accent, alone in my car or with my earbuds in walking to class.

"You know that's like, the kiss of death, right?" Eric asks him. "If you think she's 'the one' then she most definitely is not the one."

"Right," Zach chuckles. "I thought that, though. She left L.A. and I was mad and sad about it. I blamed her for a long time. How could I not be pissed that the love of my life had walked out on me? But she was doing what she needed to do, you know? Sometimes you fall apart from someone because the timing isn't right. You can have chemistry, and you can have passion and you can have common interests and all that other shit, but man, if you don't have timing, you got nothing," he finished.

It hits me like a sucker punch. He turns his head my direction again. His eyes search the crowd. I try to shrink into my seat, make myself invisible.

"Timing is a bitch," Eric says. He goes on to relay a story about the time he tried to apologize to his ex about something that had to do with her cat. The cat ended up dying during their fight. It turned into a huge thing, and they ended up staying together, only to break up over the next cat that she got. Everyone laughs.

The show goes on and at the end there is a standing ovation. Zach and Eric stand, wave at the crowd and begin to walk off the stage. But as they do, Zach lingers. And for a split second, I swear that his eyes meet mine.

CHAPTER 24

Los Angeles Jan. 2012

The first time I ever went to the Sanctuary with Alex was two years after we moved to Los Angeles. It was a Saturday night in mid-winter. There was a crispness to the air that made it refreshing even though it nipped at my skin with tiny teeth.

I'd worn a black dress and heels, unsure of what sort of thing I should be wearing. Alex wore a suit, which was his usual attire at work. He looked good. The suit had been hand-tailored to fit him, just like all his others. It was black with grey pin stripes.

On the way there, I was quiet. We parked in the back of the series of warehouse buildings that made up the street that the Sanctuary was on. Alex walked with a brisk pace, eager to get inside. I trailed behind, looking over my shoulder in the alleyway. He got to the door and flashed a smile like a kid on Christmas morning. His excitement was palpable. He'd told me a little bit about the club. It was a sex thing, as I understood it. I wasn't keen on going, but I did lots of things I wasn't keen on doing to please him. A coworker of his told him about it and got us on the list.

At the door, we were greeted by a woman in a corset and thigh high stockings. She was heavily made up and her blonde hair fell in luscious waves around her cleavage.

"Pendergast," he told her when she asked the name that the RSVP was under. She found it quickly and stamped both of our hands and ushered us to a door that had a keycode. She punched it in and let us enter.

"And remember, there's no reentry," she said as we walked past her.

Alex took my hand, and we walked down a long dark hallway. When we got to the end, we found a spacious area. The entire first floor of the warehouse was lit with red ambient sources of light, bathing the walls in a crimson that was reminiscent of blood. There were crosses that were shaped like X's on stations all around the room. There was a bar in the center that had a large metal ring hanging from it. There were benches and tables that had leather straps and upholstery that made them look like something right out of a medieval depiction of the Spanish Inquisition. Alex touched the small of my back and I had to shake off the feeling that an icy hand was wrapping itself around my spine.

My heels clicked on the floor, but the noise was masked by the booming bass of the stereo system that pumped industrial music throughout the room. The stations were empty, and a group of people had gathered at the far end of the room. We went their direction.

Approaching the crowd, I recognized Alex's coworker, and he saw me. I flashed a smile and waved. He waved back and came up to us.

"Tony!" Alex said, releasing my back and clapping his hand around Tony's shoulders.

"Hey, man! Glad you two could make it," he said.

I noticed that a meek girl wearing a mask that was shaped like a butterfly was approaching behind him. I smiled at her, and she smiled back demurely. She bowed her head and did a little curtsy.

"This is Lola," said Tony. "She's mine."

He wrapped a protective arm around her. I was relatively certain that Lola wasn't her real name.

"You can talk to them," he told the girl.

She smiled.

"Thank you, sir," she said to Tony.

The interaction between the two of them put me off. The girl pulled her mask off, revealing stunning ice blue eyes and long dark hair that was cut to perfectly frame her angelic face.

"Hi," I said, offering her my hand.

She timidly took it, shaking it.

"Hello," she said.

Tony and Alex began to be lost in their own conversation. I caught bits and pieces of it. They talked about work and Tony began to tell Alex about the Sanctuary. I was more interested in the dynamic that was going on between Tony and the girl he called Lola.

"Is that your real name?" I asked her.

"No. It's not my real name. Not very many people go by their real name here." She looked around. She had an air of innocence, and I wondered what kinds of things had brought her to a place like this. "That's Madame Leslie," she said, pointing out a woman in a dominatrix outfit. She had leather boots that practically rode up to her crotch. I noted that it couldn't be comfortable. "And that's Sparkle," she said, pointing out a woman who was topless, her breasts covered in glitter. She was shaking them at another woman who leaned her head down and put them on her chest. A man watched them, nodding his head as though he approved. "You'll meet everyone soon enough," said Lola. "What sort of stuff are you into?"

I looked back at her, taken aback by the question. I wasn't sure what she meant.

"I like to go to concerts," I said dumbly.

She laughed.

"No, like sex stuff. What brought you here?"

"Oh, I don't really know. Just the basic stuff. I've never really been anywhere like this," I said, suddenly aware that in this arena I was the outsider. I wondered if Alex had always been into this stuff and had just never told me. "My fiancé wanted to come," I offered.

"That's how it starts," Lola said with a chuckle. "Pretty soon, you'll be at every party."

I shuddered at the thought, both intrigued and a little scared.

"Are you doing any scenes tonight?" Lola asked me after an awkward silence.

"Scenes?" I asked.

"Yeah, it's what it's called when you play with someone."

I stared at her.

"Like flogging, needles, fire play, knife play. Any of that —all of that—could make up a scene. You'll see," she said. "I'm doing a scene with some fire play tonight. Master Tony is doing it. I'm his sub."

"Sub?"

"Submissive. I was collared by him. I belong to him. We have certain rules in our relationship. One of them is that when we're at parties, I can't speak unless he gives me permission."

I was appalled by that.

"Seriously?" I asked.

"Yeah," she said as though it was the most normal thing in the world.

I snorted a laugh.

"That wouldn't work out well for Alex," I said.

"Are you not his submissive?" Lola asked me.

"No," I barked out as a laugh. "Hardly. He can barely keep me in line."

"You'd like it," she said. "It brings me a lot of peace to be obedient to Tony."

"Do you have to call him 'sir' all the time?" I asked.

"Yeah, that's another part of our contract."

"Jesus," I muttered.

"Well, I'll see you later," Lola said, leaving me to stand beside Alex and Tony as she went to get herself a drink.

"Good to see you, man," Alex was saying to Tony as I turned to them. I smiled at Tony, having a new feel for who he was. I didn't like it.

"This place is weird," I said to Alex. "We can leave whenever you're ready."

"You want to leave?" he asked me, surprised.

I looked at him.

"Don't you?"

"I kind of want to stay and see this scene thing that they're going to do. Come on. It'll be fun," he said, taking both of my hands as though he was begging. Begging wasn't in Alex's nature.

"Fine. Whatever," I said. "I'm getting a drink."

I left him and made my way to the table of refreshments where I took in the sight of more women in outfits that I'd only ever seen in sex shops. I pushed through them and got some punch, hoping it was spiked with something good.

Sorely disappointed when I took a sip and there wasn't any alcohol in it, I groaned.

———

We took a seat on a lavish couch that was set up behind one of the stations with a cross shaped like an *X*, which I was informed was called a St. Andrew's cross. I watched as Lola went to the cross and disrobed down to nothing. I wasn't shocked by her nakedness, but by the bold nature in which she undressed. It didn't bother her at all that people were watching. She smiled at me, I thought, and then saw that Alex was smiling back at her.

Lola wrapped her hair in a towel that was dripping water and Tony strapped her to the cross. He then went to a box that had various tools in it. He got out two sticks that had tails at the end of them. Floggers. These weren't ordinary leather floggers like some of the other people were using at other stations. He soaked these in a liquid and then he lit them on fire.

"Is this safe?" I whispered to Alex.

"Probably not," he whispered back. "I think that's what makes it fun."

Our definitions of fun varied slightly, I realized.

Tony began to twirl the floggers, sending flames dancing through the air. Finally, he got close enough that they brushed Lola's back. She arched, moaned, and dig a little jig like she was trying to escape. He barked for her to be still, and she obeyed with a whimper.

I wondered how much of it was an act and how much of it was real. I wondered how much of this was a show for other people and how much of it was gratifying to the two people participating in it.

They went on like that for some time. Finally, Tony put out the floggers and went up to Lola and untied her. She was limp in his arms, and it alarmed me. Had she passed out? Was she okay?

He marched her over to the couch and sat her down next to us. She sat, almost catatonic. She stared off in space and he wrapped her in a blanket and smiled at Alex. They exchanged some words, and I just stared at Lola.

I wanted to leave and get as far away from this as I could. I grabbed Alex's hand.

"Are you ready?" I asked him.

"Do you want to leave?" he asked.

"Yeah, kinda," I said.

"Okay," he finally agreed.

We stood and he exchanged some words with Tony. They shook hands and then Alex took mine and we left the way we'd come in.

Once inside the car, the silence between us was tension-filled. I knew that he had enjoyed everything that he'd seen that night. And I knew that our life together would never go back to the way it had been before we'd stepped into that crimson room.

CHAPTER 25

New Orleans Dec. 2016

Even in the winter, with a slight chill on the evening air, the streets of the French Quarter are full of tourists. We meander our way past couples holding hands and families taking pictures outside of bars that the kids aren't old enough to go into yet. The whole place smells of spices, gumbo, alcohol, and debauchery.

"Look!" Heather says, pointing to the corner where a little voodoo shop is set up. "Isn't that creepy? Let's go in!" She offers a huge smile and drags me by the hand. She's hellbent on taking my mind off whatever was on it during the show even though I wouldn't elaborate.

The shop looks like something out of *American Horror Story: Coven*. The walls are lined with skulls that I'm not sure are real, but don't have the courage to ask about. There are cloths and tarot cards, runes and crystal balls, and then there are items in jars that I don't recognize. Most of them look like they were chopped off of an animal. I wonder if they are used in some sort of ritual practice.

"How can I help you ladies?" a woman behind the counter asks with a thick Cajun accent.

"Just looking," I say before Heather can get us into some kind of trouble that she'll later refer to as an adventure. God only knows what she would say. Probably ask the woman to make a love potion for me.

"Actually, what do these do?" Heather asks, holding up what looks like a cute little doll aside from the face that it has no eyes, nose, or mouth.

"That's a voodoo doll, *cher*," says the woman. "You can use them for good or evil. It's up to you. Do you have someone in your life that you'd like to suffer the slings and arrows of misfortune in this cold world?"

I do.

I snort slightly.

"It seems that perhaps you might," the woman says, shifting her gaze to me. Her eyes meet mine and they are an uncanny light green. They contrast with her dark skin in a way that makes her seem like a character out of a vampire movie. I force a smile at her. "Oh, I take it that you don't believe?" the woman asks with a sly smile.

"I just know that a lot of bad stuff happens to people who don't deserve it," I say. *Not that I'm one of them.* "Come on," I urge Heather, ready to get as far away from that woman and her store as possible.

"Wouldn't you like to change that?" she asks me as I turn to lead Heather out of the store. As I begin to open my mouth, Heather speaks.

"I would," she says.

The woman fixes her gaze on Heather as though she's found her evening meal.

"I'm going outside," I say firmly and look the woman in the eyes, spelling out in no uncertain terms that I most certainly do not believe in voodoo. I walk out of the store and the smells of the Quarter are a welcome reprieve from all the incense that was inside the store.

We are right around the corner from one of the more famous bars in the French Quarter and I really want to make a stop there before we leave on Monday.

I stand on the corner and watch the people walking by. Families and couples, all of them seeming to be happy. I wonder how much of it is real and how much of it is for show. How many of them are on a trip that's a last-ditch effort to save everything? I know I was never really happy with Alex after we moved to Los Angeles, but people always said how well we went together and how happy we looked. I feel sickened as I remember that smile that was plastered all over my face on our last Christmas card, sent out only a week or two before I split.

Before memories can sweep me away, I feel a tug on my arm.

"Look!" Heather says in a whisper and holds up one of the voodoo dolls with a pin stuck directly in its crotch.

"Jesus, what is that supposed to be?" I ask.

"It's Alex. With a needle in his dick," she says, as though it was the most obvious answer to the stupidest question she's ever heard.

"Get rid of that," I say. I'm not afraid of its magical capabilities but more of its capabilities to remind me of the past. Anything that serves as a reminder of him has been expulsed from my life, at least until the last week. That doll is going to be the next thing to go, and quick if Heather doesn't watch it.

"I hope someone cuts his dick off," Heather says.

"Not more than I do," I reply. "You know, let's not talk

about him. I've talked enough about him and thought enough about him this week for the rest of my life."

Heather is quiet for a moment.

"When are you not thinking about him, though?" she asks, her question so probing and intimate that my natural reaction is hypervigilance.

"Just drop it," I say defensively.

"Okay, okay," Heather says. She shoves the doll into her giant purse.

"I want to go there," I say, pointing down the street to where the bar I was looking at earlier stands. Pat O'Brien's.

"Oh, isn't that like one of the most famous bars here?" she asks, excitement in her voice.

"Yeah. They have these hurricane drinks that are amazing," I say.

Maybe I should have told Zach that we could meet up in New Orleans. Maybe I shouldn't have turned my head away when he was at the end of the row. Maybe I should have stayed after the podcast recording and tried to talk to him. Maybe I should have responded to his message, but I didn't do any of those things.

"You look lost in thought," Heather says dramatically. "What's up?"

"I'm fine," I lie. "I just—"

"Thinking about that hot comedian guy?" Heather asks with a smile in her voice.

"No," I say quickly. "God, just shut up," I reply, a smile in my voice now, too.

Once inside Pat O'Brien's, we get ourselves a hurricane each and find seats on the patio at a table for four. Even in the dark, it's beautiful. A fountain stands in the center of it all with plants around it and several flowerbeds and bushes that line the wrought iron fence. Fancy gas heaters ring the area giving off an almost romantic warmth.

"I'm so glad you came with me," Heather says. "I hate doing these things alone." Authenticity glows from her statement. A little bit of vulnerability, too, that I'm not expecting.

"Why?" I ask, genuinely curious.

"Just being in a big city that I don't know. People that I don't know. That Dana woman. She was nice, but my God, could she talk. All that shit just gets to me sometimes, you know?" she says and takes a big sip, finishing her drink. "I'm gonna get another one. You want one?"

I look at my first, almost-finished hurricane.

"No. I'm good for now. I'll get another one in a little while," I say, not wanting the alcohol to go completely to my head. If Heather is going to keep up this pace for the rest of the night, it's probably wise for me to stay somewhat sober.

Heather gets up and goes inside. I'm left to watch the couples and groups on the patio. It's loud with laughter and music and the clang of glassware. The gas-lit heating lamps give off enough warmth that I have to shed my jacket. That delicious smell that will turn sour sometime in the night permeates the Quarter. In the evening, the smell is intoxicating. In the morning, it's a brutal reminder of all the bad decisions made the night before.

Heather returns with a hurricane and two amber shots.

"Jack Daniels," she says, handing one of them to me. "To jiu-jitsu. May we keep doing it until we die!" she says, holding up her shot glass while still standing. I stand up to join her, shot in hand. I toast her.

"Hear, hear!"

I laugh as I bring the shot to my lips. Before the alcohol even hits my bloodstream, I feel a little lighter.

I sit down, letting the aftertaste of the whiskey burn my tongue. Heather quickly chases the shot with her hurricane. I smile, watching her.

"You're not gonna chase it?" Heather asks, incredulous.

"Nah," I say. "I like the burn." I smile.

"You must have had one hell of a party phase," Heather says.

"You don't know the half of it."

"You and Dan like to party, huh?"

"Yeah, sometimes," I reply.

"So, what about him?" Heather prods. "You and him ever a thing?"

"God, no," I say and laugh a little at the idea. "It would be like dating my brother."

"Is he single?"

"Eh," I say. "He's got a girl that I wish he'd settle down with, but I get why he doesn't."

"That's a shame. He's cute," she says, smiling at me.

There's a lull in the conversation in which I suck down the remainder of my first hurricane. I get up to go get another one.

"Anything from the bar?" I ask Heather.

"Shots?" Heather asks with a smile that really means *Is it okay if we do more shots?*

"Sure," I say, a mother acquiescing to the wishes of a child who has been particularly good.

I walk through the people on the patio and push through to the bar. It's packed. Once I'm there, I wait to get the bartender's attention. He turns towards me and I shout, "Hey!" making sure he sees me. He nods in my direction, stepping close to hear me.

"A hurricane and two shots of Jack!" I shout over the din.

"Got it," he says and starts making the drinks.

I take in my surroundings, something I'm always sure to do. I look around the bar and see guys sitting alone and some of them trying to talk to the girls that are coming up to the bar for a drink. I look behind me and see a sea of people flowing in and out of the bar as though they are blood cells, passing oxygen in and out of a body.

I turn back to the bar to see the bartender pouring the whiskey. When he finishes, he gives me the total. I pay in cash and take the drinks, turning to walk back out onto the patio. As soon as I do, a familiar voice stops me.

"Tash?"

I look up from the drinks to see Zach standing there, getting ready to go up to the bar, looking as good as ever. His hair is longer, to his shoulders. He wears a gray t-shirt and a black hoodie. Bootcut jeans and black sneakers.

"Zach," I say. Not a question.

"How are you?" he asks, walking cautiously towards me.

"I'm good," I say and smile. Even after so much time, his warmth feels so familiar. The way he made me feel that night still reverberated between us. I turn completely toward him.

"Let me help you," he says and takes the shots from my right hand.

"Oh," I say as he takes them. "You don't have to do that."

Shit. He'll go back to your table with you.

I lead the way out onto the patio and all the way to the table where Heather sits. She's turned around, having a conversation with a couple of guys that are sitting behind us. I tap her on the shoulder and clear my throat.

"Heather, this is Zach," I say, the tone of my voice cautioning her against saying anything idiotic. But she isn't one to disappoint.

"Oh, my God!" she squeals. "From the podcast recording!"

Zach looks from her to me.

"Yeah," he says with a smile, running a hand through his dark hair that I know smells fresh and clean. I want to bury myself in it. "I thought I saw you there," he says to me.

"Can't get away with anything, can I?" I ask Heather pointedly. She looks away, a sheepish grin on her face. She's pleased with the situation. I, on the other hand, am not sure how I feel, but I don't want him to leave.

"Is your friend with you?" Heather asks.

"Eric?" Zach asks. "Yeah, he's at the bar."

"Why don't you guys come and sit with us?" Heather asks excitedly.

I'm unamused but don't stop her.

Zach looks at me as though for confirmation and I find myself nodding my head almost eagerly. There's no reason to turn him away, I try to remind myself.

"Sure," I say. "Join us."

Zach smiles.

"I'm gonna get a drink and a shot myself," Zach says. "We'll be out in a minute."

He turns to go inside. I find myself admiring the snug fit of his jeans as he disappears into the bar. The buzz from the alcohol that I had going has gone away and I'm buzzing with something else. It's an excitement that I haven't felt in years. Not since that night when I stood on the beach with him, and he kissed me and took me back to his house. I feel an overwhelming heat gather in my cheeks. The idea of having to make small talk all night is just about too much. I grab my shot and threw it back without making any toast.

"You okay?" Heather asks.

"Yeah," I lie, trying not to be frustrated with her. "It's just—it's a lot, you know?"

Heather is quiet for a moment.

"You deserve a lot," she says, smiling like the Sphinx in the center of the labyrinth, her words cryptic and full of meaning that I don't understand.

I wonder what she means but didn't want to pursue the road that leads to drunken philosophy, so instead I sip quickly on my hurricane, abandoning my original plan of staying sober to take care of Heather. Now all I care about is soothing my nerves.

In a few moments, I see Eric's familiar face come around the corner. He throws up his arms, carrying two hurricanes which I'm pretty sure were both for him.

"Hey!" Eric shouts. Unlike Zach, it appears that Eric has done a little pre-partying. Eric holds his arms out as he approaches the table. He comes in for a hug. I stand and embrace him awkwardly. I look at Zach who looks incredibly uncomfortable.

"Hey!" I mock enthusiasm.

My speech is muffled against Eric's shirt. He pulls away quickly.

"So, how are you guys?" I ask, filling the silence.

"Great!" Eric says. I can tell that he means it. I know that Zach's career has really taken off. I'll be surprised if someone doesn't recognize the pair of them before the night is over.

I gesture to the seat across from me, next to Heather. Eric takes it and sits down, looking to Heather without missing a beat.

"Hi, I'm Eric," he says to her before I can even attempt an introduction. Zach steps behind me and pulls out the seat next to me.

"This guy," he says under his breath. "I can't take him anywhere that he doesn't make some inappropriate pass at someone's friend. You wanna take bets on how long you think it is before he asks her to come back to the hotel room with him?"

I smile slightly without looking at Zach. His sense of humor is a comfort. It makes me feel a little more at ease in this awkward situation. I don't know what it is about him—something about the way he blends the serious with the funny, or maybe it's just his warmth, his general kindness—that reassured me that he was somehow different. I feel so dangerously close to familiarity with this man that I left back in Los Angeles that I push back against it, willing it into submission and failing.

Zach and I both sit down and I look at him finally. My eyes scan over his features, trying to get a read on how he's feeling. I look over to say something to Heather, but see that she's engrossed in conversation with Eric, leaving me to make conversation with Zach. My stomach knots. I want to tell him everything. I want him to tell me it will be okay. I don't want his pity or his help. I just want to know that he believes I can make everything okay again.

"Wow," he says. He speaks quietly in comparison to the laughter and conversation of the people around us. I strain to hear him and my eyes focus on his lips, trying to read them. "It's been a long time."

I only nod. I don't know what to say. The burden to speak is on me. I wade through the swamp that my thoughts have become since Zach arrived. I struggle to articulate any of them.

"It has," I say, kicking myself, thinking it's probably the stupidest thing I could say in response to him. "How are you?" I tack onto the end of it, hoping that I sound like I'm keeping my cool.

"I'm good, actually," Zach says. "It's been busy. Crazy, too, but good." A big smile breaks across his face. He looks good. He looks like whatever he's doing is working for him. I smile, kind of in pain. I want nothing but happiness for him. What pains me is that I haven't been there to watch it happen for him.

"So, tell me about the Comedy Central thing. I saw it on your page," I say, hoping to shift the conversation away from me and towards him. The last thing I want to talk about is why we got back in touch to begin with.

"Oh, it was just a one-time thing. A special," he says, running a hand through his dark hair. It always has the look to it that he hasn't done anything special to style it, yet it falls perfectly disheveled around his face.

"That's still really cool," I say. The most famous person I've ever known was one of my friends whose dad was a funeral director that had a local access TV commercial when we were in college. It had to do with drunk driving. I remember my friend being in the commercial with this insane tagline. *Drunk driving isn't anyone else's business, unless you end up dead. Then it's my dad's business.* I've never forgotten the amount of brass balls it probably took to put that on television.

"Eh, it's work," Zach says with a smile that indicates though it was work, he enjoys it very much. "It looks like you're doing something you really enjoy these days, too."

"I am," I say, still smiling.

"Jiu-jitsu, huh?"

"Yeah," I say. "You know, choking people out for a living. Helps with my anger issues."

Zach laughs. It's a warm, friendly sound, but also undeniably sexy.

I look over at Eric and Heather. He moves a hand to her thigh and they are giggling, his forehead pressed to hers like they didn't just meet only a few minutes go. Jesus. Zach is right. I would have gambled on it taking a little longer, but damn, he's charming her right out of her panties before my very eyes.

"What'd I tell you?" Zach asks, nodding towards Eric and Heather, his voice only loud enough that I can hear him. I can't hear what they're talking about on the other side of the table. They've lowered their voices, their conversation taking on a more intimate tone. I only hear the occasional peal of Heather's falsetto laugh that she reserves for occasions just like this one.

I watch the two of them for a few seconds, marveling at how effortlessly Heather interacts with this man that's a complete stranger. I yearn for the ability to do that, to shake Alex's touch from my skin. I want to erase the memory of that night with Henry and replace it with something beautiful. I don't know if that will even be possible for me ever again.

My throat grows tight as I watch them, sipping my drink. Zach has grown silent beside me. Somehow, his silent presence is more helpful to me than any words of solace Heather has ever offered.

I finally break my gaze away from the happy new couple.

"How long are you staying in town?" I ask.

"We're leaving tomorrow," he says, somewhat sadly. "You?"

He looks up at me from under two dark eyebrows. I notice then that his eyelashes are longer than most guys I've ever met. His nose is long and straight. He reaches up and rubs his facial hair.

"Monday," I say.

"Are you having a good time?" he asks.

For a moment, I don't know if he means *Are you having a good time in New Orleans?* or *Are you having a good time right now, with me?* The answer to the latter is undoubtedly yes.

"I am, actually," I say, answering the question however he means for it to be taken.

"Did you have fun at the podcast recording?"

I chuckle under my breath.

"That was supposed to be a totally under the radar thing," I say.

"I thought I saw you when we first came out. I kept telling myself that I couldn't have. That you wouldn't have been there. That was the last place in New Orleans you'd be tonight," he says. His voice trails off at the end. He looks away from me.

The two of us are silent for a moment.

"I didn't think it was somewhere I was going to be this weekend, either, up until a couple of days ago. I saw the tickets and bought them on a whim, before you messaged me. I didn't think I'd get to do anything but see you on stage. I didn't plan for it to go this way," I say.

"I'm glad it did," Zach says, he reaches up and brushes a piece of hair back behind my ear. His hand lingers for a moment longer than necessary. I feel my insides turn to mush as he does it. His smile is all the warmth I need for the rest of this cool, December evening.

CHAPTER 26

Los Angeles Sept. 2012

After we moved to Los Angeles, Alex flaunted his money. He bought a yacht.

It was an Otam Millenium 100 that he bought after carefully considering his options. That was something I wasn't used to when it came to his purchases. It was lavish. The kind of thing that you see in movies. Alex came from money that I couldn't fathom. We had people over on the boat for dinner and often we had dinner on it ourselves and spent the night there.

On one such evening, he broached a subject that he'd been wanting to bring up since our first trip to the Sanctuary and his first conversation with Tony afterwards. We were eating dinner—takeout—and he put his fork down.

"There's something I wanted to ask you about," he said, finishing a bite of his food and washing it down with a sip of white wine.

I cut my pasta delicately, unsure of where this was going but having a decent idea.

In the last few weeks, we'd gone out with Tony and Lola

several times. Not enough for me to have learned much about either of them, but enough for them to have at least become buddies that we could double date with. It felt awkward to me, though, knowing what kind of relationship they had and not knowing Lola's real name.

"What?" I asked, an edge in my voice.

"Just hear me out," Alex said with a charming smile.

It was a smile that I was used to seeing whenever Alex had an idea that he knew I wouldn't like or wanted to do something that I knew would upset me. It didn't matter what it was, he always got his way.

I took the last bite of my pasta and got up from the table. I asked him if he was finished, and he shook his head. I headed into the kitchen with my unfinished pasta and threw it in the trash.

I stood at the counter and stared at him, my stomach in a knot, knowing that the conversation would have something to do with the Sanctuary.

"I wanted to ask you how you'd feel about me doing a scene with Lola," he said.

My face must have revealed everything I was thinking, he quickly went on.

"It's not a sex thing, Natasha," he said, as though I were the dumbest person on earth. He slumped in his chair and ran his hands through his hair. "This isn't going to work if you're going to be jealous."

"*This isn't going to work?*" I spluttered, incredulous. "What, exactly, isn't going to work? You fucking other girls under my nose?"

"Natasha," he said. "It's not like that." I could tell he was calculating his next sentence to be crafted for maximum persuasion. "I want to learn to do what Tony does with her so I can do it with *you*."

I was silent for a moment. I knew this was coming. I hadn't wanted to do a scene or play in the way that we saw the couples play at the Sanctuary. We hadn't done anything of that nature yet and it hung in the air between us, palpable as if it had a pulse.

"And you think you're going to learn on Lola?" I asked, skeptical.

"Yeah," he said, glowing with the thought that I was coming around to his idea.

I sighed, knowing that I was going to lose this battle. Since we'd started going to the Sanctuary, I'd seen small changes in Alex. He wasn't the person I'd known, at least not completely. Some of it was dark. I wondered why he wanted to do this. There was something about this that appealed to Alex that I wasn't sure appealed to the other people in this lifestyle. For him, there was something darker here.

"Why?" I asked.

He shrugged his shoulders, again acting like it was the dumbest question he'd ever heard.

"It'll be fun. Doesn't it look like they're having fun?" he asked.

I didn't care if they were having fun. I knew *I* wouldn't have fun doing that.

"Not really," I managed to say, unwilling to get into a fight with him about the nature of Tony and Lola's relationship.

"Come on," he said, standing up and walking over to me. He took my hands and brushed some hair away from my face tenderly. "It would be fun. I promise."

I turned my face into his palm, eager for his touch.

He took me by the hand and led me below deck to the master bedroom. Knowing every curve of my body, he took my clothes off quickly and slipped a hand over my breast. I breathed in sharply. We hadn't had sex in a week or two. He took me in his arms and laid me on the bed. We made love.

Lying next to him, him curled around me, he whispered in my ear, "Come on, Natasha."

"Okay," I gave in.

The next weekend, we went to the Sanctuary. I hadn't obliged Alex's requests that I buy something 'sexier' to wear to the parties. I didn't feel comfortable riding around Los Angeles wearing a corset under a trench coat. Call me old fashioned.

Lola was wearing a corset under a kimono with five-inch heels that looked like they would break her ankles if she had a misstep. Once we spotted her, I noticed that she had someone with her. A girl with flame red wavy hair.

"This is my friend, Amy," Lola said, introducing us to her.

I stuck my hand out to shake Amy's. She gave me a limp handshake that I always hated to receive from other women. I pulled my hand back, feeling like it had been dipped in something slimy.

"Nice to meet you," Alex said, stepping forward, nearly in front of me to greet the new guest.

"First time?" I asked, poking my head around my forward fiancé.

"Yeah," Amy said, looking around nervously.

"Don't look so scared," Lola laughed melodically. Tony came up and put an arm around her.

"Amy's under my protection tonight," Tony said. It was

a phrase that kept people from being to forward with new guests. Tony would see to it that nothing happened to Amy.

As the night went on, we watched various scenes. Tony and Lola did a scene with a needle corset. Someone else inserted the needles and Tony watched, looking like he was on the verge of vomiting. It amused me.

I yawned as the three of us, myself, Alex, and Amy, sat on one of the couches and watched.

"You bored?" Amy asked.

"No," I lied. "I'm just tired. Long day," I said with a smile.

"What do you do?" she asked.

"I'm a paleontologist," I said. "You?"

"Phlebotomist," she said. "But I'm looking for a new job."

I nodded, trying to pretend that I had any interest in what career path this stranger had taken when Alex leaned over to both of us.

"How would you guys feel about coming back to our place after the party?" he asked.

"Alex!" I hissed, unable to control myself. All I wanted to do was crawl into bed after this and try to forget this place for another two weeks.

"That sounds great," Amy said, looking for confirmation from me.

Annoyed, I nodded and smiled.

I shot a look of disgust at Alex as we watched the rest of the scene unfold.

———

Entrusting Amy and Lola's well-being to Alex and I, Tony left and went home, having a big case that he needed to keep preparing for the next day. I rolled my eyes as the two of them congratulated each other on the fact that they had three girls at their disposal. In the car, Amy and Lola sat in the backseat, giggling nervously.

We all rode in silence, my annoyance practically tangible to all of them. Alex turned on the radio—Christian rock—and Amy snorted.

"Something funny?" Alex asked, a smile in his voice, though his face was dangerous.

"Oh, just the Christian music," Amy said. "Nice touch."

"I like it," Alex said, and I rolled my eyes. I wondered if Amy had, too. At least she also saw the ridiculousness of it.

Amy and Lola were quiet for the rest of the ride. I leaned against the passenger side window and looked out at the rainy evening. Once we got to the house, we all poured into the living room.

"Why don't you get them something to drink?" Alex asked me.

I shot him a look of annoyance.

"Sure," I said, through gritted teeth.

"I'll help you," Lola offered.

She followed me to our kitchen and helped me once I got the glasses down and opened a bottle of sparkling wine. I handed her two of the glasses and I took two. She took her second glass to Alex which rubbed me the wrong way.

"Here you go, sir," she said to him.

I rolled my eyes.

"Oh, don't give him any ideas," I said sharply.

But Alex was already gazing down at her as though she was a meal. I was disgusted. Amy must have sensed my disgust because she sidled up to me.

"Not your idea of a good time?" she asked me.

"Not particularly," I said, unable to lie.

"It's a little weird," Amy admitted. "Sam—I mean Lola —invited me and I wasn't sure I wanted to come. It's strange, isn't it?"

"To say the least," I said, unsure that I wanted to start a friendly conversation with a woman who'd come back to my house at my fiance's request.

"I think we're going to do a little scene," Alex said over us.

"What?" I asked.

"Tony sent some floggers with me. He said we could," Alex said as though Tony's permission was the only permission that mattered.

I sighed, exasperated, not wanting to appear like a jealous girlfriend or wife in front of these girls and upset the delicate atmosphere of the evening.

"Okay," I said, gritting my teeth. "I'm going to change."

I left the three of them in the living room and went to the bedroom. I angrily grabbed some pajamas—the sloppiest that I could find—and threw them on. I grabbed my wine glass and went back into the living room to see Lola—Sam— stretch out topless on the couch, arching her back as she leaned over the edge of it and Alex swung the floggers at her, not knowing what the fuck he was doing.

"Is it his first time?" Amy asked me.

"That obvious?" I asked sarcastically.

She chuckled.

Sam giggled as Alex hit her with the strips of leather. I settled into the uncomfortableness of the moment. I realized suddenly that this was my life. This was what I'd left Nashville behind for. Dan's words about Alex echoed in my mind and I wondered briefly if he'd been right about him all along. I felt trapped in the moment, unable to breathe. Tears welled in my eyes. I wiped them from the corners before they could slip out.

"You okay?" Amy asked.

"I'm fine," I lied and went to the bedroom, leaving the three of them to their little party. I struggled to fall asleep as I heard Alex and Lola's muffled voices. Sam, that was her real name. I wondered how much of what I knew about her was real. I barely knew anything at all. All that I knew was real was the pit in the center of my stomach, an ache that would never go away.

CHAPTER 27

New Orleans Dec. 2016

The evening stretches out like a cat's arching back, wrapping me up in pleasant conversation and warmth even if there is a chill in the air. Zach tells stories about his dog, Lucy, and his life as a bachelor and I tell him stories about the jiu-jitsu school and the trips that Heather I have taken together promoting the women's program.

Around 12:30am I look at my watch.

"Damn," I say with regret.

"Need to go to bed?" Zach asks with a little sadness in his voice.

It stabs me deeply to think about the evening ending so abruptly. Responsibility plagues me.

I look over at Heather who is lost in the world that has been created between her and Eric. I haven't seen her that engrossed in a guy in a long time. I tap on the table in front of her. She finally looks at me, a big dopey grin on her face.

"We probably need to get back to the hotel room," I say. Even as the words roll off my tongue, I regret them. I want to stay out all night with Zach. I want to see the sunrise with him. I want to feel the hope that he's giving me in this midnight hour stretch on into the dawn.

Heather looks at Eric with regret and then realization dawns on both of them.

Eric whispers something in her ear.

She looks at me, a shy teenage girl asking to stay out after prom.

"I think I'm going to go back to the hotel with Eric. I'll catch up with you later," she says.

My head juts forward, incredulous.

"Seriously?" I hiss.

She shoots me a look that begs me not to embarrass her so I don't. I grab my hurricane and finish it. I twirl the straw in the ice. Zach groans. Heather and Eric turn back toward each other and I look over at Zach.

"What's wrong?" I ask.

"He always does this," he says. "He tells me we can share a room and then he winds up bringing a girl back to it with him."

"You can come with me," I blurt out, the words falling out of my mouth. "Just for a drink or coffee or whatever. Just to talk," I clarify.

Zach looks at me, unsure.

"You sure?" he asks.

"Yeah," I say, entirely unsure. "Let's go," I say, standing from the table. "I'll see you later," I say to Heather.

Zach stands up and together we leave Pat O'Brien's.

We walk, side by side but not touching each other, all the way back to the hotel. It's in the French Quarter so it isn't far. Once inside, I feel self-conscious as I walk with Zach to the elevator. I think all eyes are on me, judging me for bringing a man back to my room when I left earlier with a woman.

On my floor, we get off. I lead the way to my hotel room and fumble around in my purse for the key. I finally pull it out and my hand shakes as I slide it into the card reader on the doorlock. It flashes red. I have to try again twice before it flashes green and let us in.

The room is cool, the way I always like a hotel room to be. I slip out of my jacket and flip on the light switch. The room is dimly illuminated and I go to the coffee machine on the desk.

"Coffee?" I ask Zach, acutely aware of the proximity that we share.

"Sure," he says, nodding his head. He still has his jacket on and stands at the foot of Heather's bed.

"You can sit down," I tell him.

I hear the bed creak under his weight as I pour water into the side of the Keurig and start it up, brewing a cup of coffee for him and then one for me. I take them and stand in front of him, the space between us marginal as he sits on the inside side of Heather's bed and I take a seat on the inside side of my bed.

"I'm sorry about this," Zach says after he sipped his coffee. "He's a jackass. He always does this. Usually I just find an IHOP to hang out at until he texts me the all clear."

I laugh.

"Well, you can hang out here until he does this time," I say.

I swallow, feeling entirely conscious of the way my throat feels as I do so. I sip some more coffee even though it scalds my lips and tongue. I'm in that heightened state of awareness where things like hot coffee stop registering in favor of other stimuli. The silence in the room is interrupted by the A/C kicking on. I'm grateful.

The last time that I was alone with a man was with Henry. The memory of his hand snaking up my side makes my flesh crawl beneath my gray sweater. I roll my shoulders and tilt my head, trying to physically shake the sensation from my body. If I've learned anything from jiu-jitsu, it's that trauma lives in the body. There are times that I'm rolling, not thinking about that night with Alex, when it will hit me. I'll be suddenly aware of every inch of my skin. I can feel the other person's eyes trailing down my neck and across my chest. I will want to hide, feeling violated by the presence of another person. It feels like that now.

It's nothing that Zach does or says. It's just that he's here and he's a man.

I finally meet his eyes.

"I'm glad we ran into each other," he says, looking away from me for a moment.

"Me too," I agree. I look down at my feet and kicked off my shoes, folding my legs up under me. "Want to watch TV?" I ask.

"Whatever you want to do," Zach says with a smile. "I'm at your mercy. I'm just glad that I don't have to hide in my hotel room bathroom while Eric works his magic."

I laugh.

"Not tonight, anyway," I say.

I reach for the remote and flip the TV on. A local channel is showing the weather for the next day on a rerun of the news. I go to change it and then there is a box that appears in the middle of the TV that says CABLE SIGNAL LOST, CONTACT YOUR PROVIDER.

Of course it is.

I look at Zach, forcing an awkward smile. The last night

that we truly spent together hangs in the air between us, an entity all its own. My thought that we could ditch it by having the white noise of television on in the background is scrapped.

I sigh. It looks like we're going to have to talk to each other.

"So," I say. "Tell me some more dating stories." I try once again to shift the focus off me in fear that we might talk about the pictures, and that it will lead to discussing Alex, which will lead to discussing other parts of the past that I want to bury. I spin the ring on my right finger as I watch him run a hand through his dark hair.

"Well, as you know, Amy and I broke up right before I met you. But then after you left, we got back together," he says.

That's news to me. That means that she isn't with Alex.

"But then we broke up again," he says.

Or possibly she is.

"It went back and forth like that for awhile. It was during a time when I was having trouble finding work. Things kind of took a dark turn. I was drinking a lot, pretty depressed. That next Halloween was particularly eventful," he said.

"What happened?" I ask.

"Aside from me ending up in the hospital?" he asks with a bitter laugh. It isn't a sound I'm accustomed to hearing from him. "Not much."

"How did you end up in the hospital?"

He's silent for a moment.

"Eh, you probably don't want to hear that story. It's not very funny," he says, making certain that now I want nothing more than to hear that story. I stare at him with curious eyes.

"Come on," I say. "You can tell me. What was it, an STI?" I sip my coffee and smirk, but his face shifts. He becomes somber. The A/C kicks off and we're left with only the sounds of our pulses in our ears and each other's breathing.

"I tried to kill myself," he says matter-of-factly.

I'm silent.

"I didn't think there was any hope of things getting better. The situation with Amy was on again, off again. Work sucked. Eric and I had pitched what's now the podcast to every radio station within 500 miles. Bills were getting higher. I gave up," he concludes, looking me directly in the eyes.

I say nothing. I think of that night in the Museum of Death and his statement about the man who had committed suicide in the black and white pictures.

"I took about fifty Xanax," he says. "And drank a bottle of tequila. Eric came home early and found me. Took me to the emergency room. They pumped my stomach, and I had the worst hangover of my entire life," he concludes with a pressed smile. "And that was that."

The space between us feels entirely too small. I need air. I need the sound of the A/C in the background to break up the sound of my blood thundering past my eardrums. I need space. I need Zach to leave. I begin to breathe harder.

The intimacy of the moment strains my shoulders. It's too much to carry any distance and the only distance I want to go is to the door to show him out. It's wrong. He just opened up to me. I should be there for him, but I can't. I physically can't. I'm terrified of what I feel for him and the idea that he might have killed himself is too much. Tears sting my eyes as I choke down a sob. I think about Zach in Los Angeles, me at home and probably watching *The Exor-*

cist with Dan, unaware that 2,000 miles away, someone that I care deeply for was trying to end their life. And the only reason that I didn't know about it is because I wasn't strong enough to stay in Los Angeles.

I stand up from the bed.

"You have to go," I say, my voice full of sadness.

"Tash, what—" he begins.

"Please leave,' I choke out.

Zach stands, his eyes pained. He just opened up to me about one of the most painful and secret events of his life and I'm kicking him out.

I feel sick. I feel sick for him and sick for myself. He sits his coffee cup down on the TV stand and walks towards the door. He opens it. I stand by the bed and watch him go, feeling like a part of myself is dying. He turns and looks at me.

"Tash—" he tries again.

"No," I say.

"I'm glad I got to see you," he says.

Zach goes out the door and I hear his footsteps begin to traipse down the hall. I go to the door and press my ear to it, trying to hear the ding of the elevator but I can't. All I can hear are my own sobs. I collapse on the floor. I'm broken and no one can ever understand the shattered mess that I've become.

I sit in the silence of my hotel room for a few moments after Zach leaves—after I forced him out. The A/C kicks on again and I'm grateful for its company. My thoughts have become too jumbled and loud to make good bedfellows. I shrug out of my sweater and into my pajamas and grab my phone. I check the cable one last time to see that it still isn't working. I call the front desk to let them know. They act like they couldn't be more disinterested in my problem.

I crawl into bed and hold my phone. I open my text messages and go to Alex's name. I hammer out some text and my finger hovers over the send button.

I miss you, too.

I hesitate long enough that I delete the message. It's true, though. I do miss him. I put my phone on the nightstand and roll over to face the window. It's open, something I'll regret when the harsh sunlight comes through it in the morning, but for now I needs the lights of the city to keep me company. I lay awake, staring out the window, wondering how many other people are falling asleep that way. Alone.

I wish that Heather would come back already. I wonder where Zach had gone to pass the time. I think about Alex and the darkness that had been born inside of me, him its sire.

I wrap myself in the arms of these thoughts and drift into a restless sleep.

CHAPTER 28

Los Angeles Oct. 2012

At Alex's urging, I made a date to take Sam and Amy to lunch. I was meeting them at a little café that served coffee and pastries as well as deli-type sandwiches. I sat in a booth munching on a piece of banana bread, not really wanting to be there. My gut churned as I waited for them. When I caught sight of Amy's red hair and Sam's black hair coming through the door, I girded my loins, trying to prepare myself to be as polite as possible.

"Hey!" Sam said, her voice eager to please. She wanted to be my friend so desperately that it was almost sickening.

"Hey," I said to her and Amy without standing. "Have a seat."

The two of them took a seat across from me at the table. We sat awkwardly for a moment.

"How are you, Natasha?" asked Sam, her voice sickly sweet.

"I'm fine," I said, ice cold. I hated this. And I hated Alex for making me do it. It was ridiculous. Having lunch with the women that he wanted to fuck. I felt destroyed. Like a shell of myself.

"What did you get?" she asked, prodding the conversation along.

"Banana bread," I offered, holding up the last piece of it.

"Are you going to get lunch?" Sam asked.

"I don't think so," I replied. "Not very hungry."

We sat in silence for a moment.

The girls began to chatter about what they were going to have. Amy offered to get up and place the order for them, leaving Sam and I at the table alone. I pictured her lying naked on my couch, Alex hovering over her. My blood began to boil.

"So, I guess that this is part of the process, huh?" Sam said with a smile.

"Process?" I asked.

"Of us all becoming a family," she said.

I balked at the word. This was news to me.

"Alex has already talked to Tony about it," Sam said. "Surely he's talked to you, hasn't he?"

I nodded my head instinctively, even though he hadn't talked to me about any of it, but knowing that if I told her he had, I would get more information.

"It'll be nice," she said. "I think you'll enjoy it."

I smiled, rage simmering beneath the surface. I wanted to get home and choke the shit out of Alex. Throttle his perfect neck until his eyes popped out of his skull.

Amy returned with a number and placed it on a stand in the middle of the table. I looked at her and forced a smile. She returned it gingerly like it was a gently served tennis ball.

We spent the rest of the hour trying to force a conversation. I made myself smile and be as cordial as possible. I wasn't angry with either of them. My anger was directed at the appropriate target: my idiot fiancé.

And I was ready to kill him.

CHAPTER 29

New Orleans Dec. 2016

In the morning, I wake alone. I look over with sleepy eyes at Heather's bed and groan, throwing myself back into my pillows when I see that she isn't there.

"Fuck," I hiss.

I look at my watch and see that it's a quarter till seven. We have until ten to get to the seminar. She better hurry the fuck up. My phone dings and I grab it, hoping that it's her saying she's just down the street and to meet her downstairs for breakfast. Instead, it's Alex.

I'll be in Tennessee next week and I'd like to see you.

My heart thuds deep in my chest, sending the blood thundering to my head and extremities, making my fingertips pulse as adrenaline dumps into my system. My fight-or-flight response was so jacked that I have trouble determining good excitement from bad. I hate surprises. I hate to be startled. This does both.

I don't know what to say. I want to resolve this. I want the pictures gone. I don't know what he wants though.

What the hell could he possibly want from the girl he threw away like trash?

I debate on sending something snarky back, but fear ultimately wins out, and like a well-trained dog, I salivate at the opportunity to see my master.

When?

He responds a minute later.

Next Friday night. The Hilton.

I quickly type.

Okay.

And that's that.

There I lay, in a hotel room in New Orleans, a date with destiny in the books for next Friday night. I'm going to confront my fate, one way or another. Perhaps Alex and I are destined for each other. No one knows my heart the way he once did. I've never let another person in after him. He mauled it like a lion mauls a sickly underweight gazelle. And still, it beats for him. The thought nauseates and excites me.

Maybe Zach has been a distraction all along. Who am I kidding thinking that I could be with him? He is so good. He doesn't know me. He doesn't know my darkness. He doesn't understand the kind of person that I really am, but Alex does.

He understands that. He knows how terrible I am and yet, still, he wants me.

I should be grateful for that.

I wait for Heather to get back to the room somewhat impatiently. We have less than an hour to be at the seminar and she still hasn't shown up. Finally, I hear the door handle turn and she bursts into the room, her hair a mess and her makeup blurry around the edges looking like the poster child for the walk of shame. It's a walk I'm pretty sure New Orleans is accustomed to seeing.

I sit up on my bed and fold my arms, annoyed with her.

"Good morning," I say, my tone more judgmental than I'd like for it to be.

She looks up from under her dark hair that's somewhat in her face.

"Good morning," she says with an enthusiastic sigh. She throws herself face first onto her bed, dropping her purse beside it.

"That good, huh?" I ask, my annoyance fading a little bit.

"That good," she confirms. "Tash, he's amazing."

"Don't tell me you're in love," I say, rolling my eyes.

"Hardly," she says, leaning up on one elbow. "But he knows what he's doing if you know what I mean," she says, wiggling her eyebrows.

I laugh.

"What about you and Zach?" she asks me.

I prickle like a hedgehog going into defensive mode.

"What about us?" I ask.

"Well, didn't he come back here with you?"

"Yeah, so?"

"So...what happened?" she asks, prodding the conversation along despite my best efforts to stall it.

"I made him leave," I say.

"He get fresh with you?" she asks.

"Hardly," I say, echoing her sentiment from earlier.

"Geez, Tash. You've gotta let your shit go. He's a good guy," she says, throwing herself back into her prone position.

I need to do no such thing, so instead of acknowledging her statement, I simply say, "You smell like a brewery. Get ready."

I get off the bed, and grab my gi out of my suitcase and head for the bathroom, unwilling to take the conversation any further, though now I can't deny that Zach will be on my mind for the rest of the day.

CHAPTER 30

Los Angeles Oct. 2012

The night after my little lunch date with the girls, I sat on the couch as Alex flipped through the television. Not finding anything to his liking, he switched it off.

"I'm going to bed," he said.

I looked up from my magazine. I'd been cold and distant since my meeting with Sam and Amy. I wanted to ream Alex. I'd resisted the urge to explode on him, but now, without him even asking how it went, it was too much.

"I talked to Sam today," I said.

"I figured as much," he replied nonchalantly.

"She told me that you gave her the impression that we were all going to be in a relationship together or something like that. Is that true?" I asked him, my tone as dry and procedural as if I were someone in one of his courtrooms.

He looked at me, almost like a deer in the headlights. I'd never seen Alex caught off guard.

"Well—" he began.

"No, don't *well* me. You told her that, didn't you?" I

said, throwing the magazine off of my lap and standing. "Is that what you think is going to happen? Do you think this is some kind of game or something?"

"Natasha, listen—" he tried.

"No! You listen! I'm sick of this shit! I don't want that. I don't want to share you. I don't want you to be with other people. I don't want either of us to be with other people. Am I not enough for you?"

"I'm not asking you to!" he shouted. "I just asked her about all of us playing together and I was going to bring it up with you tonight. And of course you're enough." But the way he said the last part of that made me wonder how sincere he was. Why hadn't he ever told me this was something he wanted to do? I was so confused.

It all sounded like an excuse and a lie.

He went on.

"What if the next time I play with her, you play with us?"

"What do you mean?" I asked.

"You top her with me. Like we're both the dominant. We tell her what to do. We do it together," he stepped forward and circled his arms around my waist. "Don't you think that would be kinda hot?"

My body went rigid. There was nothing sexy about it to me, but the look in his eyes told me that this was what he wanted. And I wanted to keep him. As broken as we had become, I didn't want to lose him.

I sighed, defeated.

"We can try it," I acquiesced.

"You won't be sorry," he said, sounding as excited as he might have if he were a child on Christmas Day.

I loved Alex. I loved him with every breath that I took.

I'd left behind my family and my hometown to be with him. And here I was. In this big city without any friends besides my coworkers and a man who I thought I could fall in love with if given half a chance.

I had to do this.

I had to try to save my relationship.

CHAPTER 31

Nashville Dec. 2016

The next week at work is excruciating. Henry and I see each other in passing and avoid each other at all costs after that. Finally, it becomes apparent to Heather that something is up and she corners me in the office.

"Dude, what's the deal with Henry?" she asks, holding her hands out to her sides in exasperation, carrying contracts in both of them.

"Nothing," I say.

She rolls her eyes.

"You're insanely easy to read. You know that, right?"

I sigh.

"We went on a date, okay?" I acquiesce. "It didn't go so well. I don't want to hear about it."

Heather is surprisingly quiet. She isn't usually one to not speak her mind. There isn't any policy about not dating within the school, but I'm sure that she'll have something smart to say about it or some advice for my broken heart at the very least.

"You okay?" she finally asks.

"Yeah. I'm fine. You should be more worried about him," I say. It isn't untrue. I haven't had any conversation with Henry about what happened. He knows some things about my past but not the whole story. He thought he'd take control that night and it would be fun.

"I'll talk to him," Heather says.

I imagine Henry divulging the events of that night to Heather.

"On second thought," I blurt out. "Maybe just leave it alone."

Heather thinks about it for a second.

"I'd never get anything done if I let my pride get in the way of everything," she says, shrugging her shoulders. "Oh, well. He's a big boy. He'll deal with it."

He will, I think.

That Thursday when I get to work and walk in, I look out from behind my Ray Bans and see the entirety of the crowd sitting on the bleachers turn and stare at me. One of the moms whispers something to another one who laughs smugly. Another pulls her son a little closer to her. I pull my shades off and walk past, smiling at all of them.

Heather is gone for the weekend. She's going to Memphis to see her mom and sister and she left me in charge of things. It bolstered my confidence that she felt she could trust me with the thing she was most proud of.

I walk around towards the bathroom and shrug off the strange looks I'm getting from the parents. It's about an hour before the first adult class, most of the kids are still out on the mat. One of the other instructors is out there, teaching guard passing techniques to the kids.

Inside the bathroom, I see Amanda's back at the sink.

"Hey, Amanda," I say.

She turns to face me, her face red from crying. With tears in her voice, she spoke.

"Are they real?" she asks.

I'm bewildered.

"Is what real?"

"The pictures," she says.

My gut hits the floor. I think about the parents' eyes that were on me as I came through the door. I stumble out of the bathroom and find my way to the bulletin board. It's in the center of the atrium where everyone would be sure not to miss anything posted on it. And there are five 8" x 10" prints of me posed wearing next to nothing, and, in a couple, nothing at all.

I scramble to grab the pictures, pulling them out so quickly that the tacks that hold them up fly across the room. I hear one of the parents snickering at me. I turn to face her, knowing that if I speak, my voice will crack and shatter me into a sobbing mess.

She sits there. Her face bold judgement. She doesn't care about the time I've spent with her daughter helping her practice what to say and do the next time she's bullied so badly at school that she wets the bed again. She doesn't care about the times I've taken her daughter home from the school or who I've proven myself to be. Every single opinion she had about me has turned on a dime the moment she saw those pictures, coloring her perception of me forever.

With the pictures in my hands, I storm into the gym, the door slamming behind me. As loudly and clearly as I can, I speak.

"Class is over."

"I saw Henry at the bulletin board. He only came in for a few minutes. I thought they were pictures from the last tournament or something. I couldn't make out what they were form the mat, and, honestly, I didn't think anything about it," says Monica. She's one of the other instructors that was on duty when the pictures showed up.

I sit in the office, my hands shaking.

"Why would he do that?" Monica asks, tilting her black ponytail to the side and squinting her eyes in disbelief. She crosses her arms over her chest in a protective gesture.

"Don't worry about it," I say. "I'll sort it out."

Monica offers me a hug and I stiffly accept her embrace from my seated position. The last thing I want is to be pressed against another person, but she means nothing by it. Most people don't. I force a smile as she leaves and I follow her to the door, locking it behind her.

I punch the office door and scream, a pit forming in my stomach.

A week and a half ago I was on track to graduate. I had a job that I loved with students who respected me. I had moved on with my life. It only took a few e-mails with attachments and a photo dump on a hidden server to change all of that. And who could I blame but myself for having let the photos exist in the first place?

I don't want to call Heather yet. I know I can't talk about it. I want to calm down before I go home for the same reason. I'm not ready.

CHAPTER 32

The next night, Dan is out with some friends and I'm grateful for it. I don't know if I could withstand a question-and-answer session about why I'm wearing a little black dress and heels. I haven't worn an outfit like this one since I left Los Angeles. Buying it was strange. I'm meeting Alex and I want to look my best. It feels like a costume. I need to be alluring. I need Alex to want me and know what he's lost.

I put on my makeup and some earrings. Dab a little perfume at all my pulse points and I'm out the door. My stomach flutters with nerves as I drive, accidentally cutting off several other drivers and absentmindedly almost causing a wreck. One of the guys honks and flips me off as he passes. I turn into the parking garage of the Hilton in downtown Nashville and shut my car off. When I take my hands form the wheel, they're shaking. I have the distinct feeling that I'm doing something I shouldn't. Like a kid, watching HBO while their parents are asleep in the other room. I can't help but dread seeing someone that knows me. I know where

Dan was going but still, I imagine him popping into the Hilton bar for a drink.

I inhale deeply through my nose and push all the air from my lungs until they ache for another breath. I do that several times until I am able to take the keys out of the ignition and exit the car.

My heels clack, echoing throughout the parking garage. No one else is around and I feel myself slipping into the skin of someone entirely other. Someone who isn't afraid of Alex, but instead actually wants to see him.

In the hotel lobby, I look around nervously. My eyes flit from chair to chair and to the doors of the elevator, searching for him. I don't find him, though.

I go into the bar and take a seat. I order a Bloody Mary and I'm glad when the bartender obliges my request for extra olives. I immediately take them out and begin to munch nervously on one of them.

I sit alone in the bar for what seems like an eternity. A couple to my right chatters to each other intimately. I look to my side to see the guy caress the girl's bare shoulder. She smiles coyly and sips her drink. I watch people come and go. I look at my watch and count the minutes until 7:30. It comes and passes. At 7:33 I look at my watch again. I'm staring at the second hand moving as though it's parting a sea of molasses when I feel a cold hand on my shoulder.

I turn and there he is.

Alex.

The last three years have been good to him. His sandy blonde hair waves just below the nape of his neck. It's swept out of his face and perfectly coiffed. He's handsome, put together, and has all the makings of a man who looks like a real catch. And I had released him.

"Hey," he says.

"Hey," I say, barely loud enough to be heard. My breath catches in my throat, making the word come out only partially audible.

He pulls out the barstool next to me and for a moment I take it in. I am sitting next to him. He could reach out and touch me if he wanted to. My stomach clenches and I think for a moment that I might throw up, but then he looks at me again. His eyes are soft. There isn't the hardness in them that I'd grown so used to in those last months of our relationship. He looks like the man I fell in love with so many years ago.

I feel a pain inside my chest. It's knowing that he wasn't —perhaps never had been—the person I fell in love with. It makes it hard to speak so I let him fill the silence.

"You look amazing," he says, his voice smooth like silk and deadly as a viper's strike.

"You do, too," I say, not lying in the least.

Alex orders a drink. Whiskey on the rocks. He sips it in silence as we sit there, letting the last few years settle between us like dust after a tornado.

"I'm grateful that you decided to meet up with me," he says.

Gratitude. It's an interesting platform for him. Not one that he usually operates from.

"I didn't have much of a choice, did I?" I say tightly. Even despite his charm and the fear I still have for what he could do to me, there's something in me that's just *done*. Part of me wants to throw my Bloody Mary in his face and stab him in the jugular with the skewer, olives intact.

Instead, after years of practice and conditioning, I smile.

"I guess you didn't," he admits. "Look, I'm sorry," he says. "I didn't think it would hurt anything. It was just a joke. Just a way to get back at you for everything."

"Are you really so far above the rest of us that you can't comprehend how posting my phone number and home address with naked pictures of me could cause me pain? Let's talk about the guy who's been stalking me for the past week!" My voice grows louder and louder as I continue.

"Stalking you?" Alex asks.

"Yeah. He was parked outside my house when I got home the other night after—you know what? It doesn't matter."

"It does matter. I'll take care of it."

"I don't want you to take care of it!"

The bartender looks at me like he wonders if I'm being held against my will. I stare him down. Alex places a cold hand over mine.

"Natasha," he says. "Calm down. We can fix this."

"*Fix it?* How?" I hiss.

"Come back to Los Angeles with me. Let's start over," he says.

"Alex—"

"You're the only person who's ever understood me. And you know that I'm the only one who's ever really understood you. We're made for each other in our own fucked up way. There's no escaping it. I'll love you forever," he says. He's nearly breathless at the end of his little proclamation.

What scares me the most is how much he believes every single word that's coming out of his mouth.

"I need to go to the bathroom," I say, standing up from the bar. I feel dizzy. I grab my purse and turn on my heel. I think about storming out through the lobby and getting to my car, speeding off and being done with it. Trying to find some other way to resolve this. I know what will happen, though. I know he'll follow me.

In the bathroom I wet a paper towel and use it to cool

my cheeks. They're flushed with anger and vodka, a combination I'd grown used to in Los Angeles. I'm not nervous anymore. Rage has taken over and my common sense has come back to me. I fish in my purse for my phone. A new Facebook message is waiting on me.

It's from Zach.

Hey,

I'm pretty sure you don't want to hear from me and I'm also pretty sure that was how I started my last message to you, but some stuff has happened. This afternoon when I got back from lunch, Lucy was on the doorstep crying. Someone had hurt her. She's fine now. I took her to the vet. But something kind of felt strange about it.

There was a note with her. It said, "Ha. Ha. Ha." Wasn't that part of the e-mail with the pictures?

Zach

The black and white words blur as my vision tunnels and realization dawns on me. It isn't just about me anymore. Something in the pit of my stomach turns, thinking of Sue at home alone. Now it's about more than just me. It's about other people. People that I care deeply for. I bite my lip. I need to get the fuck out of here and I need for Alex not to know that I know about Lucy.

I dial Dan.

"Dan?" I say.

"Hey!" he shouts, obviously inside a busy bar.

"I need you to call me in two minutes and act like you have an emergency," I say.

"Bad date?"

"Something like that."

"Wait, you're really on a date? Is it with the jiu-jitsu guy?"

"I'll explain when you get home later. Bye."

I hang up the phone and look at myself in the mirror. I try to calm myself down. I don't want to look like anything is up.

I tell myself that I look natural. I smile in the mirror.

Girding my loins, I open the bathroom door and turn my charm up to eleven. I saunter back to the bar and act like I've calmed myself down. Like I'd been irrational. *Ha. Ha. Ha.* What else is new?

Alex settles into the role of benevolent dictator quite easily. He goes on about missing me for the next two minutes, making me cringe inwardly. I only nod my head in assent and tell him that I understand, that I have missed him, too.

My phone rings.

"I probably ought to get this," I say.

I answer.

"Hello? Wait, slow down. Are you okay? Okay. I'll be there in just a minute."

I hang it up and looked sadly at Alex.

"What's wrong?" he asks, skepticism behind his reptilian eyes.

"It's Dan. He's having an allergic reaction or something. He needs to go to the hospital and needs me to drive him. You know how he is in an emergency," I shrug and roll my eyes like the last thing I want to do is leave Alex's side and join Dan in the ER.

Alex nods, acknowledging Dan's shortcomings. He swirls his whiskey.

"I'm leaving tomorrow," he says, making the statement like he's declaring that he's about to be executed, like this is the last time I'll ever see him. How dare I prioritize my friend over him? Even after all this time, he remains just as predictable as I am.

"When will you be back?" I probe, wondering if he will show his hand.

"Not anytime soon," he says, a petulant child now.

"Maybe I could come see you," I offer the olive branch. Anything to satiate his need for an illusion of control over the situation.

He looks at me blankly for a moment, and for that moment his guard is down. I see the same man who told me about the effect of his brother's death. He's a child and he's vulnerable to me. He wants nothing more than to have me back and I need to make him believe he's going to get what he wants.

I smile at him.

"Would that be okay?" I ask, knowing that it will. I know as I pose the question that it's more than okay—it's the outcome that he wants.

"I'd like that," he says. "I'll get in touch with you next week. Los Angeles has missed you," he says with a wolf's smile.

"I've missed Los Angeles," I lie. I give him a peck good-bye, pressing my lips against the sandpaper roughness of his cool cheek. I shudder inwardly. "I'll see you soon," I promise.

He has no idea how I intend to keep it.

I pace the kitchen when I get home, waiting with ever-eroding patience for Dan to show up. Sue walks patiently with me, heeling at my side and I'm grateful for his presence. When I got home, I rushed in, crying out his name, unsure of whether I would find him alive or dead. It was enough to nauseate me. Finally, Dan gets home. He walks into the kitchen and right past me. He throws his jacket over one of the dining room chairs and tosses his keys onto the counter.

"What was up tonight? Did Bruce Lee disappoint you?" he asks.

"That happened yesterday," I say. "Sit down."

Dan looks at me like I'm about to launch a nuclear weapon. I rarely, if ever, ask him to sit down when relaying important information. I know from the look on his face that he thinks someone is dead.

"It's nothing like that so calm down," I say.

Relief passes over his face like sun peeking through clouds on an overcast day. His concern quickly returns, though.

"I saw Alex tonight," I say.

"What?" Dan blurts. "What the fuck do you mean?"

"Look, I know it was stupid. I had to, though. I had to see with my own eyes that he's still the same monster that he was. And he is," I say.

"No shit, Sherlock," Dan says, cradling his face in his palms. "And what exactly did this accomplish?"

"Nothing. Well, something. He thinks I'm coming to see him."

"What?"

"You should have heard him, Dan," I say. "He talked about it like this was something I brought on myself. Like it could have all been avoided. He sounded like a fucking crazy person. And Zach's dog got hurt." I look down at Sue and noticed when I look back at Dan that he's shifted his gaze to our four-legged friend as well.

"Wait, Zach who?" Dan asks.

"He's a comedian. In Los Angeles. A friend of mine," I say.

"Wait, Zach O'Halloran? With the podcast?"

"Yes, that Zach. The dog had a note on its collar. It said '*Ha. Ha. Ha.*' Just like the e-mail Alex sent to you and to him. He knows that I was with Zach last weekend. He had to have seen it on Facebook or something."

"Jesus Christ," Dan says.

"Yeah, tell me about it," I reply. "And there's more."

"Go on," he says.

"Henry printed off the pictures and tacked them to the bulletin board at the school."

"What?"

"You heard me."

"You're fucking joking right?" he asks, incredulous.

"I wish."

"That son of a bitch," he mutters. "Get in the car."

"What?" I ask.

Dan stands up. He's reaching for his jacket on the dining room chair. He walks over and grabs his keys.

"We're going to his place," he says with finality. "Get in the car."

"Dan, I don't think—"

"I didn't ask what you thought. I'm telling you what we're doing. That sick fuck isn't going to control your life anymore. Not either one of them. Now let's go."

He looks at me with pain in his eyes. He's pleading with me not to stop him. A part of me is afraid. I'm a rule follower, but if this experience has taught me anything, it's that following the rules doesn't always pay off. I bite my lip.

"Tash, I said let's go," Dan repeats.

I nod my head and grab my own jacket. I lean down and give Sue a hug, promising him that I'll be right back. Before we leave, I check all the locks on the house just to be sure and meet his eyes once more, trying to convey to him that I'll be back as soon as I can.

I give Dan directions as he drives his pickup way too fast through the streets of Nashville, rushing to Henry's apartment complex in the dark. He cuts someone off and nearly hits a pedestrian but I don't think it's the time to comment on his driving.

He whips into the complex and parks in the first spot he finds without bothering to find out which building Henry's apartment is in. I point to 103, the third building to the south. Dan nods and gets out of the truck. I follow his lead, unsure of what exactly he thinks he's going to do or how I'm going to help him. Anxiety piles up on my sternum, making it harder and harder to draw a full breath.

I scurry along behind him after I give him the apartment number. He walks up and pounds on the door.

"Open up!" he shouts.

I hear footsteps moving towards the door. It cracks open and Dan shoves his foot into the crack and pushes the door open. He backs Henry up against the wall across from the bar. I stand in the entry way.

"Shut the door!" he growls at me, holding Henry up against the wall, Dan's strength outmatching Henry's ability to use leverage while Dan is holding his feet an inch off the ground. I follow Dan's orders and slam the door, locking it behind me.

"Where are the pictures?" Dan barks at Henry.

"I don't know what you're talking about, man!" Henry lies.

"Where did you get them?" I ask.

"I don't know what fucking pictures you're talking about, you crazy bitch," Henry hisses at me, struggling against Dan's grip. I turn to the kitchen and see a knife display. I grab the largest one I can find. "Whoa," Henry says, his voice strained.

I walk towards him and brandish the knife. Its handle feels slippery in my damp palm. I inch closer and hold the knife up to his face. I let the blade reflect the dim kitchen light into his dark eyes. I bring it down to his groin and press it inward.

"Where?" I ask.

"Answer her," Dan says.

"Okay, okay," Henry says. "They were e-mailed to the school. I got them before Heather deleted them. Jesus Christ."

"There was only one in the e-mail. Where did the rest of them come from?" I ask.

"The website!" he shouts. "Calm down! Fuck!"

I press the knife closer to his balls and for a moment I imagine it slicing through his clothes and slipping into his flesh. I'm a hair's breadth from crossing a line I never imagined I'd be standing on.

I lower the knife, breathing for the first time since I grabbed it.

"Jesus," Henry hisses.

Dan lowers him down and relaxed his body language.

Then he punches him in the jaw, sending Henry cascading into the recliner in the living room, scooting it sideways.

"Get out your computer," Dan says.

Henry doesn't argue. He goes to his laptop sitting on the coffee table. He opens it as instructed.

"Open your e-mail," Dan says.

I've never seen him like this.

Henry does as he's told.

"You have all the students' and parents' e-mails?" Dan asks him.

"Yeah," Henry says.

"Good. Start writing. Explain yourself. Why you did that to Tash," Dan orders.

"Man, I'm sorry—"

"I don't care how sorry you are, you're gonna prove it. You're gonna resign right now," Dan says.

"Dude, I need this job—"

"Do I look like I give a shit?" Dan asks.

Henry glances at me and looks down at the butcher knife still hanging from my hand. I grip the handle more tightly.

Henry starts typing.

"And send a copy to Tash," Dan barks.

Henry nods.

We stand for several minutes while Henry types. Finally, he relaxes his hands and looks up at Dan like a student might look at a teacher after completing a test to determine if they'd passed or failed a class where their life hung in the balance.

Dan grabs the computer and looks at me, gesturing with his head for me to watch Henry. I do. Dan reads in silence for the next minute and then puts the laptop down.

"Send it," he says.

Henry growls.

"I said, 'Send it,'" Dan repeats.

Henry obliges.

"Congratulations, asshole. That's the first decent thing you've done today," Dan says. He picks up Henry's laptop and bends the screen back until it pops away from the computer.

"Hey!" Henry says.

"Shut up," Dan growls, dropping the laptop to the ground and stomping on it with one foot while pulling up on it with his hands. It breaks further, making a sad noise as it dies.

I watch Henry's face. He's defeated. He looks at me like I can rescue him. I only stare back at him blankly, feeling nothing.

"Let's go," Dan says to me.

CHAPTER 33

Dan and I are silent for the ride home. When we pull into our neighborhood, I break the silence.

"Thank you," I say.

He's quiet.

"What are friends for?" he finally asks.

I smile in the darkness of the pickup cab.

We turn down into the cul de sac and I see a familiar set of taillights sitting in front of the house. It's my stalker. The man who called me, breathing heavily and acting like a total pervert.

"Stop," I say as Dan gets closer to the car. "Let me out."

"What are you doing?" he asks.

"What I should have done the first time he was outside of the house," I say.

Dan stops the truck a few yards from the pervert's car. I hop out and slam the door loudly. I march up to the driver's side of the car and grab the door handle. I throw it open and reach inside.

A little guy in his forties sits in the driver's seat. He has greasy black hair and wears thick glasses. He's wearing a polo shirt and khakis. He looked like he would have been right at home working in IT and using his skills for nefarious purposes.

I grab him by the front of his shirt and drag him out of the car and throw him onto the ground.

"Hey!" he shouts.

"Hey, yourself, asshole," I say, kicking him in the stomach.

He makes a grunting noise as the air is forced out of him. He curls into the fetal position and then begins to get up on his hands and knees. I walk over and climb onto his back. I sink in a rear naked choke swiftly and he begins to claw at my arm.

Dan gets out of the pickup and comes around to the back of the guy's car. He pulls his cell phone out and takes a picture.

"Got your license plate, asshole," he says.

He comes around to watch me choke the guy out.

He goes limp in my arms and I release him. He hits the ground and begins to snore, a sure-fire sign that he's out. I untangle myself from him and stand up. I lodge one final kick to his side, hoping that the crack I hear is one of his ribs. A lasting reminder of his last visit to my house.

"Come on," I say to Dan.

Dan looks at me with a new regard.

"You're kind of a badass," he says. "You know that, right?"

I smile, a little out of breath.

We both get back into the pickup and pull it into the driveway. We're silent. The pervert sleeps peacefully in the middle of the street outside the house.

"I'm going to L.A.," I say.

"Tash, you can't do that," Dan says.

"I have to," I reply.

"You don't—"

"I do, Dan," I say. "I have to take care of this once and for all. I'm leaving in the morning. I'll buy my ticket tonight. I have to go," I say.

Dan looks at me like he knows he can't stop me. And he can't. I've made up my mind. I'm going to Los Angeles. I am going to get the hard drive from Alex's computer that has the rest of the pictures on, and I am going to destroy it.

"Be careful," Dan says.

"I always am," I say with a smile. "I'll be okay."

"I know you will," he says.

Dan reaches out his hand, giving me the opportunity to take it. I do. And I squeeze. I bring him into the first hug I've given him since I gotten back from Los Angeles and I hold him there.

CHAPTER 34

Los Angeles Dec. 2016

The plane lands in Los Angeles the next evening. The flight is smooth aside from my rocky nerves. I go from insane confidence fueled by rage to intimidated fear inspired by events of the past and the sheer magnitude of what I am about to try to do.

I decided that if I can't get the pictures removed from the website, I can get the hard drive. It was more about having the originals and getting them out of Alex's possession. Sure, he could download them again from the site if he wanted to, but I wanted the hard drive. It isn't perfect but it's better than living the rest of my life wondering what other pictures might show up on the internet at any given moment.

I smile at the flight attendant as I exit the plane. I don't need to stop at baggage claim, taking only a small carryon with one change of clothes. I don't plan on staying more time than I need to. I only need to make sure Alex is out of his apartment for a few hours. That's all I need. That tiny window of time.

I made reservations at the Roosevelt in Hollywood. It's more than I can afford for more than two nights, but I don't care. I'd always wanted to stay there and never had. I go out to the pool that night, ordering a drink at the famous bar and stick my legs in the water.

There is a couple in the heated pool, completely unaware of my presence. So in love that the idea of a stranger being annoyed at their happiness completed escapes them. But I'm not annoyed. I sip on my drink and watch them. I think about the freedom that will come if I can do this. If I can prove that I can beat him. I can taste it like it's salt on the air.

The girl looks at me, bashful. She smiles a little and then goes back to kissing her boyfriend. I wonder if maybe they're about to get engaged. I wonder where they'refrom. I take a shower that night and lay my clothes out for the next day. My plan is to go to Alex's place while he's at work. He never goes to work for less than twelve hours. I'll have plenty of time.

I go to bed that night confident in my plans and sleep a dreamless sleep.

The next morning, I wake at 5:29am, one minute before my alarm is set to go off. I dress in silence in the dark. I tie on my athletic shoes and I slick my hair back, my wavy ponytail fanning out across my back. Alex hated it when I wore a ponytail. I think it's was only fair that I wear one today.

I looked him up to see if he still lived in the house that we'd shared together. He'd moved to an apartment in downtown Los Angeles not far from the law firm. It looks like it's the penthouse, which means getting in would be tricky, but I'm up for the challenge.

I grab the messenger bag I brought with me to carry anything that I'd need. I drive my rental car the short distance from the hotel to the office building that Alex works in. I park in the garage across the street like I'd done so many years ago. I wait.

Two hours pass and he shows up.

Amy is with him, though she doesn't seem as eager to please him as she had once been. I wonder how their relationship has shifted. I wonder if she gets tired of his shit or if she eats it up with a grin. I could never tell about her.

I watch them interact. I watch her get his coffee and give it to him without a smile. I watch him work on the computer for longer than I probably should. There's something fascinating about being there, watching two people in their everyday lives, knowing that in a few hours, he'll come home and find that maybe he needs to be afraid of me this time.

Finally, I shift into drive and head out for his apartment. I park in the garage and get my ticket that I'll pay when I leave. I smile at the guard.

I walk to the elevator and say a prayer. I only remember the code from when we lived together. The one that we used to open our gate. I punched it in. 9733.

The lock on the door flashes green and I open it.

I breathe a sigh of relief as I walk in through the garage and onward towards the elevator that will lead to the penthouse. One hurdle is down, now I just have to get into the apartment. I wonder if Alex used a different code for that. I wonder if he ever thought enough of me that he would change it after I left.

There is another woman in the elevator going up. She

has a small dog with her and I smile at her. She looks like a kept woman. I wonder if her situation is anything like mine was. She smiles back at me, cold as Alex's serpentine hands. There is no happiness in her eyes.

I think of all the things that Alex was able to provide for me. I think about all the opportunities that money could have bought and I wonder if any of it was worth what I went through. No. It wasn't. There was nothing he could have bought for me that would give me back my dignity. That had to be earned all over again and at a steeper price.

I have worked tirelessly for the last three years to do just that.

I have put in the time.

I have put in the blood, the sweat, and the tears.

And now, it's my moment to cash in on it.

I smile at her once more when she gets off the elevator and continues up to the penthouse. When I step off, there is one door and I know it leads into the apartment. My stomach is cinched into a knot, and I'm dreading walking through that door, across that threshold into the past.

I walk up to the keypad and my finger shakes as I type in the password we'd used for our garage door: 1780, his day and year of birth.

The door lock flashes red.

It's wrong.

I breathe in deeply. I'm not sure what I'm going to do. I rack my brain. I have two more tries before there will be an alert to security and the elevator will lock me out, if this building is anything like other fancy apartments I've been to.

I think.

I punch in a different number: 2685. Killian's birthday.

The light flashes red.

Shit. Shit. Shit.

My heart begins to speed up. I have one more try. I can either take my chances on one more number or I can turn around and punch in the number that I knew would bring the elevator to me. I can walk out right now: no harm, no foul. I can retreat to my life and live with what he's done. I can let him continue to have the power over my life.

Or I can try one more number.

I cautiously hammer out one last four-digit date.

The only other date that I think it could be.

A date in October 2012.

The light flashed green.

I walk across the threshold and the cold air hits me like a strong wave. The scent of the apartment, a mixture of wood and cleanliness sucks me under like an undertow. My hands shake as I walk through the entry hall into the living room. The furniture is the same. I look at the end table where I had put my coffee every morning as I watched the news. Books are perfectly spread out across the coffee table.

I look them over.

One of the first that catches my eye was a photography book. I open it.

Inside are kink images. High quality photography that makes it look like art. But all I can see is the pain I endured. I cringe and shut the book immediately when I come across an image of a girl with a needle corset cinched up and down her back, her skin puckered together and blood droplets beginning to form at the puncture sites.

The other books are also photography. One of them political and the other an homage to old Hollywood. It's a surprising choice. I wonder why Alex would include something that had to do with a thing he so desperately loathed about Los Angeles. My only thought is that it has to be Amy's.

I move through the living room into the hallway. The office is to my left but the bedroom they share is probably down the hall. Curiosity gets the best of me and I wander in.

The bed is perfectly made as though no one slept in it at all the night before. It wouldn't surprise me if Alex sleeps in a coffin that he keeps sequestered away in some secret closet. I notice on his side of the bed there is nothing, but I see a phone charger and a pair of women's reading glasses on the side closest to me.

I walk over and pick them up.

I open the drawer of the nightstand and dig through it. It's full of all the amenities that someone would want sleeping on that side of the bed. Advil, throat lozenges, a little bit of pot, which I'm sure Alex doesn't know about since he detests the idea of smoking. And there is a book of photographs.

I open it.

They're all of him and Amy. Dates, concerts, anniversaries.

And finally, a proposal at the end dated only a month prior to my arrival.

I ponder the photograph, not envying her but wondering why, if he has someone else so willing to cater to his every whim, would he have pursued getting my attention again? What kind of man kept photos like that for three years and then used them in such a way? What kind of monster?

I place everything back as I found it and left the bedroom.

The eerie quiet of the apartment sets me on edge. When the A/C kicks on, I jump. I remind myself that Alex is at work. I go right into the study, wasting no more time, and begin looking around for anything that might point me in the right direction.

It's just as it had been in our old house. He has his display of weaponry behind the huge mahogany desk. There is that lamp that I imagined him sunning his corpse-like flesh under. The desk is perfect. Nothing out of place, no papers scattered around. It's creepy that a person could live in such a way.

It's creepy that I spent a few years of my life living that way.

I walk up to the desk and go around to the chair. I sit down and move the mouse.

The screen comes to life and it's a picture of Alex and Amy, her behind him, her arms draped around him. Him smiling that million-dollar politician's son's smile. I want to put a fist through the monitor.

I click on the screen and a password box pops up.

When Alex and I were together, his password had been a mashup of our names. I try it. The computer rejects it.

I look around the desk and spot a picture of his brother. I thought about the e-mail address that he used to send the e-mail with the pictures.

I type it out.

krothpenderg

Just like that, the computer unlocks.

He's so insufferably arrogant.

I breathe deeply, feeling like a cat burglar who just accessed the safe to the largest bank in all of Switzerland.

I go to his files, finding nothing but pictures of him and Amy. There is nothing on the computer that indicates Alex was anything but an upstanding citizen of California. A senator's son and perfect.

Frustrated, I begin to panic.

I dig through the drawers of the desk like a rabid animal. I claw through papers, trying to find an external hard drive that the pictures might be on.

"Shit," I mutter as a piece of paper slices between my fingers. I saw blood beginning to pool there in the web between my middle and first digits.

I wipe my hand on my jeans as best I can and keep looking. Drawer after drawer, nothing. Finally, I migrate to the filing cabinet only to discover that it's locked. I remember then that he always kept it locked, even when we were together. I knew that's where it has to be.

I look over at the large display case of weapons hanging behind the desk. Maybe the keys are in there. I slide open the glass door and begin searching every nook and crevice. I pull up the velvet bottom of the cabinet and I see, brass and dull, a small key.

"Yes," I hiss like a snake happy with a kill.

I take the key and scramble to unlock the filing cabinet. I go through the top three drawers and find nothing. When I open the bottom drawer, there it is. An external hard drive.

I pick it up like I'm Indiana Jones in *The Temple of Doom*. I don't want to disturb any dark magic that might be waiting for me. Nothing happens as I lifted it carefully out of the drawer like a live bomb. I put it on the desk and quickly connect it to Alex's computer.

There are lots of folders. Lots of names.

They are all women's names.

I click on one of them and find a stash of pictures, not unlike the pictures of me. This girl is tied up. I look at another folder. Same thing. It looks like all of them were taken here in the apartment. I cringe.

Finally, I find a folder with my name on it.

I open it.

There are the pictures. There are pictures of me in bondage. There are pictures of me naked. There are pictures of me in Nashville within the last year. And there are pictures of Zach. Lastly, there are pictures of Zach and I at Pat O'Brien's in New Orleans. I look through them, my blood running ice cold as goosebumps prickle my skin.

I go back to the list of folders, curious.

And I find her name.

Sam.

I open the file. And there they are. Pictures of Samantha Logan the night before she went missing. She is naked, sprawled across the couch. A hand to her throat, choking her as she looks up at the camera with her best sultry face. I close it quickly. Memories haunting me.

But then another catches my eye. I click it.

It's Samantha.

Dead.

It's then that I hear the creak of the door opening. My blood runs cold as I know what it means. I hear footsteps coming towards the study. My muscles stiffen.

"Well, hello," says a cold and familiar voice.

The temperature in the already cold room drops about ten degrees when I look up and see Alex standing in the doorway with his arms folded casually across his chest.

I swallow hard. I fight the Pavlovian response that is ingrained in me to cower to him. I fight the urge to apologize, as though the whole thing was just a huge misunderstanding with me on the wrong end of it. I fight the urge to vomit and I fight the urge to run. Instead, I stand, pulling the hard drive free of the computer.

"You're not gonna get away with this," I say. My voice betrays me, sounding much less brave than I want it to. "I have all the pictures here. All these other girls. Samantha."

"Oh, Natahsa," he says, walking slowly over towards the desk. He stops to play with single flower in a vase that sits on the corner. "Or should I say 'Tash'? Isn't that what your new boyfriend calls you?"

Hearing my nickname roll off Alex's tongue makes me cringe. It sounds cheap, just like he always claimed that it did. Just like he thought I was: cheap and dirty, something to be thrown out with the trash. It only steels my resolve. He doesn't know who I am, who I have become.

"Just back off," I say.

"Or what?" he laughs.

I stare at him for a moment, unsure of what to say or do next. I am paralyzed like I've been so many times before when he stood across the desk or across the counter or on the other side of the room. Even with something substantial separating us, I can feel the danger in my bones, palpable like a drop in barometric pressure on arthritic knees. I can feel how close to the surface swam the part of him that would gnash its teeth around my neck and shake me until the life left my eyes.

"Or I'll kill you," I say, possessed by something foreign and powerful. I feel it move inside of me like a snake in my gut, slithering its way right up and out of my throat. I let it take over. I know that its words are true. I know that I will kill him if I have to.

He laughs outrageously.

"You'd know all about that, wouldn't you?" he says

when his laughing fit subsides. "What is this? Something you learned from your women's groups? You think you're some sort of survivor That I *abused* you?" he says the last with a tone in his voice that indicates how silly he thinks that is. How predictable of me, such a stupid, stupid girl.

"You raped me," I say, stating it for the cold fact that it was. My words hang in the air between us. I want him to reach out and take them, acknowledge them.

"Tash, really?" he says, acting like I'm a child recounting an incident on the playground so that it was in my favor. "Even if that was true, don't you think you deserved it? After everything?"

It's like he's punched me in the gut. All my suspicions about what had happened are confirmed with that question. The only person that can validate what happened that night is denying it. I rack my brain.

"You—you did," I say, faltering.

I think of that night. I think of his hands around my throat. He's clouding my conviction. This is his game and he's a professional at it.

"Fuck you," I whisper, a tear leaking from my eye and rolling down my cheek.

"Oh, did I touch a nerve?" he asks.

"You don't get to touch me at all now," I say.

Alex laughs bitterly. Even as he plays it cool, I can tell that the dark part of him is only becoming more and more agitated, waiting for the moment to rear its head. The thin sheath that housed the monster was growing thinner and thinner with each thunderous beat of my heart.

The tendon connecting his neck to his shoulder twitches, giving him away. He lunges across the desk, reaching for me and I dodge him, making a dash for the front door. I get into the hallway and feel my foot being ripped out from under me. I fall to my stomach on the cold, hard marble tile. I turn back to see him attached to me like an animal desperate to kill its prey, having not fed for days. His bared teeth flash in the light from the living room. I turn only long enough to see the fire in his eyes and then begin to try to get up.

He claws his way up my calves and I cry out when he bites down, slowing my progress. He reaches for my hips and pulls me towards him on my stomach. I feel him straddle my hips, leaving only a small space between us. In that moment a switch flips. I know what to do. I've done it a million times.

I turn on my side and curl my body, covering my head and face. Alex rains down punches. I block a lot of the most violent and dangerous ones. Suddenly he strikes me in the ribs and I feel something crack mercilessly. Pain radiating through my body, I gasp for air. I flip onto my back with all the abdominal strength that I have. I sit up and glue my core to his, wrapping my arms around his waist. He grunts as I pull him to the ground, his hands splayed out around me.

I cling tightly to him and he pushes to get away from me. I pull him down again, making myself as heavy as possible. I want to stay glued to him. I shimmy upwards and slipped one arm around his head and as he rears to punch, I trap that arm with mine, punching my fist into the space between us, locking him in place.

I begin to shrimp out from beneath him, a technique I honed in the last three years. Swimming from one side to the other as quickly as I could, I finally wrap my legs around his waist, placing him inside my guard. The guard that I've perfected in the last three years. It is tight and impassable. I cling to his body, riding him as he struggles to get the leech off him that I have become. It's what I want. I want him to exhaust himself.

From there, I wait until he tried to strike again. I slip my foot to his hip, stopping his punch and grabbing him behind the bicep. With my other leg, I hook it high into his armpit, positioning myself to take him to the triangle. I move quickly and soon have him in the choke. My left thigh is wrapped around his neck and head with my right leg biting down on my left, trapping his left arm and squeezing the blood flow to a stop. He fights me like a tiger and I hold on.

CHAPTER 35

Los Angeles Oct. 2012

The last time that anyone saw Samantha Logan at the Sanctuary was a night in late October. She left with us to play back at the apartment. Amy came with her. We rode in silence. Tony and Sam had broken up and Sam clung to Alex whenever she could. It made me sick. Once back at the apartment, I assume the passive role that I had become accustomed to. I poured us all some wine and Sam stripped, ready for a scene.

"You're going to play with us, aren't you?" Alex asked me when I turned to leave the living room, fully intending on going to bed.

"I wasn't," I said. I don't even know why he bothered asking.

"Please stay," Alex said, stepping up and placing an arm around my waist. He kissed me, passionate and deep. My body didn't respond.

"Fine," I agreed.

Sam was laying on the couch, her naked body ready for whatever abuse Alex was going to hurl at it. I walked over and stood by Amy, not sure what I was supposed to do.

"Have you ever done this before?" Amy asked me.

"No," I admitted. I was past the point of trying to play games with her.

"Me either," she admitted.

We watched for a little while and Alex tied Sam up. He flogged her for a while and she squirmed wildly, satisfying whatever was inside of him that I couldn't reach. He looked up and locked eyes with me, something there that I'd never seen before.

"Natasha, I want you to do something," he said.

I looked at him, curious as to what I could possibly do to participate in this shit show.

"What?" I asked.

"Choke her," he said.

I must have looked appalled. I balked at it.

"Now," Alex ordered.

I looked at Sam.

"It's okay," Sam said to me, seeing the timidity in my body language.

I walked over to the couch and leaned down beside her. I wrapped my hands around her throat. I barely applied any pressure. She laughed at me.

"Choke her!" Alex said.

I dug my hands in deeper.

"Yes," she hissed, enjoying it.

I felt strange and awkward, participating in something that I didn't want to but only doing it to please that man that I'd bound myself to.

"Harder!" Alex barked.

Sam's face went red and then purple.

"Alex, I—"

"Keep choking her until she passes out," he said.

I released Sam's neck.

"I'm not doing that," I said with finality, standing up and facing him.

"Yes, you are," Alex said, approaching me. "Get back over there and choke her."

There was something in him when he said that that scared me. Something about him said not to cross him. It was clearly something that Sam enjoyed. I shrugged and placed my hands back around her neck.

"Is this okay?" I whispered to her.

"It's fine," she said with a smile.

I began to apply pressure. She turned red and then purple. My hands trembled.

"Keep choking her!" Alex shouted.

I did. I held my shaking hands in place. Her eyes bulged from her head and I let go.

"Alex, I think—"

"Dammit, keep choking her!" he screamed. He approached, right behind me, his breath on my neck and he put my hands back on her throat and with his own on top of them, he squeezed and squeezed.

Sam fought against him, and then she stopped moving. She began to convulse. I fought tears.

"Alex!" I shouted.

"Goddammit, she's not done yet!" he shouted.

I began to cry. She stopped shaking. The color drained from her face. He let go. I placed a hand on her throat, feeling for her pulse.

It was gone.

"Oh, God. Oh. God. *Oh, God*," I murmured, my voice growing more and more hysterical. "She's dead!"

Alex threw his arm into the air and backhanded me hard across the face. He slapped me again. He pushed me out of the way, grabbing Sam by the shoulders. He shook her. He slapped her hard across the face.

I looked away and my eyes met Amy's.

She stood, her arms folded across her chest.

"We have to do something with her," Amy said, her tone feverish.

"We have to call the police!" I said, my voice clogged with tears.

"No one's calling the police!" Alex shouted.

He turned from Sam's limp body to face Amy and I.

"Amy, get a sheet off my bed," he said. "We'll wrap her in it and get her in the car."

"Alex, what the fuck?" I muttered. "We have to call 9-11."

"And what? Go to prison? Fuck that. You fucking did this, you little bitch. I'm not going down for you."

I shuddered. The realization that my hands had been on her throat and taken her life only a few moments prior washed over me. I looked at my hands. They shook.

Amy returned from the bedroom with a sheet. She held it up, desperate to do something. Alex took it from her and spread it out beside the couch.

"Help me!" he barked at the two of us and we did. Amy in order to please him and get rid of evidence; me because I feared for my life.

We helped him roll Samantha off the couch and onto the sheet. We wrapped her in it. Alex and Amy maneuvered the body into the garage and into the trunk of his car.

"Get in," he said to both of us.

His captives, we obeyed.

He drove us to the dock where the boat was. It was the middle of the night, and no one was around. Under street-lamps, we took the body out. If anyone had driven by or been in the parking lot, they would have seen us. We got her onto the yacht and left her on the back deck.

Alex started it up and took us out to sea, off El Matador.

Once we anchored, he came to the back where Amy and I waited with our dead friend.

"Unwrap her," he said.

We did as he instructed. He reached down and picked Sam up. He carried her over to the edge of the boat and released her. Her naked body went over the railing and I ran in time to see her begin to sink, her face turned up to the moon, her eyes two lifeless pools of blue and black.

I turned back from the water. I threw up on the deck.

"Jesus Christ," Alex said. "Clean that up," he told me. "And if you ever say anything, I'll fucking kill you."

I began to weep as he motored the yacht back to the dock. I found a mop and got most of the vomit over the edge of the boat. I sat on the back deck.

I sat there, shaking and alone.

And I watched as we left El Matador Beach behind and the girl who would become a missing person in the days to come.

CHAPTER 36

Los Angeles Dec. 2016

"Fuck you, you bitch!" Alex mutters. His free arm flails at me, failing to land a helpful strike. I grasp his wrist, keeping his arm out and I clamp down with my thighs and press his head down on my abdomen, muffling his epithets.

His curses and the blood rushing through my veins thunders in my ears in the otherwise quiet apartment. I hold him there. My breathing is ragged. I'm tired. Six seconds. He slows. Ten seconds. He quits moving and his body relaxes into mine. Fifteen seconds. I want to be sure. Twenty seconds. Nothing. Thirty seconds. He begins to twitch. Forty seconds. If I hold on much longer, he will be brain dead. Forty-five seconds.

I think about all that he's done to me. I think about Samantha and that night. Tears flow freely down my face. I think about the way he thinks he's untouchable and that he's entitled to whatever he wants. I think about that night.

I can feel him slipping my pajamas from my body.

I can feel him breathing down my neck telling me to choke her harder.

I squeeze tighter. Fifty seconds.

I can kill him.

I can end it all right now.

He would be out of my life forever and no one would miss him.

Fifty-five seconds.

There's a crash and the door flies open. Zach comes stumbling in.

I stare at him, unsure of how he got here or what's going on. I hold the choke. By now, Alex has wet his pants, unable to control his own bladder.

"He's done! Let's go!" Zach cries, kneeling beside us. I concentrated more than ever. A few more seconds and the bastard will be brain dead. "Let him go!" Zach's voice echoes in my ear, the sound lost on me as though he's shouting into the Grand Canyon. The twitching stops. "Tash!" Zach shouts.

I let go and shove myself as far away from Alex as I can. His head hits the floor with a sick thump and he lies there, still.

He's dead.

Zach reaches over to get his pulse. Suddenly, his lifeless body moves. His head twitches and his mouth falls open. He begins to snore.

I breathe rapidly, finally allowing myself to catch my breath. I stand up and look down at the floor, seeing blood coming from my wounded calf that he bit. The reality of what has just happened hasn't sunken in. Instead, it crashes over me. My tormentor lies helpless in the floor and at my mercy.

I feel tears sting my eyes. More and more of myself realized with each breath. I look finally at Zach and feel my heart swell into my throat. I choke back a sob and collapse into him. I throw my arms around his neck and hug him as deeply as I've ever wanted to. I can feel his heart pounding his chest and his arms snug to my side as he holds onto me.

I hold on to him for what felt like forever, my tears soaking his shirt. Finally, reality comes back to me.

"We have to get the hard drive and get out of here," I say.

We went back to the office and gather it up quickly. I shove it into my bag.

"Let's go," he says.

Zach runs a hand through his hair and looks at me. Together, we rush towards the door and close it behind us, leaving Alex to the mess. I reach out and grab Zach's hand as we walk to the elevator. He looks over at me and down at our hands.

I smile at him and squeeze.

CHAPTER 37

I read once that being raped is like being murdered but having to live at the crime scene afterwards.

It's a grief. A letting go of who you once were.

Even in moments when no one is talking about it, it's still there, a constant ache inside of

you. Even when you're not thinking about it, you know that part of you is gone.

I've lived my life like that for three years. Caught in a perpetual limbo between this life and another, hellacious nightmare-fueled dream-state. I never felt alive, only on guard. My adrenaline dumped into my system at random intervals. My fight-or-flight response was alerted by the slightest trigger. I went to bed so exhausted that I couldn't sleep some nights, and other mornings woke up so groggy that I could barely slog through the day.

Despite that, I went back to school, and I learned jiu-jitsu. Depsite that, I carried on. I hunkered down and circled my wagons just enough to survive. And survival was all I needed until I got to this point.

I ride shotgun in Zach's car back to his house. I'm in a daze. Elated by the idea that I've beaten Alex, but terrified at what will happen when I take this hard drive to the police and tell them what I know about Samantha Logan.

I keep picturing his limp body lying there in the hall-way, drool beginning to pool beside his mouth. He was so helpless. And it occurs to me that he's always been helpless. Doing something like what he did to me and what he did to Sam didn't take power. It took cruelty. It took nothing in the realm of strength. What takes strength is the going on afterwards.

My heart races with excitement at the prospect of a future where I don't have to look over my shoulder, but I know that isn't entirely possible. A little black cloud hovered over me as I thought about what would come of all this once it was in the LAPD's hands.

We pull up outside a gated house with high bushes. I guess Zach is a bigger star than I gave him credit for. He punches in a code and the gate opens, leading down a short driveway to a modestly sized house for Beverly Hills. He pulls into a clean garage and gets out of the car, quickly coming over to the passenger side to help me out.

"Thanks," I say, cupping a hand on my ribcage, not wanting to touch it but also not wanting anything else to bump into it without a buffer. I grimace.

"We should go to the hospital, don't you think?" he asks.

"Nah, I'm good," I say, my voice a bit above a groan. "I've had a broken rib before. There's nothing they're gonna do for me there." I smile and it isn't forced.

"Well, come on then," he says, dipping under my arm and half carrying my weight to the garage door. He opens it and leads me inside. We go past a big kitchen with a large bar and into a modern living room. He puts me down on the couch.

I settle into my seat. He helps me lift my feet onto the couch and position myself so that I have a pillow under my head and a blanket draped over me.

"We need to call the police," I say.

Zach looks at me, a little puzzled. It pains me to see him like this. And it occurs to me it might be the last day I ever spend with him. Finally, he nods, not questioning me and hands me his phone.

I dial 9-1-1.

I tell the dispatcher I have information about the disappearance of Samantha Logan.

And then we wait.

It's not long before they show up and I tell them everything.

Against my wishes, they force me to go to the emergency room to get treated, and then

they take me to the police station to sort things out. I tell them everything, leaving nothing out. I give them every bit of information I possibly can to nail Alex and I don't attempt to absolve myself of guilt.

One of the officers, a woman, says, "It sounds like this was a very abusive relationship. And you feared for your life?"

I nod.

"Every day."

I don't add that there's a part of me that's terrified nothing will come of this. That they won't arrest him. That it won't go to trial. That there isn't enough evidence.

The other officer comes back into the interrogation room.

"The picture is on the hard drive. It's her," referring to Samantha.

The two of them look at each other and leave the room for a while.

I sit there, terrified of what might happen next, but feeling like a weight has been lifted off me. Like a gorilla has climbed off my chest.

Finally, they come back and I feel a sense of peace, okay with whatever comes from this.

"I believe you," the female detective says. "However, in California, you are legally obligated to report a crime, including murder. That being said, I believe you were under duress. That will have to be proven legally, but I feel that with the corroboration of accounts of your relationship with this man, you'll be able to do that. Tonight, I have to charge you with failure to report a crime."

I inhale sharply.

"I understand," I say.

The weeks and months ahead are a blur full of meetings with my attorney and court appearances. I explain everything to Zach and he offers me support but I refuse it. I know that I can't even consider anything with him until this is resolved, and there's no guarantee that it will be.

But finally, my case is heard.

The revenge porn, plus the threat Alex made to me, Amy's involvement, and the case against Alex work in my favor and they rule that I acted in imperfect self defense,

The Flannal Doctrine, which basically states that I was in fear for my life after Sam's murder and was afraid Alex would kill me and make good on his threat.

I cry when they read the verdict. My attorney congratulates me and gives me a hug and together we go to face the reporters. All my friends have shown up for the verdict. Heather, Dan, and even Monica. But it's when I see another familiar face that my own lights up.

Zach.

I run to him, jumping onto him and wrapping my legs around his waist. He kisses me. And I cry. I cry and cry and cry. And finally, he takes me home with him.

I'm exhausted and he gets me settled on the couch, curling up next to me and telling me how proud he is of me and how brave I was.

"I'm just gonna close my eyes for a few minutes," I say. Grogginess making my voice less clear and I can feel myself slipping into sleep. I fight it, jolting forward several times only to see Zach sitting on the adjacent side of the L-shaped couch. He watches television. It's turned down low, barely audible, and when he looks at me looking at him, he smiles.

I smile back and let the tiredness that I feel pull me into its warm arms like a swimmer being sucked into the undertow.

I wake in darkness.

I rub my eyes and lift my watch to wake it. 7:45pm. I've slept all day. I sit up to look across the living room to see if Zach has left his post and realize that I'm not in the living room anymore.

I feel a soft mattress beneath me and realize that my

shoes were gone. I throw back the covers and feel instinctively of my clothes to see if they are intact and covering my body. Nothing is out of place. My heart hammers in my chest but I breathe deeply, slowing my pulse and calming myself down. I'm safe.

I get up from the bed and stumble to the hallway in the darkness. There I find that my path is illuminated by motion sensing lights that line the floor. I pad the only way I think the living room could be and soon turn the corner and see Zach sitting where he was earlier, watching TV, dimly illuminated by the blue glow of the television light.

I stand across the room from him, hidden in the shadows and I watch him for a few moments. He fights sleep, nodding off now and again. The television is still turned down to almost nothing. He did that for me, I realize. It's such a small thing but it meant a lot. He took me to his bedroom, and he let me sleep. He didn't come in with me.

I stay there for a few more moments and take the scene in. Peace radiates off me. I could feel my heartbeat in a way that I haven't in more than three years. Instead of pulsing in my veins and trying to beat down my eardrums, it's a steady and rhythmic flow of my life force, slowly bringing me back to what I once was so many years ago.

I step into the living room and take a seat across from him on the other side of the couch. He looks over at me, sleep turning down the corners of his eyes.

"Hey," he says, a smile in his groggy voice. "How do you feel? Did you sleep okay?"

"Yeah," I say. "Really well, actually. Probably better than in a long time."

"What a day," he remarks, shaking his head and rubbing his eyes. "I'm just glad it's over and you're okay."

We sit in silence for a moment and then something dawns on me.

"How did you know where I was?" I ask.

"Your roommate messaged me on Facebook this morning. He told me where that guy lived and he said you'd be there," he says.

"How'd you get in the building?"

"I waited for someone else to go in before me. Acted like I'd left my keys in my apartment and slipped into the elevator with them. Easy as that," he says with a snap of his fingers and a smile.

I smile back at him.

"I came really close," I say after a long pause. I look away from Zach and into the television screen.

He says nothing.

"I could have done it. I really could have," I say. "I could feel myself getting so close to crossing that line. I imagined never having to worry again. I imagined never having to look over my shoulder. I imagined how simple it would be to just snuff him out like that," I say with a snap of my fingers. "And then you came in."

"My timing isn't usually that impeccable," Zach says.

I chuckle in the darkness.

"When I saw you beside me it reminded me of how different you are from Alex. I knew that the first time I met you," I say. "I realized how far I'd fallen from who I was and how long of a crawl it would be to get back there if I did it. I don't really know how to describe it, but something clicked, and I let go. It was enough to know that I could have done it. And if I ever have to in the future, I will."

"I hope you don't have to," he says.

"I really don't think I will," I say. Alex's trial is in another month. He's behind bars and there's no chance he's going to walk. Too many people have come forward, too many other women with stories like mine and Samantha's.

It's almost over. Something inside of me knows, without a single shadow of doubt, that I have come to its end. I don't have to worry anymore. I don't have to live in fear. Even though Alex isn't dead, something else died in that apartment. All the fear that I had for him was gone. To see the monster lying in a puddle of his own piss and drool was enough to make him fall from his pedestal.

I smile at Zach.

It's the part of any regular date in which I would have excused myself to go back to my hotel. Any other time I would have found an excuse to leave. I would have pushed him away and I would have sunken into myself, trying yet again to keep the world at arm's length.

It was better to be alone than to be hurt ever again.

That's what I thought.

I thought that by keeping everyone else out, I could keep someone like Alex from ever hurting me again. It only made his place in my life bigger. It gave him this dominance over my other relationships. I compared everyone to him. They were damned before they'd even stepped into my life. I had let Alex control me even when I thought I was free of him. I was living in the shadow of what he could possibly do. And I knew that I was still dancing in that shadow.

I'd always thought that maybe if I worried about the bad things enough that they wouldn't happen. That God would reward me for understanding just how bad it could get, but I'd had no idea. I'd had no clue of what was to come.

Sitting in the dark in Zach's living room, I'm glad that I hadn't.

I'm glad for how things turned out.

And I'm glad that I'm there. With him.

Then I catch him looking at me and there's something that stirs inside me. That freedom I've felt possesses me to reach for him and I pull him into a kiss. He pulls me onto his lap almost immediately, and stands, my legs wrapped around him, and he takes me to the bedroom.

CHAPTER 38

We crash through the door when it opens. A tangle of arms, he backs me up against the wall. I can feel the fire in his fingertips, how much he needs me. He holds me up, kissing me deeply. His hands run over my curves, stopping on my breasts and squeezing ever so lightly.

I moan and reach for my waist, pulling my t-shirt over my head. I throw it across the room into the bathroom. Zach kisses my bare neck and makes his way down to my chest. He expertly unhooks my bra and it falls to the side. He kisses the top of my breast, the sensation driving me wild. He cups my breast with his hand and takes my nipple into his mouth. The warmth and wetness covering me melts me into a puddle. I gasp and whine for more. He carries me over to the bed and sits me down on the edge of it.

He pulls his hoodie off and his t-shirt over his head. He kicks off his flip flops, leaving him in only his black denim jeans. A trail of hair leads from his belly button down into his pants and my eyes follow, interested in what lay beyond. I crawl back onto the bed, holding myself up on my elbows.

He slinks onto the bed and crawls between my legs. He

reaches for my hips and pulls my jeans down. Then he reaches for my panties. My breath catches in my chest for a moment, wondering if I'm really going to go through with it. I reach out a hand to stop him.

"Is this okay?" he asks, his voice ragged. His eyes are practically black and his breathing is heavy.

I nod my assent. It's okay. I'm ready. And I want it to be with him.

He slips my underwear off and tosses it aside. He wraps my legs around his waist and bends down over me. He kisses my forehead, then one eyelid, then the other. He kisses my cheeks and finally my lips. He presses himself against me and I gasp, feeling him hard and restricted inside of his jeans.

"I've wanted you from the moment I met you, Tash," he murmurs as he kisses my neck. "I wanted it to be right, though."

"This is right," I say, bringing his lips up to mine.

As I do, he brings a hand up my thigh, teasing its way between my legs. I gasp when he strokes me right between my legs. A thousand sensations explode there and sweep me away. I arch into his touch, wanting more of him than just his hand.

"Please," I say.

Not able to stand it anymore, either, he unzips his jeans. He stands and kicks them off and then he slides out of his boxer briefs. I take in the sight of him, and he positions himself again. He makes eye contact with me and slowly sinks into me.

I gasp and grab his bicep.

Zach groans and leans down on top of me. His hair falls around my face, smelling clean and fresh and just like I remember. I run my hands through it and dig my nails into his back as he increases his pace.

I can feel myself getting close and I tighten around him, wrapping my legs around his waist and digging my heels into his ass. I moan and arch my back, shivers running up and down my body.

That's all it takes.

He looks into my eyes, his black with need. He shudders and climaxes.

The next morning I go back to El Matador by myself.

I walk the beach almost in its entirety. I leave Zach sleeping in the early dawn hours. On the beach, I take off my flip flops and put them in my bag. I let the sand sink in between my toes, cool and soft.

I watch the waves break around the rocks. I walk through the rock formations and find one to sit on.

Gulls and pelicans fly out to sea and back again. I see a boat in the distance. Sitting there alone, I think of Samantha. I think of what Alex did to her. I think about the fact that he'd taken the most precious thing he could have from her.

I don't know how I could make it up to her, but I will.

I get up from the rock and walk the beach. I realize that I was happy. I'm madly in love with the man that was waiting for me back in his bed.

And for the first time in more than three years, I feel safe.

JOIN MY NEWSLETTER

Sign up now and get a free horror novella, The Body Snatchers. You'll also get updates, freebies, news about me and my dogs, plus book discounts and sales!

Sign up here:

https://BookHip.com/PZGBMZT

ALSO BY MARNIE VINGE

SHOP NOW

www.marniewritesthrillers.com

Psychological Thrillers

The Getaway

Swingers

For Rosie

I Remember Everything

Cold Blood

Women's Thrillers

The Way It Ends

What We Did That Night

Manspreader

The Blair Graves Files

The Haunting of Solomon House

The Holloway Hoax

The Vampire's Game

One Night in September

Short Horror Collections

Thicker Than Water

In Sheep's Clothing

The Reunion

Romance

Gunshy